Praise for Brian Christopher Moore

Labyrinth of Dreams

"The four novels of *Labyrinth of Dreams* comprise an epic fantasy reminiscent of Charles Williams at his best. Moore's tale is beautiful and mysterious, and great fun even as it plumbs metaphysical depths. A *tour de force!*"
—Jess Lederman, award-winning novelist and founder of The Works of George MacDonald (worksofmacdonald.com)

Beneath the Silent Heavens

"Brian Moore's historical fantasy of Noe and the building of the Ark is, at times, almost more poetry than prose. Playful, profound, delirious with reality, Moore's book felt like reading 40 pages, not 250. I have to say at the start that this gem from Angelico is a must

read for all lovers of literature, regardless of their faith."
—Julian Kwasniewski, TheImaginativeConservative.org

"With melodious prose and marvelous metaphors, Brian Moore guides us through the right doors, tapping the ancient sap of our longing for Eden and probing the trials piqued by a great chain of creation that groans for redemption. He mixes high fantasy and playful comedy, traditional storytelling and novelistic philosophizing."
—Joshua Hren, founder of Wiseblood Books, author of *This Our Exile: Short Stories*

"Writing in the great Christian tradition of fantasy pioneered by Tolkien and Lewis, Moore's *Beneath the Silent Heavens* nevertheless leads us into new spaces of the Christian imagination, which is, as we know, inexhaustible."
—Michael Martin, author of *Transfiguration: Notes Toward a Radical Catholic Reimagination of Everything*

Arcana of the Twisted Diadem

Labyrinth of Dreams, Book 3

Brian Christopher Moore

Cover art and design by Alexander von Ness, nessgraphica.com

ISBN: 978-0-9986030-7-0

Contents

Chapter One

The Book of the Dead

The mystery of the sign

T he Australian writer of the metafiction was raised Catholic, though he lost his faith many years ago. In spite of this loss, he retains a stubborn interest in the strangeness of the image, which is more correctly, the strangeness of the sign, which may be taken for the exotic nature of the word or what the early fathers in the East called *logoi*. For instance, he meditates upon an ex-priest who abandoned his vocation to become a fashionably strident moralist and writer of forgettable stories. He also relates the confession of a woman who left the Church after having been drafted to type up the particulars of the clerical abuse of a young parishioner.

These figures are rather pitiful, though one should not be distracted. The pith of the inquiry is elsewhere. Contemplating his contemporary, the priestly author of tawdry ephemera, the writer puzzles over the change between the ardent youth depicted in the thinly disguised autobiographical narrative and the blandly secularized adult. "I intended to ask what had become of the imagined presence or personage who had ruled the life of the young man. I am not judging the writer but rather marveling that a powerful image-in-the-mind could thus seem to have lapsed into irrelevance."

Some critics of the Australian writer are dismissive, discerning a form of obsessional autism in his recursive reflections teasing out seemingly idiosyncratic memories. Yet this is obtuse — akin to those who easily diagnose Joan of Arc as the victim of epileptic fantasies or schizophrenia. What the metafiction explores is the mystery of the sign which exhibits tantalizing equivocity. It may reside in self-evidently inadequate representation, like the popular line drawings that illustrated the writer's childhood missal. Yet oddly, in spite of the limits of such pious art, a crossing occurs. Realities are invoked so transcendent of finite capacities that even the most genius savant is reduced to meaningful silence. How could one repudiate an experience of that kind with a shrug or even a forgetting?

His own commonplace, seemingly inevitable dropping of religious belief wrestles with perplexity. The writer draws attention to the nebulous, unfinished character of so much that passes for knowledge. A little colored blot upon a map becomes the only tangible connection between a distinct geography and the subject who will never encounter an authentic inhabitant of a land remote and destined to remain so. Here, too, the placid equanimity of the subject before massive ignorance is countervailed by what? Science, charts with numbers, graphs, popular romances?

Rather than dull resignation, he probes memory, distant personal glimpses, wondering about the metaphysics of the image which is also the metaphysics of light. "I have learned to trust the promptings of my mind, which urges me sometimes to study in all seriousness matters that another person might dismiss as unworthy, trivial, childish."

These concerns are not separate from the initial, seemingly quaint expression about "guarding one's eyes." There is a primal terror lost to complacent secularism that the writer deftly acknowledges in oblique manner. Thus, the comical and impractical non-linearity of his investigation of the small Protestant Church and the mystery of its glass windows. The author contrasts the iconoclastic Puritans who destroyed the stained-glass of the old religion with the drab, yet somehow mysterious presence of chromatic glass in the oblong windows near the door of the Protestant edifice. This leads to an imagined afterlife of the destroyed artifact, the beauty of the stained-glass windows with lucid signification now an opaque yet hermetically vital prism. "Did children carry off handfuls of many-coloured chips and afterwards squint through them at trees or sky or try to arrange them as they had formerly been or to guess whether this or that fragment had once represented part of a trailing robe, a radiant halo, an enraptured countenance?"

These isolated, seemingly mute and dehistoricized fragments are like the discarded images that once conveyed contact with realms of the spirit. Yet the writer, unlike his apostate fellows, cannot comfortably dismiss the image. An enigmatic signified, something alive and other haunts him, even as he recollects the vacuity and childish limitations of his own adolescent imaginary. "I mentioned earlier that I guard my eyes. I do this so that I might be more alert to what appears at the edges of my range of vision; so that I might notice at once any sight so much in need of my inspection that one or more of its details seems to quiver or to be agitated until I have the illusion that I am being signaled to or winked at."

The import of a satyr

According to the vates Isaiah: "I will make a man more precious than fine gold; even a man than the golden wedge of Ophir." And shortly after he is declaring the destruction of the City. "But wild beasts of the desert shall lie there; and their houses shall be full of doleful creatures; and owls shall dwell there, and satyrs shall dance there. And the wild beasts of the islands shall cry in their desolate houses, and dragons in their pleasant palaces: and her time is near to come, and her days shall not be prolonged." The feckless and dim scholars grew embarrassed of the vates' words. The *Zijiim jiim* and *Ochim* intend the djinn of the desert. There is no doubt the vates was pointing at a vital dimension beyond mundane vision. Yet the scholars sought to obscure the message, offering a screen of ordinary beasts to hide the scandal that they had lost their innocence and could no longer understand the import of a satyr.

Mrs. Wherryweather's picture

Mrs. Wherryweather stood at the vanity and peered into the glass. She was sixty-four and a widow. Her husband, Frank Wherryweather, had been a banker. As she liked to tell everyone "retired ten years, dead six." Her two children had grown and flown the coop, Elspeth to Hollywood where she worked as an assistant to an American film producer and Joss to London, where he was an unhappy factotum for a literary magazine. Elspeth called once a week to complain about her love life. Joss did not call. She did not know why, but on the rare occasions when they met, she suddenly felt shy and could never ask and Joss acted as if it were nothing strange to see one's Mum for the first time in eight or twelve months with no communication in-between. Perhaps this wasn't strange. Perhaps this is how young people were nowadays. She did not know. The world outside of Dare Wicket had an odd unreality to her.

In spite of her two children, Mrs. Wherryweather had retained her figure. She was straight and tall and walked like a soldier, shoulders back and head unbending. The round of her hips swayed ever so slightly, that pelvic twist that some women are ashamed of. She vaguely associated this shame with feminism and anger, but it had never been her way.

Mrs. Wherryweather was not proud, but she was serene. She took everything, even her hurt about Joss, and wrapped it in a little place she thought of as an invisible sack, small and made of translucent satin. The sack fell between her breasts and when she walked, she sometimes felt its presence. Then she would say, "not now, later" and the tiny burden would obediently fall away into some secret room below the depths of her consciousness. She put a little cake of powder over her face, though it was only because she somehow felt obligated. Her face was weathered. "My face and my name match," she'd say to herself with a dry, ironic laugh, though there was no bitterness in it.

She'd been a beauty in her youth, stunning actually, but it hadn't held up. It was a quick beauty that bloomed and then tanned and grew leathery, rather than fat and saggy. Now she was *interesting*. The bones, always good, showed through and strangers would stare and try to see the ghost of the ingénue she once was. She smiled at herself in the mirror and shook her finger at her image for no particular reason. Then she stood and wondered what she would do with herself.

"Someone will come by," she said.

She had a retinue of hangers-on who found her strangely alluring. There was Rym, a refugee from the Iraqi invasion of Kuwait who was married to Tom Watt, the grocer. Rym would come for tea and hope to coax a story from her; and there was Ewa and Hal, the twins, who had extrasensory perception. They always showed at her door on the days she decided to make bread. Mrs. Wherryweather was very good at making bread.

Lately, however, her occasional friends had begun to drop off, either moved away or married — except for Rym, marriage seemed to make her off-limits, God knows why. Some few died or disappeared. There used to be an old man called simply Frost, who would appear at her door driving an old-fashioned baby buggy and wearing a decrepit top hat, its band green with mold. When she opened the door, he would swiftly raise his hat and in one continuing motion turn the crank on an ancient Victrola nestled in the carriage. She never called him Frost, but Jack, and he never got the joke. He played mostly Mozart and Chopin. He sometimes brought Brahms, but only reluctantly. Mrs. Wherryweather used to give him biscuits and tea, until one day, several years ago, he simply stopped coming. "He's probably hanging out with Frank," said Mrs. Wherryweather, laconically. Her guests laughed and she felt no sadness herself, but that night she lit a candle.

"You!'" she exclaimed.

It was Robin's cat, Pasquali, at the window. Robin had been Joss's childhood friend. The two boys still talked occasionally, though Robin had stayed in Dare Wicket and manned the pub, handing out pints to the needy. Once she'd asked Robin, ever so casually, about her son, but he'd only shrugged his shoulders, then added, rather awkwardly, "He said he'd write. Hasn't he then?" Robin seemed uncomfortable for some weeks after which rather ruined the friendly intentions of a pub. She carefully ended the experiment of intermediaries.

The cat raised himself on his hind legs and scratched lightly against the pane. He was a ginger tabby with piercing blue eyes.

She had never heard of that combination and would not quite have believed it possible, but there he was, demanding entry. Mrs. Wherryweather had apparently been placed on the regular schedule, though she rarely fed him and only sporadically scratched behind his ears. The tomcat seemed indifferent to her relative lack of adoration. He would bound into the room, follow a circuitous route of no formal consistency, though it always made a stop at the grandfather clock which no longer worked because Frank had always done the winding, and then the path paused in front of a large framed poster of an Atget photograph of turn-of-the-century Paris. Once there, Pasquali would establish himself, assuming a somewhat regal pose, like a lion resting on the Serengeti plain, and stare intently at the picture. He would do this for some ten or fifteen minutes, whereupon he would yawn, satisfied, and beg to be let out to continue his rounds.

Only once had she been away since the vigil had begun. The neighbor across the street had asked for advice on making a sweet, dark Bavarian bread and she had waxed eloquent and then it had rained and one thing or another, she was an hour late. She'd found the cat soaked and waiting at her window and he hardly stayed, though she toweled him dry and whispered "poor kitty" at him until his coat shimmered. It's true, she also berated him for having no sense, as justice required, but he paid her no mind. "That cat is incapable of guilt," she thought. That morning, the tom only glanced for a minute or two at the picture and then was off, but strange to say, it was this episode that caused a brief frisson to cross her spine.

She spent a good half-minute herself looking at the picture, yet could find nothing to dazzle feline interest. The Rue Blondel in the Bonne-Nouvelle Quarter. Tall, narrow four-story edifices, the vertical lines of the buildings shown with a sobriety adamantly opposed to the picturesque view. The Hôtel de la Seine, a poster-board for what appeared to be Alsatian Green Meadow Mustard, four posters of a flying dragon arranged like a packet of stamps, one of which was covered with an advertisement for a sporting event. Across the street there were a number of shops and a round clock reading one fifteen in the afternoon.

What else? A row of carts brushed up against the edge of the sidewalk on one side of the street. There was a mild rain, though insufficient to palpably trouble the few people captured like statues in the camera's gaze. People were somewhat unusual elements for Atget, whose main subjects were commercial and architectural. Photography had been her husband's interest. Hearing of Frank's hobby, a client from Brazil — or was it Switzerland? – had made a gift of the picture. A man and a woman stood talking. Another man, hands in pockets, looked out at what must have been the photographer preparing to engrave his passing moment in the permanence of silver nitrate. At the deepest point of the street, a blur of shadows, men walking too fast for the long exposures of Atget's plate camera. For a long moment she mused upon it all, and then forgot it.

Had she troubled to study the picture as religiously as Pasquali, she would have noticed what interested the cat.

The random demon

For some time now, Joss had gotten out of bed in the morning. Many people did this routinely. He would then remove his pajamas which were a blend of cotton and polyester. It would have been silly to jump into the shower beforehand. At first, Joss had not wanted to shave. This was not a decision to cultivate facial hair. It was not a decision at all. He simply felt a need to protest, though this rebellious spirit was counteracted by years of habit and a deep-seated sensibility that abhorred stridency or the loss of civilized custom in the face of peril. So he continued to shave with perfunctory routine mixed with persistent chagrin. After his shave, Joss often dressed. Aside from a few idealists, it was generally thought appropriate to cover the body with fabrics. This saved everyone embarrassment and frequent eye pain.

The radio was transmitting a message. The voice was helpfully suggesting that if he saw any cracks along his windows and doors, this might be a sign of foundation troubles. Fortunately, there was a company that would come out for free to determine if his house needed repairs. Joss did not own a house. He sat at the table and mechanically ate burnt toast and marmalade. Everyone did these things as a matter of course. No one seemed to find it strange.

The radio was now informing him that for four out of five people, the first sign of a stroke is a stroke. Another company helpfully suggested a very inexpensive screening to discover if one was likely to suffer a serious bodily malfunction. It was uncanny how much he noticed Claire now that she was absent. He would walk into a room and look for her. Sometimes he even imagined he saw her. He would be struck by a thought and begin a conversation directed at her ghost. Though he continued to go to work dutifully enough, he occasionally discovered to his dismay that he had been sitting for fifteen or twenty minutes vacantly staring at the wall — or he would suddenly start laughing for no apparent reason. It was embarrassing and difficult to explain how pain could be so blank, and numb, and pointless.

Having cultivated a penchant for perhaps confusing anachronism with style, Joss continued to use a landline to the chagrin and bafflement of his peers. His phone was an imitation of the old candlestick models, though the rotary dial was a sham. One pushed the buttons. It was an inoffensive piece of fakery, but lately it had become complicit in an annoying mystery. The bell would ring ominously at all hours of the early morning. When Joss answered, static crossed the line. He could not hear breathing, yet he sensed a presence on the other end. Neither entreaty, nor curse had any effect. If Joss did not hang up, the call might continue for the space of mere seconds or prolong minutes of static. Why anyone should stay on to verify this experimentally was another sign of his fragile, slightly unhinged state.

After a week of the haranguing candlestick, Joss called the phone company. He was told that there was no record of calls on his line at those hours. He felt both angry and foolish. He was not imagining the calls, but how does one dispute the mindless accuracy of a computer?

He tried taking the phone off the hook. He was then harried by the irrational certainty that just when he had made himself unreachable, some dire need would arise requiring an appeal precisely during the interval of chosen isolation. After several nights of bad conscience, he returned the errant machine to operation. Three evenings and mornings of uneventful peace gave Joss hope that he had beaten the random demon. Alas, on the fourth the odd persecution returned. Sometimes, he'd lift the receiver and ask in a sad, wistful voice, "Is it you?"

One should listen for the hum in the walls, informed the voice from the radio. The wiring was apt to go bad and become a fire hazard, though someone would come inspect your domicile for free.

Amorous dough

Mrs. Wherryweather could not help feeling that Joss was lost. Her little boy was lost, and that is why he would not seek her out, because his vulnerable spirit could not face her and ask directions. Men, of course, were far less hardy than women. Women lived longer, built for endurance and childbearing. The world had always been something of a mess, but bitterness had taken hold, a rotten, distorted quest for justice that hated everything sweet and innocent. She couldn't help thinking the suffragettes were to blame. Mothers, wives, lovers, women had previously wielded influence indirectly. Of course, there were always exceptions like Bodacea.

Joss used to tell her that even though Spenser wrote a great poem to the virgin Queen, there was probably something perverse about the first Elizabeth. If she was virgin, which was questionable, it was likely because of physical deformity, not virtue, and besides, she was not the powerful figure of Whiggish imagination, but rather the useful tool of Protestant new money eager to consolidate the gains realized by confiscating the wealth of monasteries.

All that history was certainly beyond her and could easily be a romantic invention, Joss had that penchant. Yet truly there was something arrogantly stupid about modern women. They said a woman needs a man like a fish needs a bicycle, a jeering boast. Yet women did need men. They only spoke that way because it was so crying obvious that men need women. Even monks exhibit passionate devotion to the Virgin Mother.

A kind of poem once said the truth of human beings. "They are made of amorous dough. As soon as they turn twelve, love has begun to take them somewhere. They see its glowing torch from afar and follow it through the half-light of childhood . . ." *Though now we are all out of sorts*, she thought unhappily.

The visitor in the garden

Mrs. Wherryweather opened the old French doors of her kitchen. A little stone path led from the cottage to the bit of garden she sometimes tended. It had been a typical English garden with yew hedges, spring flowers like daffodils and purple hyacinth. There was spotted dead nettle as ground cover. Her husband had admired the silver leaves. Sweet pea vines delicately ascended a lacework of wooden trellises. In the summer, there was yarrow and the stately, but poisonous foxglove.

Change had come because in his teen years, Joss had grown sullen. He had always been close to Frank, but now he could barely tolerate his father. It had pained them both. Frank racked his memory, searching for some failure on his part, some inadvertent betrayal that had separated him from his son. Mrs. Wherryweather had secretly begged Joss to be kind to his father. There was nothing really. It was just wayward time and generations and hormones. Then Joss became fascinated with Japanese anime and Frank saw his chance. The garden had a shallow pond and a nearby willow that hung tremulously over the water. Frank deepened the pond and built an arched wooden bridge over a narrow neck of the enlarged pool. He planted with great care a lovely Japanese maple whose blood purple leaves radiated an exotic beauty.

Joss was thrown out of his funk. He conspired with his father to populate the pond with koi, an ornamental carp that sometimes lived for over two hundred years. Joss knew all the names, but Mrs. Wherryweather only knew them by their appearance. There were koi of glittering, metalic scales and some that were light blue on top and red or cream below. There were others with red spots on their heads and some that changed color with the seasons. Her favorite, however, and Joss's too, was a large, tea-colored fellow, who was clearly the king of that piscine realm. Gregarious, he would come to the bridge and poke his head near the surface in greeting. They called him Solomon.

Now that Joss and Frank were gone from her, she made it a ritual to stand upon the wooden arch and wait for the great fish to greet her. Mrs. Wherryweather reached for her straw hat, and then stopped. There was something funny, but she couldn't quite tell. One sometimes feels this way, subtly, vaguely watched. Sighing at her non-sense, Mrs. Wherryweather walked over to the edge of the garden. She peered out upon the flowers, the yew hedge and the roses, the willow hunched like an ancient mother over the fish pond and the stone bench where she sometimes read. Of course, there would be nothing there. Of course, though for some unaccountable reason, there was.

Standing near the Japanese maple was an impossible creature. The head was pleasing, rather heart-shaped, with a small, pointed chin. A feminine face with a gamine, bemused expression, looked back at her, its almond eyes somewhat larger than a human's and deep amber in color. A set of horns, like an antelope, protruded from the skull just above the temples. It was tall, perhaps six feet in height, and lithe as a fairy. The creature blinked. The mouth twitched. Did she imagine the slight bow of a smile? Then, with a graceful, dancing motion, it turned from her. Another second and it was gone, vanished.

Mrs. Wherryweather hurried over to the maple and looked about. Not a trace. Exasperated, she stood upon the bridge to complain.

"Did you see her, Solomon? Was she real?"

On this day, Solomon kept himself to himself.

"Well, but what a strange way of going mad," she said.

The hirsute infant

Time seemed to function differently now for Joss. Everyone else was continually busy. True, there were homeless individuals, elderly, and young children who mainly lived outside the grind, each in a different respect. Were they free? Not really. The vagabonds were frequently subject to mental delusions, drug addiction, loneliness, and desperate vulnerability. Some of these were also dangerously violent. The elderly and the child lived in a liminal state, witness to the odd symmetry between the womb and the tomb. In different, but parallel ways, they touched lightly on a mystery beyond choice. Society, however, confined itself to producing useful citizens. Otiose wisdoms that used to address the care of the soul were now more concretely directed at minimizing pain.

The political slogans of the era were attached to rights and the outrage of victims, but Joss believed all that was surface camouflage that masked underlying apathy. Amidst these useless thoughts, Julian was insistent about a walk. And by walk, this meant mainly Joss carrying the dog like a particularly hirsute infant.

He was contemplating an addendum to the pajamas hypothesis. It seemed to Joss that everything had grown first dull and then wildly garish sometime after the 1940s. Fashion, if cinema was to be taken as an indicator, still prevailed so long as hat and gloves for women, fedoras for men ruled the day. Hollywood was still a civilizing possibility in the era of Greer Garson, Myrna Loy, and the deliciously bad Mary Astor. But then things went to seed.

Audrey Hepburn was a lone princess in a desert of vulgarity. A whisper of biblical admonition teased the corners of his memory, something about head coverings and the angels.

Complete strangers, it turns out, feel that the presence of a small, furry quadruped is an open invitation to initiate conversations. Joss had stopped visiting his friends and acquaintances. They all reminded him of someone. A gnawing pit would emerge in his abdomen and he'd start hyperventilating. Anyway, he was tired of them, regardless. So now some scourge of justice, whimsical Furies, invoked the fawning and oohing and aahing over an entirely ordinary bit of fluff and tongue and moist eyes. Domesticated dogs were surely commonplace for millennia, yet Julian bouncing on his shoulder continued to astonish them and make them ask perversely simple questions they could not possibly care about, nor remember five seconds after having asked them.

To escape the implacable regard of the *hoi polloi*, Joss darted into the nearest door which so fortunately belonged to the sort of boutique that sells lava lamps and tarot cards. The overbearing crush of potpourri immediately informed him of his mistake.

A young woman with multicolored hair and eye black that would bring envy to a raccoon asked him if he needed assistance. She deigned to ignore the redoubtable Julian, which was a surprising point in her favor.

"No, sorry. I'm afraid I've wandered in by mistake. Thought this was the tobacconist."

"The errant path is often destiny in disguise."

Joss felt a surge of anger at this fortune cookie metaphysics, but he resisted venting distaste. He feared himself. He sensed, but refused to acknowledge the witless combination of outrage and shame that was slumbering in his heart.

"There are many unique items here. Look about before you leave."

It was difficult to refuse such a request without appearing rude. With a sigh of impatience at his own softness, Joss made a circuit among the wares sufficient to oblige the girl. On a table next to a vase filled with peacock feathers, he saw an eclectic supply of occult paraphernalia. By chance his hand brushed against a small box made of ebony and covered with a mirror engraved with the image of a dragon. A handwritten card was placed before it. "A vision of your heart's desire is contained within."

You had to give them credit for audacious promises, though it would make the inevitable failure a risible event. Still, it was a practically irresistible temptation. A dragon, after all, is good luck. So Josiah opened the box and looked within. Then his hands began to tremble. There was Claire with her ocean blue eyes and that long equipoise that made even a girl like Dee say, "righteous."

He felt as if he was drawn into the scene. For a long time, he just stood off by a tree and watched her. She was reclined against a park bench reading. When he got up his nerve and came closer, he saw that it was a copy of Nietzsche's *Birth of Tragedy* — not a very Claire book, that. He decided it was one of the dragon's little jokes. *One must lie to oneself in order to act.* That was Nietzsche.

Again, a malicious wave of emotion swept over him. Josiah felt a great desire to crush the box, to gut out its absurd, dreamy confection. Yet he did not. With the care of someone handling rare, expensive china, with the delicacy of an expert defusing a bomb, he laid the package down before him. Malice was followed by nausea and then prolonged self-pity that wet his eyes with an embarrassing shine. Like a punch-drunk pugilist, he stumbled from the room. Julian followed at his heels, her compassionate glances lost upon the large creature she was tasked to look after.

"There's nothing in there I want," he said to the attendant.

"You sure?" she asked.

"Nothing matters."

"You are wise," purred the attendant.

Josiah laughed bitterly. "Hell, anyone can know that. Everyone does."

The boy who danced

Rym came by with the new child. The infant yawned, and reached out to toy with the dazzle of a small broach resting on his mother's breast. A gentle picture, the guileless babe intent on the ornament recalled the masters of the northern Renaissance. Such a sweet child, at once serious and playful, he never once lapsed into bawling discontent. Mrs. Wherrywhether was charmed, yet a shiver unobtrusively entered, a subtle, devious creature. She couldn't say why, but a worry came to her, a worry for the child. To ward off the strange fear, she praised.

"Such a wee, perfect thing, so quiet and mild and not at all a blob or ugly."

She had laughed then, because folks are afraid to say a baby is peevish or already plain. The child favored the mother. Rym, a jewel of a girl, with limpid dark eyes and a soft smile — and Tom Watt with his long mulish mug and slow, ponderous silences. Folks didn't see how they sparked. Rym's father had been a medical doctor. A missile had struck the hospital where he was tending the wounded. She went to the hospital and discovered him lying on a gurney and thought "that's not so bad." Close up, she came to speak kindness and relief, only her father could not hear. A gaping wound where his heart should have been mocked her. The young woman rarely talked of it, such perverse, almost anonymous wickedness falling from the sky. She'd look at her hands as if they somehow held an explanation.

Mrs. Wherryweather was telling Rym a story about Joss. There didn't seem to be a point to it, but it had come rattling out of her of its own accord, how they'd once gone to a pub, the kind with a little family restaurant attached. Someone had put a coin in the juke box and played an old tune. They hadn't changed the records in a generation or two. Joss couldn't have been more than four. He was wearing his plaid hat, the one that he was always losing, that or the stuffed bear, and they'd have to make a trip back to retrieve one or the other, so that Frank suggested tying a string between boy and spirit guide. The hat was harder to solve. She'd bought a spare, but he always wanted the old, rumpled hat. The new one was a false hat and he looked upon it as an intruder of dubious morals.

Well, so the song played, it was Patsy Cline, and Joss danced with utter abandon. He was an odd child. Sensitive and pensive, but then he'd just forget everything and lose himself in the moment. Afterwards, people had thrown coins at his feet.

Meeting without absolution

Claire's murder brought inquiries. Joss answered some questions, but they were brief and perfunctory. He was just a friend. No one imagined he was bewildered by grief and self-recrimination. A week later, when the police tape and journalists had disappeared, Joss visited the small museum. The photographs of Henry Ellwood were still on display. Joss was alone. He walked from one print to another, gazing with the intensity of one looking for answers to perplexities that shelter in the gut and gnaw away.

They were remarkable, unsettling images. One had the sense of a mask peeled half-way back, with something both terrifying and wonderful waiting to announce itself. The camera was not laying bare an object, but glimpsing interior space. What he really wanted was Claire, her forgiveness, her presence, for the promise of life she had been. He waited a long time, but there was nothing but silence and the haunting pictures and the scribbled notebooks of her dotty, lost father.

He thought again of that day she'd asked him to come by, brought them to him with a shy demand. For what? That he keep them, read them, understand the secret she could not discover.

The alam-al-mithal

Mrs. Wherryweather wondered if there was memory in things. Her old mixing bowl, for instance, had belonged to her mother. Did it compare the old hands now with the young hands of her mother long ago? Did it make observations on changing habits of cuisine? All that was non-sense of course, but she felt affection for the bowl and couldn't help feeling that it responded in kind. She added the dark corn syrup to the tablespoon of brown sugar, coffee granules, and caraway seed to the cup of rye flour and the cup and a half of water. She mixed in the cider vinegar, the pinch of fennel seed, and the dry yeast.

She worked slowly and methodically using the dough hook to push back the rising tide of the batter. Then she added the softened butter. Vague recollections of tales she had heard in her childhood flitted like a soft hum along her fingers. There was a hut belonging to the witch, Baba Yaga, which moved about on chicken feet and knights that arose from the sea. It was possible the Russian black bread would be fine without these stories, but Mrs. Wherryweather believed they were as important as the sprinkle of coarse salt or the bit of egg white she would brush on the dough before baking.

Just then, the shining eyes of Ewa and Hal peering in from the open kitchen window greeted her, each bestowing that odd smile that invited her into their own special world.

"You've come early. It won't be ready for awhile," she said.

"We're not early," said Ewa.

"We just stopped by on the way," said Hal.

"It will be scrumptious when we return," said Ewa.

Mrs. Wherryweather smiled. "You've got it all planned out. Return from what?"

"Oh, the Fay folk are gathering. Haven't you seen them?"

Mrs. Wherryweather considered telling the twins about her mad encounter in the garden, but she suddenly felt tired and unwilling to be drawn in.

"Is there any special reason?" she asked with a tone that was cagily curious under pretext of mere polite.

"They come through mirrors and sometimes pictures," said Hal, as if this were a straight-forward answer.

"But why Dare Wicket?" asked Mrs. Wherryweather, in spite of herself.

"This is one of their high places," said Ewa. "We don't know what they want yet."

Mrs. Wherryweather sighed. Joss would know what to say to them. Joss would probably join them and bring back a report just in time for delicious new baked bread. One day, Rym had told her of the mystical thinkers, Ibn Arabi and Mulla Sudra. They said that all creatures of the imagination came from a world hidden from us, the *alam-al-mithal*. But not all of them were safe or festive. Some brought arid emptiness, despondency, and barren earth.

"Take care, take care," said Mrs. Wherryweather, her voice trembling, but already the twins were gone and the windows flush with the banality of morning sun.

Life in prison

People's lives most often did not come off. Things went badly. Disappointment was normal. And yet, everyone wants to be happy. And after awhile, once you'd lived long enough, you would know that happiness is always somewhere else. A placard in the museum explained that the photographs were the product of glass plates — Ellwood used an old camera and some unknown process that resulted in the eerie, strange images sent back from the middle of a supposedly pristine rainforest. They arrived, some years after his disappearance, on random cargo ships following untraceable mediation of diverse vehicles and polyglot instruction. It was, indeed, the nearly random fortune of adventure that seemingly devised this mode of bearing so resistant to clarity. A ludic logic of mousetrap ingenuity conveyed the messages from a man long dead, depositing a cache of images that appeared not possible in this world. No one had an explanation.

For Joss, Claire was just as surprising. Claire was a beckoning universe, promise opening onto a new land. He'd been afraid to mention it, even to Claire. He knew what the others thought, mainly. That hormones and emotional gushing deceive. Soon enough, the beloved turns out to be a harpy, an idiot, or maybe nice enough, but just plain dull, even at best, not a universe of perpetual exploration. Perhaps the trick was that Claire had been taken from him before the possibility of disillusionment could arise. Yet Joss could not accept such cynicism. *Claire was real.*

Joss understood the full inarticulate ridiculousness of his position. How could any metaphysical weight be placed upon so flimsy and common an experience? But he could not deny the thrilling shock of her. When Claire was alive, everything mattered. He saw with new eyes. Whatever secret they might hold in reserve, Henry Ellwood's photographs were not telling.

When he turned to leave, Amanda was standing at the edge of the exhibit. It was impossible to pretend not to have seen her. Her expression was severe, anger tinged with fright, and something else; shame, he thought. A cold horror gripped him. Joss passed close enough for words, but it was evident what Amanda desired most was his immediate disappearance. He hastened to comply, feeling poisoned, guilty, a victim of inexplicable violence. Each step was hopeless, a departure that was ever after into further sorrow.

Shortly after this, Joss began to write his unpostables.

Pressed from all sides

And Pilgrim Kheen was anxious, but unwilling to let the others know. For long, they had kept within their own kingdom. Adorned with powers sufficient to the burst of life, the long-lived who have numerous names, the most important of which remain unknown to human history, were content to follow their own paths, to seek what seemed right. They regarded with wry amusement those come and gone in a blink of time. In the past, that species used to fear them. Respect was their modicum, their small share of wisdom.

In recent centuries, however, growing pompous with their new methods, human acolytes sought mastery that more often than not led to unanticipated consequences. They were unable to learn much before expiring. What tradition they attempted to pass on generally failed. The lessons were ordinarily pretty dim to begin with and subject to degradation in the transmission. Nonetheless, even this was somewhat bearable. Hiding behind the screen of quantified data, the realm of Elementals remained free.

Yet there were darker spirits unknown to Kheen by name, but he sensed them. These, too, sought mastery, and perhaps were even allowing or nurturing that science of experiment mankind so prided itself upon. These watchers were drawn to electricity and the mysterious energies of life. Sometimes they appeared as lights in the sky, or took a random biped, invariably from a remote location. Were they also searching for answers, or working out confident plans based upon their own smug certitudes? If the subject was returned, the human experts would explain away claims of abduction. Crop circles, sometimes faked and dismissed as a hoax by the credulous, were one of their gnostic puzzles.

Arrogance was common coin. The human engineers were building large language models, a new virtual tower of Babel, hoping to exceed the limits of their finite, mortal condition. Never did they suppose that the observers from dark dimensions might inhabit and make use of their cleverly devised and curated machines. So, Kheen surmised the dark archons intended purposes other than the utility of mankind. The Balance was in jeopardy, but how to defend or restore it? In their new grown fear, some of the sprites of forest, the river nymphs, the lesser lords of fields and lower hills contemplated making compact with the secretive power.

Yet there was an ancient promise, something different and joyous. Ironically, it was rumored buried seed, some impossible secret carried in the fleshy soul of the ignorant bipeds. Heretofore, the faerie had felt no need of it, happy enough to tolerate foolish men.

"We are pressed, pressed from all sides," sighed the Faerie king and he pondered how one might test the winds and measure the immeasurable.

An unpostable

Something I wanted to tell you. I am always wanting to tell you. I can't explain, exactly, but certain events interest me. Most people live very dull, inattentive lives. They live superficially, even children. Though my friend Lafferty reports that "children, though apparently so grubby and squalid, are each of them absolutely exceptional and excellent in their invisible trailing appendages. There has never been a common child." Well, he then notes an exception. Lafferty is good for a laugh and a lark, especially when he's serious.

A lot of what matters, what is most important, is hardly noticed. To be more precise, it isn't noticed, except by a few. I just now went rummaging through your father's notebooks. It was suddenly necessary that I tell you about Hopkins. But I am out of breath and perhaps I have lost the report.

They walk strange

So mischief, you want to know what they are like? I will tell you, before the sun rises in the porridge, before the calf with two-heads decries the riddle, I shall speak three truths and two lies. First, they are the bumptious, the tactile, the wobbly flesh, knowing everything in the body, falling against the boundaries of the crib, gumming greedily the milk breast, scraping knees, riding bicycles, staring into lover's eyes, washing the bodies of their dead. This is their way, to know and not know, to feel with hearts cold, but not blithe like ours, they are the odd.

And yet you wish to know more, my glowfish, my dandelion smile? They are short, very short, their soul stuff runs a little, even their long is short. A mountain will barely register the tiny bipeds walking like fleas upon the hard surface of a great ape. They are tiny that way, but mark, they walk strange. The spine is a tree. They wonder at the stars. Every burst forward is filled with a look back. They are constantly telling stories, carrying the time that was and peering with their prophetic flesh into time that will be. They are thus haunted in the ever present, nebulous ghosts who believe we are the fay. Don't laugh, that is their faith, by gum.

What more can I tell you, sweet queen grown sour, you who run from the heartbroken Kheen? It may be that they see when they are not looking, from out the corner of their eyes, what I know not — and neither do they. They were born in breath, that is the rumor of them, that they bear the deep silence dark rooted, the unspeakable that is the sap of language. If they do, they have rundled it, whiffed into a vapor of non-sense. I have made them dance with rank lust and reek with hate. They are dunces, by gum, but this you know.

Now they are grown so dull, the language in them runs dry, gribbles into grasping, sneering, rotting with dim speak. Such tepid stuff, we should let them die into oblivion. Still, that is the madness of it, they are somehow the crux, these grubby louses, arrogant, murderous, foulness, brief, but pungent.

Dribbling, mewling, for old times' sake, I'll steal a natal flesh for mirror. We shall see what it foretells.

The day moth

I discovered the Hopkins report about the destruction of the ash tree in his garden. "It was lopped first: I heard the sound and looking out and seeing it maimed there came at that moment a great pang and I wished to die and not to see the inscapes of the world destroyed anymore." And this put me in mind of Woolf who writes so poignantly in her essay "The Death of the Moth."

Attend, dear friend, such music in words. *"Moths that fly by day are not properly to be called moths; they do not excite that pleasant sense of dark autumn nights and ivy-blossom which the commonest yellow-underwing asleep in the shadow of the curtain never fails to rouse in us. They are hybrid creatures, neither gay like butterflies nor sombre like their own species. Nevertheless the present specimen, with his narrow hay-coloured wings, fringed with a tassel of the same colour, seemed to be content with life."*

Virginia peers through a multi-paned window upon the rich tableaux of the downs. The ploughman scores the earth and the rooks sweep the tree tops. And the obscure day moth dances upon the prism of glass, sharing in small manner with the larger wave of life transmitted in the passage of light through the pellucid curtain. *"He flew vigorously to one corner of his compartment, and, after waiting there a second, flew across to the other . . . That was all he could do, in spite of the size of the downs, the width of the sky, the far-off smoke of houses, and the romantic voice, now and then, of a steamer out at sea. What he could do he did. Watching him, it seemed as if a fibre, very thin but pure, of the enormous energy of the world had been thrust into his frail and diminutive body."*

Some folks like to focus on the end of this kind woman who observed with such skill, grace, and empathy. They contemplate with chagrin or prurient fascination as she drowns herself with rocks as anchors in her pockets. They make of her a martyr or shake their heads at madness. All I say is intelligence is tender or it is nothing at all. The day moth begins to struggle and the writer turns from casual observation to concern and futile intervention. She prods with a pencil, and then desists, for none of us has the power against death. The tiny creature fights with heroic energy the unknown darkness . . . *"after a pause of exhaustion the legs fluttered again. It was superb this last protest, and so frantic that he succeeded at last in righting himself. One's sympathies, of course, were all on the side of life. Also, when there was nobody to care or to know, this gigantic effort on the part of an insignificant little moth .*
. "

The story ends, as it must, in resignation to the bitter triumph of our mortal enemy. Claire, there is something in all this that is more than frivolous. We are meant for some ultimacy, destiny, call it what you will, I know not what, but this is what begins to be lost.

Canticle of the elements

Swift, invisible Ariel, you were first to arrive. Then *Hermes*, burning, unhappy just then to be still. Next came that many voiced one, the chorus of *Nyads* that live in rivers and wells, daughters of the sea. Finally, waking, because already there, the rough soldier **earth** yawned and said that they were late. And the Wanderer of Fairie entered into their midst.

"Name yourselves," said he.

Sometimes I play upon their chimes, breathe music to waken dull minds, I swing the wide paddles of their mills, bear tidings from afar.

Sometimes I shelter in chimneys, I warm their iron kettles, I heat the pot where they cook the potatoes for the pigs and in the same pot the good ones for themselves.

Sometimes they come, intrepid and bold, immodest or giving due veneration, either way they crawl like worms into the hermetic depths searching for sun and moon, the splendorous gems.

Sometimes I give them rest, I touch the parched lips, refresh the tired beasts, I babble in springs, brood with secrets and good destiny in the sacred wells.

I burn and dance upon the little mountain, I sing light, I cast golden shadows so they may read their letters, so they may study their books, they coax me by laying out a repast of delicious tallow.

I slumber, I stick, I resist their trudges, I dam the flow, I am bone beneath the loam, I give hardness to vegetal life, so that the moist limb may hold, so that the soft bud may beckon.

I flow, I enter into the roots of things, I burst into flower, flourish the grass, plump every gourd and fruit tree, I lie serene, mirror beautiful forms that descend from the sky.

I whisper, I gently nudge the bloom of the rose, the star fan of the daisy, I kiss with dew the boots of the early rising, I flutter grass for the playful kitten, thunder from the heights.

And sometimes, yes, I rage, I paint across the sky, I dervish their forests, I dwindle their bridges, their houses; I consume all their dear, to remind them that I am free.

And sometimes, yes, I quake, I tumble every tower, I widow every wall, into rubble I crash and tremble all their works, cause lament to rise, to remind them from whence they came.

And sometimes, yes, I flood, I cross over the safe lines, I cover the plains, I carry downriver their beds and their tables, sweep away their livestock, their very lives, to remind them in this place no abiding.

And sometimes, yes, I howl, I thunder and smash every fragile birth, I destroy in a blink a lifetime of devotion, keen over the soft, innocent life, to remind them, to remind them, how precious what they cannot keep.

Human nature

"*She's not coming,*" said the gnarled one.

"*Of course she isn't, we told you,*" shrugged the mercurial youth.

"*It is uncertain, she may or may not,*" answered the chorus of waters.

"*I tremble, I misticate, there, and there.*" Ariel seemed to indicate points near and far, so the others glared, made angry, though it was clear enough to the vagrant spirit.

"Silence," commanded the Pilgrim Kheen.

How she came amongst them, no one knew. Suddenly, yet with cool indifference, lazy to dismiss a cloak of invisibility, the ancient one was simply there.

"What are they? Torturers and rapists, nothing else," snapped Uhraine.

Report on memory

There are several things I need to report today. I've been thinking of them for some while. I wanted to tell you. It might matter where you are. The first is noted by a fella who grew up in the southwest of the Americas. I don't think he was a cowboy, per se, but I like to think of him that way on account of your love for horses.

When I was still young enough to see the shine of things, I had a photo album with a herd of mustangs on the cover. I used to try and imagine where they were and the thrill of running wild. I had a momentary sense of moving amidst the many horses, but it never lasted and I was pulled back, left with an odd sense of restless ennui. I wouldn't have expressed it that way, of course. Only now that the child I was is dead do I have the words. But what I'm really after is the strangeness of memory.

This fella tells about how as a boy in the Texas Panhandle, he herded cattle in a particular arroyo, and how when he recollects that time and space "the endless space of the voices of silence ... speak from the peripheries of absolute solitude." However, were he to visit that same geography that swells in significance in the depths of boyhood fermented by time and distance, what would he discover but a "shrunk reality" just as the house of childhood revisited in maturity appears tiny and pulled back? The secret passages of imagination recess into nullity or forgetting. The wild joy and abandon that hearkened in the spiritual landscape of his youth is betrayed by the dull record of so-called facts. Yet I believe we are meant to trust that memory, as fragile and open to distortion as such reverie may be.

My other investigation has to do with Traherne. Traherne speaks as if he never lost his early delight in the earth. He is like a child who lives perpetually on Christmas Eve. He may not have been like that at all. He has these lines, though, these words spoken into the disappearing time. If you catch them, you can hear them. Let me know if you hear them. Perhaps you can tell me what they mean.

The anchoress

The anchoress at St. Julian's was the original mistress. Whether his memory went back further, the cat could not say with certitude. He believed it did. On certain days with the wind just right, especially if he found himself near a river with a bronze sun, the cat felt the ancient song of Egypt thrumming in his blood. But his sense of beginning was later, in the cold of England. At that time he was a gray tabby with amber eyes named Methuselah.

The cat was fond of the lady who lived in the little cell with the one window that looked out upon the people and the other that looked inward towards the chapel and the garden in-between. She was a wise woman who nearly died. While she was nearly dying, he waited near. Flailing on her fever bed, the others were sure she would turn mute and diminish, putrefy and rot into the earth, but she did not and the cat knew she would not, because he could see that her aura was not yet destined for the dark portal. So, the cat stayed and when she recovered, she told him stories of what had been revealed to her and the cat said, "why don't you write that down, that's good?"

There were many reasons that he had decided to visit Dare Wicket, not just because spirits were coming through the picture that belonged to the woman who made bread. Mrs. Wherryweather resembled, and reminded him of the wise woman at St. Julian's. Sometimes he forgot himself and asked her if it was still true that "all manner of thing shall be well?" Then she would look back at him with a wondering, slightly baffled expression, because she heard him in her soul and did not know the answer.

Time's arrow

Report: Claire, I have been going over your father's notebooks. Two distinct handwritings are extant. I take the bulk of material as belonging to your father, but some not inconsiderable remainder is the work of your grandfather, Lucien. They were on to something, I am sure, though what I cannot properly say. There are scraps of paper that appear to have been thrown haphazardly into pages, though it is possible Henry intended some connection — or perhaps he sensed some relation he could not yet name.

There's a scribbled bit on the back of an envelope, for instance, where he talks about the philosopher, Bergson, who said that it was wrong to construe motion as a sequence of distinct states — an arrow piercing the air at positions $x_1, x_2, x_3 \ldots x_n$ at successive times $t_1, t_2, t_3 \ldots t_n$ because one was implicitly presuming a frozen state like a still frame pulled from the cinema as the normative condition by which one proposes to understand movement. But such a mechanical way of conceiving is external, from the outside, when the reality is that all those hypotheticals are an alienating abstraction.

Arbitrary designations are possible stopping points only recognized as such from the interior of movement itself. It's rather like life, and why the stillness of death might also be a fabrication from the outside, as it were. The reality of motion evades conceptions shoehorned to conform to a mechanical mode of action. In a different hand, on the back of a bill for dry cleaning the name of Goethe is written in large letters, then scribbled in hasty hand the following. "*The movement of metamorphosis is in the way of seeing*, and a change in the way of seeing *transforms* what is seen without *adding* to the content."

All this is pressed against a leaf in a notebook where he quotes a linguist or perhaps a philosopher, some fella named Rosenstock-Huessy. "In a man's first love, he also discovers the time-continuum of all love; the continuity of history, the order of the universe, the destiny of man, all stand disclosed to the soul who falls in love for the first time." And then, "To be loved by one other person means to know every phase of time."

Claire, Claire, Claire.

The angel speaks

"The problem with the modern world is that it lacks an *omphalos*," said the Elder, sipping carefully on a pint of Guinness so as not to disturb his beard which was white as a daisy. "Lots of folks to blame. That avid politician, Bacon, for one and Descartes, the thin, sickly knight of pale and famished reason who sucked the meaning from the cosmos like a greedy cerebral vampire. Worst of all, that proud cretin, Galileo. And then the pope goes and apologizes to his fatuous ghost."

"It is a very fine day, but himself is keeping to himself," remarked Robin looking askance at the cat and wondering about the newest stranger to enter his establishment.

"The angels cover their tracks," said the Elder by way of explanation. Robin had no idea what was intended and shrugged his shoulders, irked to always be at sea. The Elder frowned. "Our guest has always rested within the House of Mnemosyn."

Robin stared hard then at the solemn fellow warming his hands at the cup of cocoa with marshmallows ordered most particularly.

"This is a pub," Robin had reminded to no avail.

Though for an angel the guest did not inspire any hint of awe, his dark cape dripping still from a morning shower. A silvered fur, thick and short like the pelt of a seal covered his pensive head. The patron's face was oblong, the golden brown color of chestnut. There was something vaguely simian and mild mocking in the expression, twinkling sapphire eyes offset by the scratch of a wry smile.

"Allow me the observation," began Rhodion-el in a voice warm, silken, musical in a fashion that seemed incongruous with the physiogamy of the stranger. "There is heedless into the country of your people a new foe; rather, something ancient, long forgotten, tripping most pleasing, calculating, knowing more than you, desirous to use you, to make use of you, observant, prevaricating, persistent, utterly pitiless, wishing to find you in stealth and disarming, full of guile whitened in false innocence. It is determined and you know it not."

"Thanks for that," answered Robin. "Yes, yes. Perhaps it is you," he added in his thoughts, but not his speech.

"Perhaps. I have come from the far that is near; but the cat has seen them, the vile Malchariat and their followers; the sharp-eyed harpies, the foul nagfalami, the lilītu with sucking hearts breathing in the air while it is barely warming in your lungs. Trust, it is not their perverse delight to be recognized. They would much you kept them in books for children, silly tales ruled out-of-bounds by your regnant science."

Robin was agape. Had he spoken, after all? Then, suddenly taking in the import of a bit of the stranger's drift, he looked hard at Pasquali, a surge of irrational fear entering his voice.

"What do you mean the cat has seen them?"

"It is long, long since such has happened," answered the stranger. "And yet, it is only today it has begun."

Rhodion-el's speech puzzled, doubtless a result of translation from the richer realms of the alchemic tongue. Most likely, the world you're in is not the world you think you're in.

Description catalog number 3

Visions of these eternal principles or characters of human life appear to poets in all ages; the Grecian gods were the ancient Cherubim of Phoenicia; but the Greeks, and since them the Moderns have neglected to subdue the gods of Priam. These gods are visions of the eternal attributes, or divine names, which when erected into gods become destructive of humanity . . . For when

separated from man or humanity, who is Jesus the savior, the vine of eternity, they are thieves and rebels, they are destroyers.
— William Blake

Bad Queen Mab

And Hal said, "Queen Mab is misbehaving."

And Ewa said, "That is not Queen Mab."

"Well, she's definitely trouble," said Hal, "whoever she is."

Providence

Dear friend, a rather extraordinary thing has happened. I am sure it can be explained well enough, though the series of causes necessary for what appears serendipitous is beyond ordinary calculation. I suppose an actuary is the sort that could give one odds. Here is the short version. I received a package from my mum the other day. I can't imagine what possessed her. Within, a long coat she discovered at a church jumble. She says Hal and Ewa told her to send it to me.

I don't suppose I told you about the twins. They are rather spooky, but beneficent. At least, they have an aura of innocence that inclines one to trust them. Of course, they might be especially clever devils, there's a thought. But here is the really impossible part. There was a tear in one of the pockets through which some folded papers had fallen into the interior lining. Out of curiosity I went through the trouble to retrieve them. Not hundred pound notes, alas, but rather notes in a cribbed hand I have come to recognize. It is your father's coat, I am sure.

More on the notes later, which I shall call the magnum pallium codex, MPC for short, how nice.

The angel ponders

Rhodion-el knew what they were up to, for angelic intelligence naturally pierces the veils of Elementals. They were going to take a child. It was their old game, for they were still trying to puzzle the Incarnation. The Fay were of the opinion that you could figure that exalted mystery out, which was their own particular obtuseness.

What to do? They would replace the bouncing babe with a simulacrum, of course, a sort of toy of their own making. The parents wouldn't notice for a while. When they did, if they were wealthy, doctors would be consulted. The physician, unless an old country practitioner, would send the thing on to specialists who would run multiple tests and then throw up their hands. The mothers would find something to blame — vaccination, too many sugars in the diet, some such ersatz reason. The rural doctor might know, but you can't tell modern people that faeries have stolen their child.

Regardless, normally the toy wound down in short years, so everyone would sadly lower the mechanism into a grave and silently conclude with a guilty relief that it was for the best. If they did live, they were sure to be an imbecile. Many of them became successful politicians. The angel considered telling the twins. Mercurial, too curious, perhaps.

In the end, he decided upon the cat.

MPC Part One

I am not sure what to make of this, dear one. There is a cipher that I can only partially unravel. Why your father should have written in such a fashion is unclear. Who he wished to guard his words against, for whom they were intended, I cannot say. It takes all my powers to discern the strange sayings, so I leave them naked of any interpretation on my part.

This is the forgotten, the plenitude of anamnesis. We shall struggle and curse, bitterly, weep and pray for death, yet all are called, all chant the Beauty, we come from the death that is Life, and know not ourselves.

Here follow several paragraphs apparently using a different code that I have been unable to crack. In the middle of the third paragraph, the original — and to me, easier, because obviously, I have attained some access to its operation — resumes . . .

Let them take it for a hypothesis, then, what Ravaisson says, the introspection of human subjectivity reaches the heart of every being from stone to swan, from cypress to faithful dog. Habit is the art of nature, the gift of desire that longs for love. In our flourishing, we act without deliberation or struggle, we leap and dance, virtuosity beyond thinking, because the intellect of flesh understands more than solitary reason.

There follows an inventory of disparate realities: The cube whose shape entails understanding the sides invisible from the angle of perception, the back of your head, your person separated from relation to others, then a sentence attributed to John Milbank: "Imagination is the medium in which the *judgment* of the higher soul swims." Then this:

Often you feel you are alone, that the world is flat, circumscribed by the lucid empirical, confined to appearances, or deduced from mental principles, a tautology of logic. Trapped in agony, lulled in dullness, the demonic renders obeisance to the fact; confined to narcissism and despair, it is the enemy of imagination.

I confess I often feel alone.

Imbecile changelings

Those who have despaired of human meaning, who acknowledge no duties save their momentary whims, who pride themselves on not being charmed or enchanted by the master hypnotists of piety or affection or moral duty, whose curiosity or greed or lust is both unlimited and unimportant even to them, are living out the life of fairies. Whether their real human souls are somewhere else or not, what acts in them here is, in effect, a fairy. Such fairies are unaware of fairyland: to them it is the ordinary human heart that is uncanny, that is not bound forever in the circles of this world.
— Stephen R. L. Clarke

MPC Part Two

My Claire, this appears to be something in the hand I have identified as belonging to Lucien.

Einstein said this presumably, though it may be apocryphal, that the solution to the problem is not to be found on the same plane of consciousness in which the question is asked. Mystery is not even properly conceived as problem for solution does not countenance aporetic conundrums, the lure of beauty, the feeling for goodness. Only in God is their certitude, yet no one approaches truth apart from the risk of shadows. My son, hear the word of the vates Claudel: "Do you take account of women? All too easy without them. And I — I am a woman among women. I cannot be reached by reason alone and you cannot do as you like with me. I sing and I dance." Here in the darkness of the underworld, the hidden sun.

Bartleby

There's no way to send this. Bartleby the Scrivener just stopped because he preferred not to — the earnest teller of Melville's tale already knows in his gut that his Enlightened, bureaucratic, mercantile optimism is a fraud. There is the coldness of abstraction, and the oafish, often cruel stupidities of procedural reason that drives its benevolent, ineffective altruism. He concludes with a rumor of his erstwhile copyist, a story that he had once worked in the dead letter office, custodian of a thousand futile essays against chance and malice.

I would also prefer not to.

The cat's literary precis

Notes for the Life and Times of Pasquali the Cat:

Mrs. Wherryweather, maker of bread, her garden, her daughter, the unhappy son.

Of the unnamed Mother, the glorious Hal, of Quintus, Ewa, and the lost boys.

What Hal did not know.

The glory of the Mother, a descendant of King Solomon's favorite cat. The secret ability, falsely understood, but intuited by humans, which is the explanation of the fear of familiars. The cost of the gift (three lives and one must speak in one's true name).

A Deplorable Conversation

On Myself.

The mask of Pasquali and my secret face. Why all cats are independent and not subject to the power of the vulgar name. (To be included only in privately published exclusive edition.) Last names first. Eight plus one. Pasquali Sebastian Aloysius Montgomery Boots Murphy Methuselah Thimblefoot . . . the pleasure of not knowing. A cat is not curious, that is a libel. Curiosity, as any moral philosopher of minimal competency may tell you, is a sin, for it produces vanity and obsessions after the trivial. It is better to say that a cat is indifferent, not in the sense of apathetic, but as open to the possibilities of a Providential destiny.

The story of St. Sebastian

The importance and art of napping. The parabolic meaning of Mary and Martha. Contemplation and napping. The high dream.

On My Human

On the false charge that cats are deists, materialists, atheists, natural idolators, incapable of humility.

On the excellence of Smart's poem, "My Cat Jeoffrey."

Why Shakespeare was just an amanuensis for his cat.

The feline temptress in the window (Philomena).

One day I was particularly practicing indifference. I would have liked to have been indifferent with greater vigor, but the window I was interested in was four stories up and neither the sickly vine on the wall, nor the rusting drainpipe appeared anything like Jacob's ladder.

The secret of feline wisdom: the cat has not experienced Original Sin, hence the cat is not abashed. Moreover, the cat knows that it comes from God and that it is loved by the All-Father.

In rare moments, the cat may recall the knowledge that it carries in the womb, which is a consciousness shared by all cats from the beginning of time. Because of this spiritual participation, all cats possess excellent historical knowledge, know the length of Cleopatra's nose and of Pope Urban IV's yen for cheese, etc.

The spurious charge that cats are lazy and self-serving is the usual libel made by extraverted, babbling dog lovers. In truth, cats are patient, adaptive, natural educators to impious men, forgetful of their past and careless for their future. Because of this knowledge, the cat is an excellent reader of souls.

The stranger in the cafe. On the affinity of souls, spectral time, and how this is misinterpreted by theosophists.

An Unfortunate Party.

On the erotic fecundity of the cat, not to be confused with the tawdry licentiousness of humans. (Recollect the sermon plagiarized by Parson Yorick.)

Mr. Bantam and Professor Fishhead

The art of Peter Breugel the Elder. The importance of play. The weakness of the cat for coffee table books.

Why *Breakfast at Tiffany's* would not be the same without the cat.

The truth about nine lives.

Reginald, a bull mastiff.

On the war with dogs and the possibilities of ecumenicism.

On the false demonization of the cat, its association with witchcraft and reputation as a familiar. Do not forget that Hitler owned a dog.

On taste, morals, and the finickiness of the cat. The confusion of Lord Shaftsbury.

The lure of flight, the sensual delight of shimmer.

On Tragedy or Why Thomas Gray is the Aeschylus of cat poets.

On the warrior and the saints. A story about St. Francis.

The ninth name

Today was his hemlock

"My old cat," said Robin, sadly.

"He was a scamp,'" said Mrs. Wherryweather, who suddenly discovered a lash in her eye and kept having to put a kerchief to it.

"A glorious rogue," said Ewa.

"Too bad today was his hemlock," said Hal.

"He stood outside the nursery window and would not leave," said Rym, bouncing her infant boy who smiled, oblivious to the sorrow. "He raged in the twilight and I scolded him, but he was intent," she said. "I looked for another tom, but nothing. And now —."

The strange envelope

When Joss got the envelope, he nearly threw it away. It was tattered and faded, though it must once have been ornate. There was still a glimmer of gold-embossed filigree along its border. Looking at it more closely, the missive appeared to lack both indication of for whom it was intended or from whom it was sent. "It's a gag. Possibly a mistake," said Joss to himself.

Yet it was sufficiently close to a message in a bottle that vague curiosity was stirred. He took the small silver letter opener in the shape of Excalibur that Aunt Imogen had given him when still a lad of seven or eight and gently pried the dusty packaging. To his surprise, a plane ticket to Athens, Greece in his name fell out, along with a brief note in a neat, masculine hand. Was it not similar to the MPC?

The note asserted that the ticket was to facilitate a journey to the island of Patmos where "all would be explained." Appended to this cryptic invitation, in a flourish of calligraphic art, was a rather dire proclamation: "The one who has the seven Spirits of God and the seven stars says these things: 'I know your works — that you have won a name for being alive, yet you are dead.'"

Perplexed by the oddity of the thing, Joss brought it with him to the offices of *Ulysses' Attic*. The editor, however, betrayed not the slightest surprise or consternation. Rather, he winked at Joss as if it were a sly joke.

"Ah, the bishop of Ruritania," exclaimed Peabody with a chuckle. "Still alive."

Chapter Two

The People of The Land

One

"In the *Sepher Yetzirah*," said Rabbi Naftali, "it is understood that One is first and foremost the quality of uniqueness which is also that which is unsaid in any saying. One is beyond conception and cannot be counted, so those that say that the One is the all are mistaken for One is infinite frontier."

The daring of the God

There was always that difficulty, the nature of the request posing something of an incomprehensible demand, the Shema Israel: "You shall love the Lord your God with all your heart, with all your soul, with all your strength." Though often enough it was not felt to be a risible situation, folks didn't wallow in a feeling of abject, nearly hilarious despair because what was asked so infinitely beyond the capacities of human effort.

On the contrary, the impetus of being chosen, that odd election going back to Abraham and the patriarchs and renewed by the Egyptian, Moses, once things turned out the way they did, well, why not? He was secretly a Jew, surviving by the wit of a desperate mother and the care of the God, then there was anguish in the desert, a generation lost to anguish, why they didn't just walk in, it wasn't easy; some say they never left, that the Canaanites are the Jews, the skeptics always have a shrewd tale to dismiss the miracles, but the greatest miracle they cannot confound with minimalist historicism, try as they might. It was already that sign of awareness beyond the normal pagan sensibilities.

Of course the nations had their gods, their goddesses, frequently enough there were, shall we say, accommodations, borrowings sufficiently modified, nothing happens in a vacuum, after all. Allowing for human banalities, there was still that naive confidence, the others, the nations, they shook their heads at the eccentricity or accounted it wayward arrogance, those wandering folk who thought ridiculously that transcendence had made itself known, that there was revelation from beyond the cosmos, and they alone had been chosen to bear that revelation — inscrutable, baffling even, yet this insistence that by some incalculable measure both intended and achievable the contact could be made good.

And so the sons of Israel translated the immense abyss between partners in that mysterious and easily profaned dialogue into a navigable list of religious prescriptions, the proliferating inference of which iterated what was to be done, what was to be refrained from, what redress for mistake, for willful misdeed, etc. culminating in a complex rubric devoted to prayer and sacrifice that, though evidently an arduous task, they'd grant that, seemed within reach. Few stopped to ponder whether it might not be from the start a loser's bet, partly because in good faith they presumed the offer of reciprocity, the covenant and all that, implied the possible, otherwise it was a cruel joke, and life often seems a cruel joke, but the ones who put two and two together probably kept their mouths shut.

Perhaps those few, the silent wise, reckoned that their ineluctable finitude might prove an insuperable barrier to the virtually unspeakable, because practically unthinkable conclusion — that the desire in all their fumbling attempts to accomplish something truly memorable was haplessly aimed, failure baked in no matter what. After Exile, one of their poets placed words of anguish into the searching prophet, Job. . . .

Yet if the impossible were impossibly possible, it might be something else altogether. If, foolishly, the God were somehow to consent to become himself a creature, an idea so inexplicable many find it both blasphemous and inane, though if the God is not bound by the limits of what finite logic allows, this would entail more than simply the immanent transcendence that sustains in existence every contingent being. The daring of the God would suggest that heretofore, prior to the advent of the fool venture, well, that no one had fully discovered the depths of ignorance in the human race regarding the nature, specificity, unique tang and strangeness of what is involved in that action upon which the promises were predicated, the necessary ardor, that plenitude of soul, and strength, and thought intended by relation with the God that would transform the entire cosmos into divine ecstasy.

An interesting man

Certainly, he's an interesting man. And while with the passage of time, the shock of it has worn off, you can't quite finish him. The hypersensitive tried to lessen abrasive awareness, changed the numerical designation to Common Era, etc., though it's just euphemism. Those Frenchies tried to fix the calendar some centuries back with the Revolution, rid us of the entire root and branch, but shall we say the excesses of the demotic temper ruined the effort.

Have you seen those reconstructions that purport to show the face of history with verisimilitude? Robespierre comes across as a pock-mocked monster filled with rage. Cleopatra dons a parrot's beak, no beauty. The Christ, the one I saw, though based on what assumptions you can guess, appears a short-haired, copper skinned Neanderthal.

Naturally, there are obtuse scholars. There's a special dumb you can't get with plain ignorance. You have to study hard and hang out with the proper sorts to achieve the higher imbecility. Well, some of them think it was nothing very remarkable. The claim to be the anointed had happened before, and it happened afterwards, too. Men had been publically tortured, humiliated in just that fashion. Lots, actually, even a few women, but not so much. The Caesars, of course, and rulers in the ancient world in general had a habit of asserting divine provenance, if not radical deity. You might be an avatar of some blessed being from the celestial realm. It was useful and political flattery unexceptional.

That the Nazarene gathered about him an enclave of the disaffected and powerless, that he had peculiar charisma, history is rife with his kind. The times were ripe, anyhow. A concatenation of circumstances turned a local happening into a world event. It's possible to think of it that way, but then you forget just how dangerous he is.

Nicodemus

Ten are the numbers out of nothing, and not the number nine, ten and not eleven. From out of the darkness of the Cloud upon Sinai, from the UnKnowing, Moses spoke. "I am the Lord your God, who brought you out of the land of Egypt, out of the house of bondage, you shall have no other gods before me." We came out from the land of the flooded river, of crocodiles, mummified lords, and dog-headed gods.

The Greeks and the Romans cannot understand us. That is because for them a doctor of law is something very different from a healer. For the People, it is not so, we who bear the burden of nearness to the Giver of Life. But since Moses and the victories of Joshua, of David, the wealth of Solomon, we have known exile and the lament of prophets. One thinks a proud warrior trained for battle superior to a child who knows nothing. In confronting evil, best to know the tactics of a tight spot, what strategies hold best in the long run. That was our way, we doctors. It was a careful business. You had to anticipate dangers, figure acceptable losses.

I'd seen him before, you see. Of course, everyone was talking of the young prophet. They said he was surprising. You couldn't nod off and pick back up what he'd been saying. It wasn't the expected thing. So we sent a few scribes, some of the brighter clerks to test him. We wanted to sound him out. Well, their reports were . . . unsatisfactory. He wasn't following precedent. They got all balled up trying to explain. They're sharp fellows, but narrow. I asked if he was like John of the desert. Some jumped at this, but others were adamant he was a very different kind of cat. I understood that I would have to hear him for myself.

He had a way, I grant you. It was the manner in which he talked about *Life*, as if it were something other than the living. He acted as if we were a bunch of dullards who had read everything in a book while he had had adventures, knew it all from experience. But he said all that without a trace of brash callowness. Why? He was always speaking of his Father. When he spoke of himself, it was only because he was the envoy of his Father. And that's when I remembered that I had seen him before.

I was a green fellow myself then, barely older than the clerks sitting at the feet of their masters. One day, a boy wandered into the Temple Court where the scholars gave forth. He seemed very comfortable among us. Not casual, but courteous, like a young prince offering hospitality to well-regarded guests. He listened well to our disputations. To speak about God, it entails no small risk. Yet when the boy asked us questions, when he dared to make assertions — it was with the boldness of intimacy. Well, his parents came. Apparently they'd assumed he was with relatives in the caravan. The youth was some rustic from the north. I'd sometimes wondered what happened to him.

And here I am, wrapped in the care of one acquainted with dangers, meeting in the secrecy of night. No doubt, he will be disappointed that I am still quite stupid.

The lawgiver

One of their great misnomers still carried as a talisman against the fear of the unknown: the concept of law. So, the law of gravity, of non-contradiction, the law of conservation of energy, an eye for an eye, and so on. Naturally, when they tried their hand at theology, they considered the God in these terms. The God, also, was a giver of law. Did not Moses say as much? And when the divine right of kings followed in the wake of voluntarist notions of freedom and nominalist reckonings of the individual, it was not surprising that law turned into the capricious will of the absolute sovereign.

Only later did some speculate that the law was a translation, something handed on through angelic emissaries and perhaps nothing more than a rough palimpsest of an altogether different action. The worldly powers, however, preferred the myth of law for once the kings had devolved to the concept of the will of the people, everything was permitted.

Subversion

The rabboni was speaking. It's important to remember that it was one story. He insisted upon that. I don't think everyone understood, not at first, anyway, but upon the elders it began to dawn, what he was saying. You could see it begin to flicker just below awareness, and then they began to shift a bit, shrug their shoulders, betray signs of agitation. It was a lovely story. He was shrewd and learned. You could pick up on the allusions. Sometimes he shoved them right under your nose so he could remain quiet; he shouted quietly. But there could be no doubt the young rabbi was aiming high, very high. It was the founding story he was telling, only it wasn't quite right. It wasn't a pious, clever rendition. There was subversion in it — and even the venerable ones, nodding sleepily, opened an aged eye and wondered at him.

A charming story

"The story begins," he said, "with a lost sheep." I myself have never trusted shepherds. They are a devious lot, showing up from Lord knows where, often enough drunken louts, and stinking of their flock to boot. But there was a certain charm, I admit, the way that fella told it. Their elders were listening hard. You could see that there was a subtle conversation, something besides the literal surface. He was shrewd, I guess, that fella. Sheep, of course, are dim. They get themselves lost, in a fix, and what do they do? They go all wobbly, crumble into themselves, can't move at all, just sit there bleating so the wolves know where to find them. Sheep are imbeciles.

This fella was clearly casting himself in the role of the shepherd, though he often winked at his audience, as if he knew shepherds were scoundrels and he was talking to a bunch of them whilst telling his tale about a dim sheep. There was something in the economics I couldn't follow. Why would you leave ninety-nine sheep to go after a smelly, not very bright straggler? But he made you feel for that wooly creature, said something about David and the prophet Nathan and a lamb kept not for meat, but as a cherished pet. In itself, a ridiculous image, and why should a poor man spend what little he has to feed what ought to fill his own belly?

Still, that young rabbi had them sitting on the edge of their seats. Some Greeks I know might have asked a pertinent question or two I'd like to have heard him answer. Once, he even looked my way. It was almost uncanny, as if he sensed an outsider, a skeptic. I don't know, really, except that he seemed to be saying that the shepherd was not primarily interested in what was useful, that he did not calculate value apart from love, and that every fool sheep was important, so that expedience was foolish and foolishness wise.

I heard he came to a bad end, which is predictable. The machine swallows up the interesting whole and spits out the gristle.

Listening

Soren Blake had rented a domicile in a working class district, though because of the age of the place, it retained an old world charm. Iron work, dark green awnings and flower boxes outside the windows marked the residence as a respectable member of the neighborhood. It was located on the second floor above a bakery. In the morning, the smell of pastries whispered suggestively to the sleeper's stomach, entering dreams to plea for a happy tryst. Not to be left out, the hours after dusk also wished to serenade the house. On certain nights, accordion music from a dance hall drifted up with the amiable assurance of a Saint Bernard puppy that one could not possibly object. A train line carrying vegetables from the nearby farms to the city added its own comfortable syncopation, mixing in with the worker's dance steps.

Many evenings, Soren remained in the house listening even unto the wee hours. However, he was not listening to the festivities or the rhythmic hum of commerce. He waited for something he'd heard in the desert where silence is palpably greater than the absence of noise. In the desert, Soren had made a strange discovery. It would seem that death is quite egalitarian. For long it had been treated as commonplace. How leveling it is to be quenched into nothingness. It might seem that way from the outside, just as motion in the abstract could be stopped at any hypothetical intermediate point as reified stasis, an action separate from the richly woven event that precedes all our memories, discursive reasoning and history, apparently continuing on even after we have left the stage. From within, however, though they say dead men tell no tales, perhaps it is a matter of listening. Nothingness as nullity, as absolute metaphysical zero may well be outside the aptitude of the creature.

A faerie kingdom

It was the day after the traitor had left. There was a silence about the whole place. Everyone was looking sideways at each other, to see if it had really happened. We knew, but hardly anyone believed it all the same. It just didn't make any sense. Not to them. I was not surprised. He was bad seed, always was. Of course, I didn't say anything. There was no need. It would have been — undignified to remonstrate, to express, in a soft judicious tone, that this is what comes of indulgence.

He must have known. I found him puttering about in the apiary. It's one of the places father goes when he wants to relax or meditate. He likes to watch the bees, to care for them. When I was younger, he once spent a charmed hour showing me the tiny entrance to the oblong shelters, rows upon rows of them. He'd almost caress the mud walls as if he were casting a spell of protection upon the industrious inhabitants within.

I saw that he heard my steps, the slightest acknowledgement, a tremor of movement in the dark brows wintering beneath silver locks. But he didn't look up. That time, when I was yet a child, he told the Egyptian story that made out the bees to be divine creatures, tears of the sun god, *Re*. That was all a fable, but father found it amusing. He pointed out that when we took with us the wealth of Egypt, part of those riches was the craft of caring for these "divine little beasties."

After the betrayal, he was silent a long while as I watched him play with his village of winged nectar. At length, I wasn't quite sure he was speaking to me or to himself, the soft way he spoke, he said, "Look here, though Moses and Joshua announced a land of milk and honey, the Syrian bee is small and nasty, unwilling to cultivate for the gentle queen." Then he raised upon his finger like an ethereal signet a singular faerie tenant and laughed. Yes, with mirth that made one forget he had men posted at all the watchtowers, lest the ingrate bring with him a bought army to storm what remained of the kingdom. He looked at me with delight, as if he were conveying a great gift in announcing it.

"This bee is fat and docile and generous . . . and from Anatolia!"

The Akedah

"Listen, Sky, the *Akedah* is the binding," said Rabbi Naftali. When the UnNameable called out to Abraham, the Father of Lights was asking if the aged patriarch was yet up for the Great Work, the daring love, creation. The Mystery always beckons. From out of the whirlwind there comes the necessity of consent. That the creature who is nothing, raised up from the dust, must nonetheless respond with willingness, that is the strange kindness, the fearful courtesy.

And Abraham said, "*hinneni*," that is, "Here I am, ready my Lord."

Into the Wild

The problem was fraught with difficulties which he could not share, even with the woman. They were thrown like seed into the wind. Some family caught them. They came forgetful and ignorant, still trailing the penumbra of worlds. How he would rejoice to embrace them, his brothers and sisters, to gather them together to dwell in the House of the Father.

But they would not have it. Such fragile, jagged, willful tormentors of themselves and others, mistaking the shallows for depths, turning their face from honor, mouthing a desire to be free whilst fleeing with all their heart the call to liberty, how to tell them when they could never understand?

He would have to bear their incomprehension, bring it with him, carrying as a treasure the misshapen lives that were almost nothing, the tiny, savage thoughts of a shrewd animal, their anguished hearts and vicious actions. He alone had not forgotten. She would want to understand, to help him at least. The others did not wish for this, though they believed themselves open and honest folk. They were lying as they could hardly help themselves. And so the anointing had come as it must when he entered those dark waters, rising from an abyss none could fathom.

Blinkered by dullness, they only perceived the mud brown waters of the Jordan. The forerunner had to point it out to a few of his chosen, this event that was the beginning of the transformation of the cosmos. Already it was death, death at the beginning, which they never guessed. And so, ignorant of this, the disciples of the great friend left immediately for the only true adventure, unfortunately beset by miseries. The scribes would find that interesting, the bit about cousin John, might consider it all a convenient bit of nepotism. Later, their guild would discover much more elegant ways to remain unimpressed.

She was the only one who had an inkling having stored in her heart little moments, all grown from the silent, trembling majesty of her consent. Everything great begins in silence. It grows invisibly and slowly in the spirit, so that no one notices, not even the one who broods like a mother hen upon the gift. Then one day a man acts and people are astonished.

"Where did that come from?" they wonder.

The meaning of being chosen

The question of God is something they had stopped asking, because they thought they knew. Oh, they were not lacking in trepidation. They still blanched before the Holy of Holies, before that great absence that the blaspheming pagan general mistook for nothing at all. Yet still, all things considered, they'd rather started to think, not in egregious complacency for the most part, though there was that, but simply as settled fact, the God was theirs because the God had chosen.

To be chosen was nearly to possess, at least, to have a special privilege, to know things from the inside, not half-baked and dim like the vile idolaters. And so, it became a tradition, this interpretation that was an abiding, sometimes barely conscious awareness, the relation, the covenant, the treaty with the Unnameable. Later, millennia later, after horrors far worse than Babylonian captivity had occurred, after the destruction of the Temple was so far away it was half myth, that glorious boast of Herod's, philosophers spoke of modalism and middle knowledge and possible worlds. To be chosen was conceived as a sort of selection from half-real imagined permutations, the way a gamer settles upon an avatar.

All that was forgetting. It was forgetting to distinguish between the unique singularity and an individual. The latter may indeed be found indexed, stored as one potential inflection of assorted characteristics, but none of that approaches the hidden chamber of divine largesse that does not consider possibilities, but only the beloved in all her irreplaceable splendor. Here, we return to the original, nearly innocent presumption, for the quality of being chosen is deeply related to the uniqueness of the divine. And if the Jews had understood all that — well, who does understand all that?

The good son

My brother is dutiful. That's what everyone says, especially my brother. He is a fine son, a very font of rectitude. The servants, yes, but even the freemen respect him, because he is quite irreproachable, always doing what is expected and right. True, they don't like him very much. Folks don't go out of their way to tell a joke in his presence.

I know him better, better than he knows himself. He believes what everyone believes, so he does not grasp that he, too, pricks against the goad. All his obedience seethes with irritation and is likely to erupt in unaccountable fury, like that time he lashed out at the water boy who tripped and disturbed his game of droughts. He is tamed by the approbation of the folk, balm to his pride, yet no ways is he zealous for our father's honor. He thinks of that far less than I, which is the irony in it all. And then sometimes he is not bothered because, well, a certain native dullness.

The blockhead

Lampides boeticus, a small sapphire butterfly with gossamer wings, as a boy, he had often seen them in his beloved mountains of the north, near Mount Hermon. There from the middle of July to as late as September, one might discover the daylight flight of such jewels, but never so far south in the barrens. Yet a single such Longtail Blue as they are known to lepidopterists hovered like a flower's dream above the dried out husk of a fallen tree.

A certain sort of nasty child (it is usually a boy) lusts to capture the glimmering flight, to pin the poor creature into agonized stasis . . . this refusal of the gift often ended in display cases filled with wings precariously preserved against the light of the sun and prone to desiccate into dust. The Man called to the butterfly and the sociable creature danced gently above the fingers of his right hand. A soft shock of azure velvet covered the thorax. It radiated a burst of color that became indigo and violet held by a border of golden mocha at the outer margins of the wings. It was in the lightning flux of the moment, glowing eternally in the Father's regard. Fluttering softly into the air, it suddenly took flight, seemed to sense the spleen in a questioning voice.

It was a jolt when the voice said, "Son of God, if you are the Son of God, haven't you forgotten them? Tens of thousands have died in misery since you came out here to brood. Not that I blame you, their sniveling is a bit much and they are so stupid, though one shouldn't wonder at the dim bipeds, really. What a misfortune to grasp their mortality. What an earthquake in a tea cup, eh? So of course they want assurances. For starters, you might put an end to blind need. How much violence and selling themselves, how much abuse from sheer hunger."

The Slanderer was always the most tiresome moralist, smugly certain of its rectitude and of the cogency of its logic. "If you are the Son of God . . . ." The Man could barely hear the noxious buzzing of the voice. One had to attend carefully to parse out the semblance of language in the self-regarding tirade. Was it spite, disingenuous uncertainty, the atrocious vulgarity of thinking it had produced a goading ploy by shifting into the subjunctive? The entire tissue of absurdity was one blockhead misapprehension after another. As if the Father gloried in creating a cosmic prison house, delighted in handing out death sentences . . . .

The injustice of time

An Egyptian monk tells the story of a young man condemned to die. It is one of those unfortunate narratives where it appears the youth was repentant of his crimes; I forget what they may have been. The witnesses to his execution were sympathetic to his lack of years, attentive to the apparent reformation of his character. They were heartily saddened that he must die.

It was probably unimaginative and perhaps rather callous that they could see no way around the law, but that is not the fundamental interest. One day, maybe years later, having lived more fully, an old man would have equally found death. No, it is the words the young man delivered to those watching the event of his passage through an invisible frontier that persist. He said to them, "I am more than my life."

The youth had grasped in an instant of profound insight that time could not do justice to his unique being. The imminence of the gallows concentrated his spirit. And this is also true for the nonagenarian and the gravely cheated who are aborted in the womb. But how could he have known this?

A throw of the dice

I wanted to show him, because he refused to turn from an impossible, reckless action. From the beginning, he had set his face on Jerusalem. He had this way. When I talked with Caiaphas, I tried to explain, but that fellow was all grim politics. The dreaming Nazarene had to die. It was as simple as that. Rome wouldn't tolerate anything else, and besides, like a lot of those charismatic yokels from the countryside, he had bizarre ideas. Interesting, yes, but foreign to Moses, which for that calculating fellow was a euphemism for the decorous, prudent way.

Well, he *was* always shocking them, those fishermen from the north. There was a gulf between us. Iscariot and his book learning; they'd roll their eyes. I tried to be amiable. It just didn't take. A man can't force himself to feel differently than he does. Oh, they loved him in their rough, dim way. Later, you know how they are, the fishmongers put out a common story, convenient and sure to please. Iscariot must have done it because he had his hand in the company purse. Those city boys are sharp that way. Cheap village gossip, that's the sort of cowardly stunt that came readily to their minds. Two thousand years and the folks are still satisfied.

Now Caiaphas had entirely forgotten that the high priest was the embodiment of the Temple. *He* remembered. He was telling them who the genuine high priest truly was. Or maybe Caiaphas just pretended to miss the point. Maybe he saw too well, refused to acknowledge rivalry with some hick upstart. Oh, the Anointed was clever, too. I counted on that, his capacity to surprise and astound them. He was a born tactician. It was the strategy that was all wrong. A ludicrous endgame, it could only conclude in ruin. So I risked everything on a throw of the dice.

Domestic mystery

The next episode, remember, it is one story, each an iteration of the other. A woman has lost a coin. Over the years, this story more than the others, folks don't know, it translates the least.

First, know that the house the Anointed imagines is the house everyone would have understood. It is not a cozy residential affair, a place out in Santa Monica where you invite the neighbors over for barbecue. The intense heat of Palestine was part of the equation, but so was building material. What was cheap and abundant was stone. And the way to adapt to conditions, all things considered, was to build low, digging below ground, with narrow doors and tiny openings like arrow ports in a medieval castle covered over in fabric for windows. Domestic life was dark, even in the day. Lose a coin in a house like that; it wasn't a matter of looking under the seat cushions!

Remember, he'd told of a fella in the outlands. Now, he tells of a wife and life close at hand. But in that house, light is rare commodity. What does it mean? Because maybe it's just ordinary time, understand? Amidst doing the wash and fixing meals and taking the kids to football practice, and also, probably, parents grow old, friends die, the job goes bad. And a woman has to hold the house together, that's what she signed on for, but she's lost the coin.

That coin, it's the kingdom, that is what recurs, it's what every-one dreams of when they accept the challenge, an infinite yearning hidden in building a family, raising children, so the joy of finding it in *that* house is learning to see aright which is seeing amidst the anguish and the harried times, as much as the births, the weddings, the festive seasons.

Yet this is still a bit short of square: when the woman recovers the coin, she invites in the neighbors to celebrate. And everyone thinks they know what *that* is about. Some dimly see it as a sharing of good fortune; others, more acute, that the woman can now be seen because radiant in original bridal honor. There is more. Every beat in this song is provocative, the shepherd who leaves behind ninety-nine to rescue the forlorn lost one, the father who provokes his industrious, responsible son by rejoicing at the return of the ungrateful spendthrift, each illustrates a subversion of ordinary economy, so if you want to get to the heart of it, there's likely something foolish at the core of this tale, too, and it can't be the simple reclamation of lost wealth. It might announce a mysterious expansion of what is taken for granted, the times trivial, neglected, the so-called unheroic moments not even treasured in the store-house of memory. A home is a foray of the original garden into exiled lands.

The lost coin

"We have lost much, nu?" Rabbi Naftali looked so intently at Sky that she shook her head in agreement lest she offend. "There are ages when wisdom is free and open, when the babe babbles a lullaby carried from the springs of the Sephiroth and old men dream dreams. But we are far from that, dear one. It was once common coin, the midwife and the peddler knew as much as the sage, how to read a symbol. Today, try to explain that gold, and the sun, and honey are the same music played by different instruments. All will look at you as daft, then turn to important matters, their wars, their love affairs, how to make money."

The unloved middle

Some vates begin with the end. I mean, that's what they see. Then they get a glimpse of the principals and connect them. Or it might be the other way around, that's pretty popular, too. It might be an image, a phrase, anything, really, provided it grabs you. From that speck of agitation, the poet keeps brooding, secreting little bits of soul, portions of finite, irretrievable time until the pearl of some artifact arises. Or to change metaphors, start at the beginning and pull, see where the thread takes you.

The second part, it's the middle of the story they say is difficult. Lots of artists treat it as a necessary chore. The interest isn't there, but naturally, you can't have a beginning and an end without a middle to justify the difference. Though, there is another type who is skeptical. They don't quite see that there is properly speaking anything like an origin at all. Rather, it's arbitrary, you could start a thread anywhere, but strictly speaking, the idea of a beginning is false and probably an imposition of will. Any founding, by that calculus, is already guilty.

The same goes, ipso facto, for ends, which attempt to make of temporary, finite conditions a teleology thrown out of time altogether, a kind of fascist eternity. The hippie version of this philosophy is that arrival is illusory, only the journey matters. A reversal of judgment suddenly makes the unloved middle the point of it all — though all that is nonsense, pseudo-clever, Mumbo Junkie fakery that never gets beyond an either/or, so never suspects a more generous mystery.

The nature of an icon

The feeling Soren had, the more he thought about it, was that she had come to him from the realm of story. It was not that she simply told him a story, no, she came from story. Without the story, there was no Rachel, she was born in the story. Men were apt to find this utterly marvelous; a story was a made thing, a lesser realm, lacking the substance of reality. Still, how often the dull and repetitive individuals encountered in so-called real life paled in comparison to the most finely wrought characters of fiction. Why should the latter attain a vibrancy lacking in the supposedly living?

In those early years in the city, Soren was only beginning to hear the music of silence. The nature of an icon eluded him. He did not yet know that light is shattering revelation, the invocation of Spirit. He did not know that *the life of God is the womb and guardian of everything that exists*, or rather, he was in the forgetting where the pleroma is shielded from our eyes lest vision render us so still that only the Vendakar could regard one.

The Spirit of surprise

Sarah's laughter, how human. She mistook time, thought that the lost past was not living for the Ancient of Days. No miracle, to make an old woman fecund. It was not the tired, sagging body that bore fruit, but the young womb, for nothing good is rendered to oblivion by the Spirit of surprise. Like Hannah who bore Samuel and Elizabeth who gave birth to the angel man, the springtime of barren hopes announces the coming of a prophet. The fluidity of times enters into the heart of the new babe; but all men are capable of prophecy if they honor the silence.

Martha's Confession

What you can't imagine, not properly, is the waiting. People got it wrong later. They thought he had a bad flu or some disease. It wasn't like that. My brother was always . . . different. He didn't get on. He wasn't good at life, you know. We were well-born, of course, or it would have been a disaster. Eleazar would have bottomed out, I suppose. But as it was, he could go on. He was a dreamer. That's what everyone thought. They could smile about it because money. If you have it you're eccentric. If not, they've all kinds of words for you and none of them good.

Things changed when we met rabboni. Well, everything changed, but for Eleazar, life suddenly made sense. That's what you have to get clear above all else. I'd listened to Eleazar's stories my whole life. They were charming, sweet, and sad. Sad, because you knew he was going to be hurt by life, even though we were rich. And sad because only a gentle, kind heart would notice the beauty he would in small moments, the way cook hummed to the cats in the morning or a wild fern reached out through a crack in the wall.

All those little enigmatic, half-hidden beauties that were luring my brother, the way he saw things, the sort of idea that excited him and hardly anyone else, they clicked when the Anointed entered our lives.

What you don't understand is that he wasn't sick. My brother didn't have a fever. It was the invisible flame consuming him from within. His entire existence had been a seeking and then he suddenly found this incredible friend. Yes, friend. Do you know what it is like to be the friend of God? It's fire. Your soul is scorched. It was as if decades of slow progress had been compressed into a few weeks and Eleazar's body couldn't take it.

But the worst, no, the strangest, is that none of it was a surprise. They'd worked it out, you see. The Master knew he was dying. Eleazar was supposed to die. That's why he'd waited and my brother wanted that. I think it was some kind of initiation. When he came back from the grave, called by the Lord of times, of course, everyone was floored, dumbfounded. The clerics didn't like it a bit.

Did he say anything? You'd think, but he didn't. I suppose he didn't have the words. Some folks said he was silent because there wasn't anything but black on the other side. Just nothing. But

I don't believe that. There was something in his eyes and when he spoke, people would jump a little, like they were scared he was going to surprise them with a pronouncement that would be upsetting.

And then, you know, we went to Marseilles. My brother shocked us all by becoming a leader.

Naftali

One day, Soren Blake strayed from his usual paths. There was something in his heart that told him to take a different way, so he turned left where he usually turned right and kept on going. He chatted with a fellow in a kiosk that sold colorful balloons artfully compressed into odd shapes, poodles or dirigibles, for instance. Then he followed the sounds of joyous celebration until he came to a gathering of Hasidim. A marriage, perhaps. It wasn't clear to Soren, but he looked on wistfully. One of the young men in their number stood out from the rest. He leapt high into the air in a kind of dancing on the edge of flight.

"Careful, friend, or you might forget to come back down," shouted Soren.

A week later, a group of young men were entering a brownstone which contained the home of their chief rabbi. One of them struck Soren as familiar. It was the dancer. Probably a student at yeshiva, the youth listened carefully to a learned disputation taking place amongst his elders with a quiet, serious face; you had to know him well before you'd see his child like grin and appreciate the innocence that made him a natural adventurer of the soul. The young man happened to look up in the vague direction of where Soren was watching them from the window of his apartment. It was likely a trick of fancy that he seemed to nod. Why should the Jew recall a passing stranger from seven days ago? Three days after that, the Hasid stood outside his door and knocked.

"I have a message for you from *En Sof*," said Naftali.

The stonecutter's art

"You're a long way from home," said Soren.

The young man shrugged. "It's not Shabbat. I rode my bicycle. I left it next to the bakery."

"You should try the éclairs."

"There is nothing more important than the discovery of reality," declared the Hasidic youth.

"I quite agree, start with the éclairs. Is this your message?"

"In a way," said Naftali, who suddenly felt the need to introduce himself. "My father and my grandfather are rabbis. Before that, we have some artisans who merely studied Torah."

"I have been listening since I got here," said Soren. "It's hard, with all the noise, though I think the God rather likes all that, everything a bit wild and full of hijinks."

"Yes," said Naftali. "But you have been angry with the Un-Nameable. You do not understand the bliss of the Holy, but allow yourself anger."

"Don't you?"

The Hasid peered with guileless eyes, they were sometimes more green than brown, a changeable hazel. "I do not understand the Holy, that is why I am asked to trust," he said. "How can we find Him if we do not cry out to Him? Why would we cry out if we did not seek? Why would we seek if we were not lost?"

"Folks don't like to think they are lost," said Soren. "They like to think they know where they are."

"When I entered your house, you spoke wisdom. We are far from home," said Naftali. "You are going to start the work of stone. You have been thinking about it. You should start. The stone cutter is an ancient art. You will find that you must create, it is the only way one comes to know. All our rabbis understand this."

Soren was surprised. He *had* been thinking about it. "I don't have any experience with it. At least, I don't remember it," he said.

"We are one," said Naftali. "The gnosis is held by one for all. But you have this *techne* in your past; the past you have forgotten."

Soren had actually been thinking of Rachel, about her mystery. And then he had thought, he had this knowledge too from his past, that etymologically there is a connection between *charakter* "image" and *charax* "to sharpen into a point" and *charasso* "to engrave," but to carve an image into flesh and blood, that is not so easy, a work of the intimate eternal.

Why am I even speaking to you?

And he said to them, "You are from that which is below, I am from that which is above; you are from this cosmos, I am not from this cosmos. Therefore I said to you that you will die in your sins, for if you do not have faith that I AM, you will die in your sins."

So they said to him, "Who are you?"

Jesus said to them, "To begin with, why am I even speaking to you?"

Night in his pocket

"*—an animal hunted, stopping in some ill-chosen covert to consider the wickedness of man.*"

And they said that he carried night in his pocket. How else to explain it, how he could be surrounded, caught in the crush of people — or led to the edge of a cliff, yet escape? He was like that; provoking. Even in Gethsemane, that droll, sad quip about a kiss, about how he was readily to be found preaching, both in the north and in the city, surrounded by crowds of curious or adoring folk; and sceptics, we sent our lot, maybe even secret followers, there were those, too, but available, though they waited for dwindled numbers.

It was a boast about his popularity, that's what some thought later, but it could hardly have been more wrong. He never courted or desired the approval of men. He knew them too well, the value of their glory. No, it was a different joke, that they had come into his night, yes, *his night* I tell you. That night is baptism, communion, divine abyss. He was telling them, even then, that they would never have caught him had he not wished it so.

Paradoxical word

What it was, Soren still could not fathom, he would probably never fathom, yet he began to have a feel for it, like he'd gotten it round to the tip of his tongue, but it was in his fingers, in the chisel and the scraping and the listening. He couldn't work without listening to what the stone was saying. And what did it say? It said naming is unmaking, which seemed counter to his efforts, but the more he was obedient to that paradoxical word, the more the form would emerge from the chaos of rough matter. You do not start with form. You do not discover form. Utter human pomposity, to believe that in thinking one gains control, that an idea is sufficient.

A Portrait with a Cat

A little girl looks at a book with a picture of a cat
  Who wears a fluffy collar and has a green velvet frock.
  Her lips, very red, are half opened in a sweet reverie.
  This takes place in 1910 or 1912, the painting bears no date.
  It was painted by Marjorie C. Murphy, an American
  Born in 1888, like my mother, more or less.
  I contemplate the painting in Grinnell, Iowa,
  At the end of the century. That cat with his collar
  Where is he? And the girl? Am I going to meet her,
  One of those mummies with rouge, tapping with their canes?
  But this face: a tiny pug nose, round cheeks,
  Moves me so, quite like a face that I, suddenly awake

In the middle of the night, saw by my side on a pillow.
The cat is not here, he is in the book, the book in the painting.
No girl, and yet she is here, before me
And has never been lost. Our true encounter
Is in the zones of childhood. Amazement called love,
A thought of touching, a cat in velvet.
— *Czeslaw Milosz,* "A Portrait with a Cat," Berkeley, 1985

Symbolon

They made it out to be a simple platitude, the kind dear to moralists, as if it was still calculation. They were always pretending, seeing how far they might suppose themselves able to dare, a game of chicken where they sought the very last moment one could progress into the abyss without abandoning the hope of return.

Decision then became retreat into safe quarters, though it was nothing like that really. Revulsion, despair, near disbelief that life could turn out that way, yes, but not calculation. It remained desire, thirst, yearning for freedom, because in the end, that's what we are, or at least, not less, not separate from the heart's search.

I kept hearing those words father whispered into my ear when I left: "Everything, my boy, is symbol." It was an odd thing to say, no? What could he have meant? When it all went sideways, I thought about it.

Far-seeing, he knew the path I chose could not but disappoint, and *then* temptation would come. Note: *then, after,* just when the moralists think the turning vindicates them. Everything would appear miserable, priced, worthless all at once. But if I recollected, I would know that father's kingdom is *symbolon*, not to be calculated or discerned by ordinary reckoning.

Eden

Long ago, so fresh, and new, it was before time, there was a garden. So remarkable was this lush earth, this fragrant enchantment of play and delight in discovery that it was nearly forgotten, its beauty so radiant, so innocent, full of child-like joy and promise, no one could bear to think of it as lost, to admit the exile that had come to them. "Nostalgia," they spat, a pathetic legend. And further, the trace of the unremembered, so perhaps an unfelt pain, he was sure it was still there, in their embraces, which were always both driven by pleasure and threaded with pain, every touch a wounding, never pure of harm, no matter how sweetly intended.

This duality is the mark of Cain, the devastation, so that every psyche, emerging from the soup of maternal oneness, knew in its bones the fear, the danger to emerge, to be was to be towards death. And yet, that appalling nihilation, the drop in the gut that cuts off speech, should not be. "No, no," the heart says in despair before the doom of the dear one. Eden, what then was your time? Something unique, sourced and flowing differently, not inexorably yielding to the gravity of pain and loss and mortality, some other future, for the future was meant to be life, not death. Stories in that garden did not cower, knew not shame.

Singular adventure

What was so hard for them to understand, truly coming from the nothing, so that if they looked down like Simon Peter on the Sea of Galilee, they felt their weight, they felt the body as weight, as separation, and they did not know the water as mirror, as receptive between, the chthonic roots rising to the surface to meet the divine kiss. Naturally, Peter began to sink with the thought that after all, he is not a god, but deathbound and trying something crazy.

But really, those roots are nearly phantom, the sophianic tap root where everything is open, porous, a divine dance. What was intended as invitation to joy was now encountered as vulnerability, as something to be defended against hostile forces — other men, disease, the natural world. Hence, the tiny figment of self, that first, almost somnolent acknowledgement, yet so far from destiny, from Uncreated Light, reaches out, learning as knowing danger, suspicious. This is what they all take to be the way of things, their wisdom.

Only he knew differently, not emerging from the dark womb of slumbering content to discover daunting rivals, but rather adventuring forth from the mysterious plenitude to invent in time the eternal verities. Behind every feeling for life, sometimes it was more like a dream, that this grain of sand should sing, that the gems buried deep radiated from soulscape, there was an intimation that etched in each being was a face that gifted every face its eyes, its mouth, its vision, its word. Its kiss was the face of faces.

Sand in the shorts

What did they expect? They thought, that is, they believed that they were the keepers of the promise. That is what the covenant between themselves and He who shall be who He shall be intended. The strange openness of that revelation they remembered, but labored to forget. Every time the Law was invoked, every time Moses was named, they clung to the history of that pledge that constituted the people. Surely, the long suffering of Israel was the sacred price, the sign of privilege that preserved an intimate knowledge of the singular, unique One who otherwise was utterly beyond naming. Indeed, the wisest of them held within their hearts the secret of their longing ignorance. They alone, those forgotten ones, the *anawim*, kept within their hearts what even the priests for the most part had somehow failed to endure.

The prophets, well, they had fallen silent, before that desert hermit, that shouter caused a ruckus, touched a political nerve. And yet, the promise tenaciously held through desperate years, lives stretched out into seeming abandonment, this promise is what the prophets gave. The human heart reached out and some unspeakable power, it felt like death, you couldn't get near it, you started to unravel, to break apart into dust and grief and shame, but then there was the beauty, and joy, and — odd, kindness, but not like human kindness — burning, but so lovely, incandescent beauty; no, love, just love, as if you never knew that word before, so that if only you could forget yourself, die without falling into the fear of reflection, that proud cowardice, you'd find yourself past it, past all that, soaring into the song of life.

But now, the promise was well established, codified. The priests and the scribes had tamed it, made it manageable, something you could accept. It was hard, often, yes, and yet not so hard. It didn't ask of you the unimaginable, the impossible. And so, the promise had shrunk to a proper sized ambition. Until he came. He came and told them they had not reckoned upon the promise at all. He told them, no, he just appeared and they knew, that was the galling sand in the shorts, that embarrassment, that cruel, humiliating realization. They knew that they did not want the promise, not on those terms, which were the only ones there ever were.

The spy

I know him still. A devious, spoiled child. Father is overjoyed. His love blinds him to justice. That bedraggled, stinking, grasping, ungrateful actor — is still a poison barb, subtle spearhead. Does he think I do not know he is yet spy, biding time till the gates lie open to the armies of the dead?

The language of nard

And what did they think when he said, "Amen, I tell you, wherever these good tidings are proclaimed, in the whole world, what this woman did will also be told, as a memorial to her"? They thought her extravagant, tormented, emotionally unhinged. The room was filled with emotion as fragrant as her gift. Embarrassment, incomprehension, disgust, at best in some, vague, puzzled sympathy.

How understand when they could only see in my beloved an arrogant upstart, addled prophet, something smaller than themselves made to fit within familiar boxes? Good tidings might mean wealth, honor, a copious harvest, or the overthrow of the Romans. Whatever they surmised, it wasn't the kingdom. And so the prophecy that the perfume of nard would be remembered unto the Age could only strike them as senseless.

They did not hear in it a pledge of love. My tears, my long, lustrous hair caressing his feet, the broken glass and aromatic unguent were my own sibylline tongue. He answered with a promise, an oracle legible only to the loving heart. And yet, one did hear, if not the truth of it, the strangeness. Later, for crude ears, it was made into a simple tale fit for supposedly simple peasants. Iscariot was angry because he was greedy, a thief. No. Judas felt the Mysterious Unknown and his spirit balked.

Where the other is found

He saw her in his dreams, Rachel beyond the stars. Already, he sensed that she came to him from the heart of eternity, only there, the true beginning. She might yet be only a story, though he'd held her hand and felt her breath upon his neck. *I have always loved you*, he thought. *Before loving you, I did not exist.* He knew this as indisputable truth, though he could not find her in the times. She was hidden from him, yet calling his name. *You must shatter, break into pure fragrance where the Other is found*, she said. The God is not captured in moral teaching, to be picked up and dropped at the whim of some convenient persona, a *jiva*, the mask you wear journeying the ages.

Vates through and through

"No, I do not understand him, but I know him a little," said the Elder. "Enough to know that those who claim to believe him often get it wrong. They think of him as walking through a pre-ordained role, as if there were no risk and all he had to do was get his lines right. But the way is shown in the faring. The faring together of the human and the divine is receptive anticipation, the gift of energies. '*We love we know not what . . . There are invisible ways of conveyance by which some great thing doth touch our soul and by which we tend to it.*'

Was it simply that mankind's crying need and its dreamless contentment wore him down? What did he seek in the high places and in the desert? The life that does not show itself in the world. '*Do you not feel yourself drawn with the expectation and desire of some Great Thing?*'

To be sure, whatever Father means, it is no thing. Nor an idea, a static principle, something easily demonstrated. He seeks the high places because he is telling a story by living it out. The Father is known and discovered through creative likening. He is finding his way as he goes. Whatever else, he is Vates through and through."

The new eyes

There was a physician, Swiss perhaps, around the turn of the 20th century, not so far away, but does it matter? He'd performed an operation on a blind boy. The boy was born blind, a congenital condition. There was a man in the gospels said to be born blind. When the Anointed healed him, it was a process. At first, it was like trees walking. Maybe that was natural, the man had nothing to compare it with. But over time, and rather quickly, it is said that the man understood, he saw, one imagines though who can say, like other men. It was something of a scandal. The elites, the Levites, the keepers of lore found it questionable. They didn't approve, going outside the prescribed order, but they say it happened.

Anyway, complaints were made, they asked the old parents, folks are sly, always looking to game the system, but deep down, the investigators had to admit that if the parents and the fella were acting, it was better than Olivier. It was different with the boy healed by the Swiss doctor. No one said it was a miracle, exactly, though modern medicine was certainly clever. Only the result wasn't the same. The lad didn't like it.

The eyes worked fine, the mechanics of the organ restored to operational, but the boy couldn't make anything out. It wasn't even trees walking. Everything was a mash of color, weird, shapeless assault. The visual data was not assimilated as information, but rather a riot of meaningless chaos. It wasn't a world that meant. The boy refused the eyes, went back to the dark, where the world was available again free from the monsters.

What no one had anticipated was how much nurturing plays a role in the capacity to interpret and to know. Turns out meaning is not mechanical, the mind did not have a default setting apart from culture, the thousands of ways, often implicit, by which one learns to perceive the other. And what if there were greater eyes bringing dimensions of the real that disorient, put in question the narrow band of comfortable certitudes?

Wisdom of the vates

If the world you are living in is actually quite different than what you think it is, your reasoning could be wildly mistaken. It might be that what is commonly honored or what is deemed desirable may suffer from distortion, perhaps to the edge of madness. Every man and woman is a storyteller, carries with them like sacred images some memory or a word borrowed, whispered, often enough proclaimed in cinema or glossy magazine. Learning to discern, to remark the roots of the image, the path of the narrative, that is the wisdom of the vates.

It may be that he imagined differently than the rest. He was telling a story no one had told before, so that his listeners failed to recognize the logic in it, a unique logic, perhaps the primal *ratio*. And now that centuries have passed, that initial, compelling, gentle meaning is now perhaps covered over by our own concepts, our own forays into history and forgetting. What he told them was that they did not know the Father, that when they spoke with authority, they were stealing, because they did not know. They came from nothing, after all. And when they rebelled in spite or sullen ingratitude, these too, did not know.

Even today, when the priests and the sages and the common people try to figure out what he meant, they likely forget that he said that his actions were ever only a dance that mirrored the radiance of a hidden sun. When he told that story of an anxious papa, he was telling them something of what *he* was doing. And when the father forgot his dignity and ran out upon the road to meet the miserable ingrate that was a significant beat in the story to consider. And so was the resentment of the tolerably dutiful son who could not abide festivity and honor wasted on a scoundrel. It never entered his thought, no, his heart, that the kingdom might be so different, that when his brother returned, his inheritance was not thereby less, but increased.

Moreover, it may be that the audience was intended to contemplate that he knew humanity, and this you will not properly guess, that he knew it intimately in a manner unique to himself, and so he understood how far along the road he would have to travel in order to meet each one of them, how deeply into shadows, into monstrous hells, how far into death some might request he journey in order to bestow the signet ring of love.

Last judgment

The ambiguity of the poetic act is rooted in ontological equivocity. The living came to one as gift, as inspiration, literally, something breathed in, the soft kiss as free and ungovernable as the wind.

Only dead things could be commanded. And thus, the Elder understood that the claim to command one's identity was not only tyrannical and fraudulent, he suspected a surd element in such assertions, a mad stupidity. And that is why the eschatological reckoning is not properly reduced to an assessment of finite acts, but the discovery of one's hidden quest, the gift of unique being. Only there, from the lips of another, may I discover who I am meant to be.

An enigma

Those folk of the north and the entire matter of the tribes of Israel dragged off, dispersed, disappeared into the dust of nations, as invisible and fecund of imposters as the lost island of Atlantis. Now, Africans and crackpot cults with stockpiles of rifles in remote Idaho pass along a tract to let you know what had happened to them. And what of Mary Douglass who discerned in the priestly caste something very different than the zealous returnees from Exile? Were the people of the land an impurity, a rabble of harlots and con men, and what should the fiery, never to be captured and enigmatic divine name have to do with them?

Properly reflected upon, the enigma transcends the usual categories of nations, eras, geographical frontiers. Something both intimate and beyond, whatever one made of the People of the Land, the Jew was implicated. Was the Jew the pure remnant to be brought away from the dross of the world or was the Jew the secret antidote to the poison of sin and death? Was he there to condemn or to rescue? So many had concluded the former, and from anger and resentment, the lost had perpetrated upon the strange ones who sang and wondered upon the ecstasy of being chosen such agonies of torture, murder, rage, and profligate scorn.

And then the Elder said this: "Sheep, coin, child. Wilderness, home, the outlands. Nature, artifact, the frontier creature lost both far and near, yet more lost near, because thinking itself already of the kingdom. Betrayed by false shepherds, by carelessness, by family; the finding is both invitation and weaving. The latter is storytelling of the robe seamless, lacking no one and nothing. You know, the one the soldiers cast lots upon."

Chapter Three

Patmos

Interpretive prerequisite

S ergius Bulgakov, following the tradition of common author-
ship, which we deign to also follow despite the reservations of
scholars, asserted that it was the same John, the same son of Thunder, *Boanerges*, who penned the luminous, mystically rich portrait
of the gospel and before that, the stark, frequently appalling dream
vision of the Revelation. Bulgakov goes so far as to suppose the
latter written first as a kind of fifth gospel. The apocalyptic is
necessary if one is to properly assess the meaning of the event where
humanity glimpsed something altogether shocking. Not least, one
is confronted by the local stability of certain notions. The principle
of non-contradiction, for instance, which melted into vanishing
when the attempt was made to apply it to the infinite.

The Johannine gospel is bathed in the wonder of Paschal light,
whereas the furious fire of the Apocalypse threatens to overwhelm

everything, to burn the cosmos into ashes. Bulgakov observes that the seer of mysteries exhibits the work of an ardent, expansive soul: "his book of revelation belongs not to old age beyond time, but to supra-temporal youth. It is a young book, although it also belongs to old age." And here, we ask one to tolerate a bit this confusion of time senses. Reality bends at the margins, it stretches quotidian certitudes. What seems outlandish turns out to be required for the ordinary to exist at all.

Notice two other points that announce the ordeal of vision. Implicitly, the seer recognizes that to properly read (this is not automatic, so more than a function of bare literacy), it will require endurance on the part of the reader. "Blessed is he that readeth, and they that hear the words of this prophecy, and keep those things which are written therein" (1:3). The sophisticate will be inclined to laugh off that sort of portentous rhetoric, assimilate the warning as typical of religious hysteria. In doing so, there is a reduction to the psychological. John refuses such criteria. He has stood before shattering reality, or been restored to breath. What the seer offers is not a coping mechanism, a fantastic recovery of history on the part of the defeated. Rather, his vision is on the other side, has crossed the border of nullity, having already suffered the negation of all psychological hope.

And this brings us to the second point. John announces that he is merely the vehicle of translation. He does not invent, but relates the witness of Jesus the Anointed, "the firstborn of the dead, and the Archon of the kings of the earth" (1:5). It is one who proclaims

"I am alive unto the ages of the ages, and I have the keys of death and Hades" (1:18) who bears the authority of such a vision.

The symbolism can only be interpreted by those who have already died.

Aunt Fish

Adam Dollinger shuffled through the new mail's envelopes, stopping at one small, obviously RSVP missile.

"What's that look you've got on your face? I do believe it's consternation. Is it a bill for last month's dry cleaning, because really, how was I to know the fondue pot was particularly there, a most unusual place, you have to admit, dahling, well, don't you?"

"Eve, what are you talking about?"

Adam thought the gods very cruel, setting him up with a girl named Eve. Every wag, and especially the stupid ones, always had a ready joke. He looked at her now, larking about in his old football jersey. Why is it a girl looks so delicious in a numbered cloth edifice large enough to be a nightshirt? Or perhaps it was just that, some surreptitious melding of sex and sport. Wasn't even difficult, really.

"It's a letter from Aunt Fish."

"Oh, do tell."

Aunt Fish was Wilhelmina Augusta Pike. The Pikes who made their money in coal and railroads, diversified to include mint, silver, china, and the occasional slave, though the last disputed and, besides, only involving decidedly more or less distant black sheep in the family, none greater than a second cousin. Despite this caveat, she had the unavoidable brashness of being American. Aunt Fish, herself, carried the moral fiber of the abolitionists in her soul. She was the granddaughter of a suffragette and had now graduated to working for the rights and enfranchisement of the voiceless masses, by which she meant, as Adam was likely to point out, "the irrational brutes that one can find stuffed and paraded at the Natural History Museum."

"She's giving a fête in honor of a secret society that worships the tadpole," said Adam.

"She is not!" said Eve, and stamped her foot, as if she were really mad.

"Well, you're right. It's in honor of Dr. Albright and Babu, an ape whom they say has learned sign language and knows more than Dr. Albright."

"Adam!"

"Alright, I added that last bit, though it's very likely true."

"Oh well, if it's about Babu."

Eve stuck her lower lip out and blew onto her bangs. It was one of her habits that Adam found strangely endearing, by which he knew that the disaster had happened. He was truly in love.

"It's sure to be dull."

"Aunt Fish is never dull, dahling."

"You know what I mean. She's going to rope us into something. We'll probably end up picking fleas off the ape. Remember last year, the Pomeranian Society?"

The previous annual tally of months, they'd been asked to bring a donation for the upkeep of abandoned Pomeranian dogs. This was a problem, as two seasons ago it had become absolute sheik to have a Pomeranian dog, but the fashion changed to Schnauzers and everyone who wasn't a maiden aunt simply dropped their domesticated fox at the local pound. Adam insisted they really were only foxes. So, in the end, Aunt Fish had adopted twenty-six Pomeranian dogs. Adam and Eve had spent a pleasant weekend taking care of the yip-yips.

"Yip yip," said Eve. "She's a silly woman, but a dear, do admit. Oh, look, a postcard from Joss."

Adam noted the photograph of a Greek fishing village with a hurried scrawl on the back that read "The Island of Patmos. Nothing much to reveal so far."

"It's a shame about Claire."

Adam tapped the card, a dark scowl overcoming his pleasing irony. "Yes."

"What is it?"

"Something Joss said. I'd forgotten. He said Claire was like a girl out in the African bush listening to a drummer sending signals towards infinity."

"How extraordinary. What does it mean?"

"I don't know, but I think Joss is trying to find her trail."

Tilt

Dear friend, I know that I stopped sending the Unpostables. Somehow I think it might be alright. Anyway, I keep writing them in my heart, so just as well try. I can see why they thought he was mad, Claire. But like you, I have come to believe in him. If there ever was an order to all these notes and scribbles, and I rather doubt it, what is left is a kaleidoscope of fragmented shards, pieces to a mosaic that whisper of a consummation that could only be discovered beyond the next visible line. Perhaps because of this or perhaps because I am coming to share his eccentricity, am I merely projecting meaning onto a random inkblot? — the adventitious juxtaposition of one thought next to another sometimes seems to suggest a larger frame, a manner of understanding lost to nearly everyone.

A scribbled reference to Sheldrake's morphic resonance and the assertion that rats in a maze in Harvard mysteriously transferred insight to a colony of rodent subjects in Melbourne which, presented with a similarly constructed labyrinth, do not repeat the stumbling hesitations of original forays, but exhibit a starting point that takes up where their distant brethren left off. The experts claim this has not been replicated or verified and that it is all pseudo-science of a Lamarckian variety. In his own hand, a comment: "*The low devils have no sense of vertical causality.*"

Then, by chance or strange providence, there is a scrap of yellowed notebook regarding a species of bamboo that flowers very rarely, once every 120 years. Yet plants separated by continents, in Russia, England, China, Japan, and the Americas all flower simultaneously, as if the life of a single plant radiated out into each instance. And what if this sort of connection involves all of us? What if humanity as well bears the imprint of hidden momentum? It is likely nothing, but a notion of unity, concrete, living — suddenly the floor tilts and all our mental furniture slides into disarray.

A goat for Azazel

What has come to me of late, it's most amusing, is just how like a beast an empire is. They flaunt and rage, know not that they are mortal. Because of this, they have a kind of megalomania about time. Everything they think and do is tinged with the febrile tentativeness of those doomed to expire, yet they aim for the long view. The shorter the span of attention, the more lasting they imagine the import of their efforts. It's very strange. They pull down the monuments of yesterday's favorites only to erect new idols whose evident destiny is blithely forgotten. So, this exile where they have flung the impure, the intransigent, all of us unable to adapt to present pieties, the abuse of language whereby lies are taken for virtue. Blind to the monstrous prodigies sprung from each of them, they spawn those whelps they call facts; the demons, they cannot hide forever in darkness. Into this prison wanders the goat for Azazel.

Return trip

Patmos may have been a dreadful place when the Romans used it to punish. The well-born were often sent there to labor quarrying rock until their soft hands bled into hopelessness. Without a bribe or some good fortune, you died there. Yet hegemony is short-lived. The rocks stayed, imperial power fled elsewhere. The site of anguish and horror was now picturesque.

Joss pondered the mute trace of the past in stones, picking up diminutive exemplars and flinging them into the sea. And though lovely in its way, Wherryweather could not easily recognize in its small fishing village or the white stones of its monastery a setting for bizarre apocalyptic visions. Thankfully, unlike Rome or Jerusalem, it was largely devoid of hucksters of cheap religious souvenirs. One could almost forget historical memory persisted apart from the remote abbey. The only concession that Joss could discover in the small store catering to residents and tourists alike was a carousel of postcards with quaint photographs of the island.

Joss purchased one he deemed suitable and hastily scrawled a boring declaration of arrival. The proprietor was also the local postmaster, so he wrote down Adam's address and was done with it.

To all appearances, he was a typical outlander of ordinary circumstances. There was nothing to draw attention. Nonetheless, as Joss stood at the counter writing on the postcard, a young mother and her children stood apart whispering. One of her little boys pointed at Joss with guileless spontaneity and said a word that may have been Greek. It was certainly not English. The proprietor met Joss' inquiring glance with momentary embarrassment before explaining that since it was not the season for tourists, the boy had simply been impressed by the presence of an outsider. This was an obvious evasion, but Joss let the fabrication pass. What could it matter, after all?

On the flight to Athens, Joss had sat next to a young woman from Korea. She was telling him a story related to the massive earthquake and tsunami that had devastated Japan shortly before, spreading radiation from their damaged nuclear plants to the surrounding region. He said she would have to be careful about food and water.

"Yes, I know," answered the girl. "My aunt bought a whole bunch of seafood. She is crazy." Suddenly, this reminded her of a story she had heard. "There are dead bodies washing up on the shore everywhere. Even in North America. There was this girl on vacation in Japan. He was from Canada. I don't know if it was a man or woman. She was killed and then, later, they found his body on the shore in Canada." She paused, waiting for the eerie fate of the androgynous victim to sink in.

"It was a return trip," he answered laconically, but the quip did not translate.

"But isn't it strange?" she said.

Roommate

A storm of particular vehemence has come to the island. Even the soldiers on the supply boats arriving at the port of Skala look about in surprise. I suppose those of us who peer out from the caves and makeshift hovels have the likeness of vagrant ghosts, so bleak is our lot. I must thank the lord of winds, in any event, for my new friend. A sea eagle, wounded in the tempest, has declared himself temporary denizen of our humble cell. For a few days after the violence, he flew near, and then one day he dropped down onto a rock whilst I dozed. He, too, had ducked his head beneath a wing. When I awoke, he stared with his regal eyes, letting me know he could be dangerous, but at this parley was open to friendship. I told him I had seen angels less imposing, not to flatter him, but to seal our mutual covenant, because I am dangerous, too.

Pious piffery

Already, there are legends. For instance, it is said that I am like Enoch, that I shall not see death. This is false, already. My heart-friend, the Lord, has promised me the journey. Still, on Tabor we beheld a baffling beauty, more than anything Enoch could aspire to reveal. And then some put forth the story that I am a kind of soft mystic, tremulously awaiting visions. I'd knock them on their arse for that. Lucky for that bunch I'm quarantined at the behest of Caesar. Peter may have secured the sword, but James and I were

the ones to bring to a knife fight. It's true, my old bones ache. A lad
with some literacy stops by now and again. He might make do for an
amanuensis. Presently, he is avoiding me on account of the eagle.

Fractional realm

Joss tried to think what it must be like for human beings to have
visions. There were normally initiatory rites in ancient cultures,
possibly involving psychedelic substances. He vaguely recalled that
the shaman experienced a kind of death and wandered in the astral
plane before returning to his body. As a child, he'd read the stories
of the Oglala medicine man, Black Elk, with sympathy, but could
not imagine the remotest possibility that any kind of opening
towards greater dimensions or other worlds could happen to him.
Only with Claire did the porosity of the flux briefly break through.
William Blake speculated that folks in prior ages simply perceived
more. Our sensory organs had atrophied and now we could only
recognize a fraction of the realm experienced by our ancestors.
It was rather difficult to determine where the line of historical
demarcation should be located. John, supposedly, was still on the
other side.

The mark of the beast

The lad is a Greek slave from Macedonia. He gives an elaborate
romance for why he is here that would make Potiphar's wife blush.
The youth is so far reconciled to the presence of our visitor from the

sea that he has agreed to write down what I dictate provided I give him a share in the modest provisions sent to me from those who live in the experience of love. The first words I spoke forth have already furrowed his brow into a study of stubborn incredulity. I saw the false humanity, how all were stamped with the name of the beast. The boy had in mind the practice of barbarous tribes that etch into their skin the ideographs of their gods. That might not be too misleading. He knows nothing of our ways or I might have explained about the signet ring and the headband of Aaron, that we are a people called to be Holy unto the Lord. I tried a bit of metaphor to explain beyond the literal bent of his intellect. I said that heart and mind are linked, favor one another. Who and what you delight in becomes the light by which the mind searches. He pondered that, or made a pretense of considering, then asked for a portion of smoked sardines gifted to me by the granddaughter of Lydia of Thyatira.

Report from Patmos

My dear friend, I have one more report to make. There is a strange fellow haunting me. He has the appearance of Captain Nemo gone to seed and follows my steps on this quaint island as if he is both hesitant to approach, and yet has something important he must tell. I dare say he wants a fiver to purchase some inexpensive inebriant.

Monsters of deceit

There is something appallingly mechanical about these monsters. When I first saw them, I could hardly understand their character. They are nothing like the antelope, the sailfish, the mollusks one finds rousing in the shallow pools that supplicate the rocky shore. Indeed, I do not believe they exist at all. Perhaps they persist as fever dreams, the demons of our deceit, wretched parasites that both lust after and fear true being. I have come to recognize that they are akin to the grim surd of nothingness. All their speech is sham, a perverse mimicry that distracts from an essential dumbness.

The name on the forehead

A strange episode begins Book Six of Wolfram von Eschenbach's *Parzifal*. The Red Knight in his adventuring confronts an emblematic display, three drops of blood upon a field of white. How this comes about is as follows: We are told that Arthur, "the Mayful man," ever experienced wonders in the flower time of early summer. Yet "Parzifal the Waleis" — in that realm of chivalric surprise Waleis can mean French or Italian or many other things, but rarely Welsh — encounters the border from which Arthur's encampment sends out knights. So, summer, perhaps, but the ground is covered in snow.

Wolfram explains that *this* tale is "of most mixed cloth . . . pied with snow's ways." It is somehow out of season, and what that intends must be reasoned out by the wise. It is snow, in any event, that provides the mirror that transfixes Parzifal. Arthur's falconers had ridden out the night before in high spirits. They were on the hunt when mishap befell them. The best falcon was lost in the forest and subsequently spent the evening "standing" like Marlow's stuff of dreams, for it was thought that falcons slept so. In the same forest of the night wanders Parzifal, both falcon and knight uncertain where they are. With morning light, Parzifal discovers that the trail has disappeared, covered over by snow. Parzifal must slowly parse his way. As he does so, the falcon follows. It's possible the bird of prey surmised in the incarnadine armor one of its own, a master from the Table Round. Regardless, discovering the occluded path is an act of discernment, reading the covert text and translating what is hidden into solar lucidity.

The forest begins to thin and a meadow appears, though crossed by a fallen tree trunk. The Red Knight moves towards this snowy meadow, as does the falcon. In this wintry summer, a thousand geese are said to roost upon the meadow. They must sense the danger. As the alarum is given, a great gaggling ensues. The geese rise into the air and the falcon charges into their midst. From that thousand, one is wounded. We are told that in its agony, the hurt bird sought solace, sheltering beneath the fallen tree. Because of this seemingly adventitious episode, when Parzifal comes upon the tree, he sees three sanguine drops upon the field of snow.

The tale is thick with the arcane signification of heraldic symbols, yet it remains hard to fathom that when Parzifal sees the trine bloodlets spotting the white ground, he immediately envisions the fair image of his beloved wife who we are told is the most beautiful woman in the world. This seems a rather incredible interpretive stretch, though perhaps for Wolfram's contemporaries it was less obscure and even admirably obvious. The artful blood may imply the Triune Mystery, and the shining snow the purity of the Virgin.

For Parzifal the splendor of the image is so powerful that he literally loses his wits. He becomes utterly rapt before the nearly forgotten beauty of his wife, astonishment subject to irony since he has chosen this path of adventure that requires her absence. Various members of Arthur's retinue challenge the unknown knight to battle and Parzifal defeats them in a fog of barely cognizant action, whereupon he returns to the compelling enchantment of the image of the beloved.

Joss lived in an age of more egalitarian romance. No one was likely to be overcome with emotion before random blood spatter in a field, even those disposed to render what most see as chance a providential and idiosyncratic allegory. On Patmos, there was no snow, though the white stones of the monastery glistened in the sun. Where he lay, desolate amidst the rocky beach, Joss did not need to seek out revelatory symbols. He had a photograph of Claire who was to him certainly the most beautiful woman, though no longer in the world.

Joss had wandered all over the island. No message had come to him. Only with disappointment did he realize how much secret hope had attended his quixotic enterprise. Exhausted, he lay down against a rocky outcropping on the shore and soothed his feet in the warming sand. Small boats danced upon the sea. His reflections grew hazy with sadness. He might have drifted into dream, when he was suddenly aware of being watched. The old drifter who dogged his steps looked down upon him now with a bemused, yet still predatory expression. As Josh bashfully returned the photo of Claire to the protective veil of his wallet, not without a certain anger, the fella asked him for five dollars.

The ugly dog

Josiah sat down at a table of the cafe in the mood of a man who throws sticks to discover his fortune or one who opens a book at random hoping to land upon a guiding passage. Unbeliever that he was, Joss had once tried this with the Bible, but after three or four tries gave it up, as each effort landed on either the wrath of Yahweh or a string of genealogies, neither of which seemed very illuminating. Even a sallie into the New Testament had only provoked a denunciation of the Pharisees by the Christ. God seemed to be perpetually in a foul mood; not that he blamed Him.

Nursing the slim remains of dark, bitter coffee, he listened attentively to the surrounding conversation, nearly all in Greek. The banality and crude oafishness of the talk translated anyhow, because it was the human tongue. He waited without hope, sighed, and rose to pay his meager bill. The waitress glared at him, for he'd secured his table on too short a fare. He did not notice her hostility, however, because he was suddenly captivated by a short, bow-legged mutt of indescribable ugliness. The dog was perhaps fifteen inches high, a mélange of grays and browns with a long tail and a head that seemed prehistoric; a hatchet-faced terrier with ebony, knowing eyes and patches of missing fur. Scars and scrapes were distributed like badges across his dappled hide.

"Dog," he said, "I have heard that a woman will bed a man if he is hideously ugly, because there is some perverse thrill in it. Is it so among your kind?"

He knew, of course, the beasts to be sometimes indiscriminate in their coupling, providing the tides be in their proper place. It pleased him to ask and the dog responded to his query with a sharp look and something that was half growl and half laugh. It was certainly a laugh, thought Joss, and he further reflected that those who say a dog cannot laugh will surely admit that a dog may cry and then it is penurious to deny laughter.

The mutt, in any event, turned from Joss and walked a short ways along the sidewalk and then stopped, looking back at his questioner. It was so much an invitation that Joss followed this haphazard pull upon the thread, whereupon the mutt resumed his smelling and poking at trash cans and snuffling, his trudging and barking and marking of territory in the traditional canine manner.

The dog went so far as to offer a brief philosophizing upon the moon, at the end of which, he stood at the back door of a little house. When he was satisfied that the man was yet with him, he curled himself into a ball on the highest step and gazed up at the stranger who had beseeched him on the aphrodisiac qualities of outstanding ugliness. The dog, too, had half a mind to tell him, to relate his dozens of conquests and his prowess in courting, but reminded himself that men prided themselves on speech and considered themselves rational, that they were a sorry lot, always chasing after dreams. Then he waited for the old woman.

Reading comprehension

I was talking to the eagle. At least there I can expect adequate comprehension. The eagle, of course, showed no surprise when I waxed eloquent upon the matter of the 144,000. The number, as anyone with a little sense can determine, is symbolic, consisting of the twelve squared and multiplied by one thousand. "Most will see that, will they not?" I asked. I feared the poor journalists, nearly always shoddy thinkers, might think an historical tally was intended. The eagle deigned not to answer.

And then I teased out a bit the unusual nature of the martyrs' complaint. I was still concerned that dim readers were apt to construe wrongly, think that one is dealing with vengeful victims crying out for retribution. But really, how could that be? Is that what the Lord demonstrated when he bled for the beloved? Who are the pure ones, but all of redeemed humanity, the perfected pleroma? And then who are the persecutors, but those false aspects, the monstrous idols that cling so tenaciously to the encumbered spirit? You are twinned, both martyr and vicious tormentor. Not to put too fine a point on it, we ourselves in our depths cry out for the destruction of the imperious idols, those falsehoods that masquarade under our names, vampiric, seductive, murderous, the very pretense of life we take for real.

After I had expounded the plain meaning, the eagle flew off and returned with a fish. I have taken this as fitting confirmation that the arcane symbols are properly vindicated.

Goldfish gematria

Having begun this elementary primer on how to understand a symbol, I am carried forth by the momentum of conscience to say a bit more. I fear that folk who come upon these words in later years may misapprehend the whole of it. If the Lord of times is not speaking to you and I, each in our immediacy, then there are better means to entertain. My uncle once pleased us with the prospect of a little billygoat from his youth that, he solemnly asserted, would dance at the sound of a shepherd's flute. Take that over the esoteric ramblings of a tired, vatic prophet if it is no more than a cipher for passing events, no matter how bloody.

The God, mysterious Father, in every instant is conceiving me now. Just now, you are baking with the leaven of grace, rising to an unknown fruition. If you should begin to hear, listen. Childhood years are thick, like the rings of a tree in a bounteous year. From season to season is an age for a child. He cannot grasp the brevity, the speed, the emptiness and anguish of so much of the time endured by his elders. There, if you will, is the nub of that puzzle regarding the number of the beast. Do not waste your efforts discerning the gematria of historical figures. All that is dressing to dangle before learned ignoramuses with less acumen than a goldfish who forgets the circuit of his bowl.

Well, here are the crib notes. Numbers are qualities. The consciousness of humankind opens or closes with the ages. When even a few truly live out prayer, the doors of perception expand exponentially and an entire civilization may broaden its horizon. Though that will overwhelm ... one will babble in symbols or keep in expectant silence a precious knowledge that waits for the parousia. On the other end of the scale are experts in efficiency who require finite objects, as close to dead as possible, in order to clarify by quantity, which is the shroud of music, the true counting.

The principle is simple and well-known. The greater can comprehend the lesser, but the darkness comprehends not the light. So, go beyond. To understand the nature of 666, look to 777. The staureological number is inscribed in Greek by that latter quality. If 777 invites equivocity, the cross putting in question certitudes regarding the reality you inhabit, then 888 is eschatological surprise, for the Anointed in Greek is signified by that number.

There is, of course, much that could be parsed from this, how each number is divisible by the prime of 37, but that is for the graduate course. Enough to recognize that the cross binds the creaturely reality to a journey that must return to the Father. 666 is the refusal to even think, a univocal stubbornness that culpably blinds itself to the signs.

The hag

Not all old women are hags. It takes a certain distribution of flesh and bone, the sinking of posture must be just so, expression needs have enough intelligence to register malice, and yet occasional kindness must show through the ravaged screen of time. Jane had this and knew it, knew it in the way the young man betrayed an involuntary shudder standing there in the sparse yard below the bottom steps leading to her door.

"Boss," she said, "who have you brought this night?"

The dog looked back at her with insouciance. He considered a tart reply such as "he is interested in ugliness and bedding," just to see how Herself would respond, but some secret sense, the kind scientists can't figure, so they say it doesn't exist, told him there was already someone in the house. Then Jane said something puzzling to Joss.

"I suppose you're the one he's been waiting for. Best come in."

The muted light of the interior displayed a quaint décor. There was a fine white dining table, a pair of plush Queen Anne seats the color of sea coral, and a two-tiered corner table crowned with a large lamp adorned with tear-dropped glass crystals that hung like iridescent fruit from its bronze arms. Standing behind the dining table pouring a glass of port was Captain Nemo. The twinkle in his eyes showed recognition and humor at the private joke of their earlier meeting. Joss managed to mouth some awkward introduction to which the Elder gave gnomic reply with words Joss had recently read in a notebook: "It is useless to teach those who do not expect to be transformed."

Contradiction

There is something shocking about reality. If you think otherwise, you have not yet faced the fire. Here, I'll tell it straight. When you begin to be seen by the beloved, your heart melts. Part of you trembles. Is it the fear of the bride before the last veil falls? I do not know. There's something terrible in it. You want to run away, that's for sure, but your feet have already turned to cinder. Lost in ashes, the flesh is transformed. I suppose our brother Paul meant something like this when he talked of the pneumatic body. On the way to that translation, there might be a lot of dark turns. At the same time, it doesn't seem possible; everything in you yearns for that consummating union that must destroy the mortal flesh. It makes for contradiction and you are it.

The memory of God

Joss and the old man fell into a wordless tracing of the path from the beach to the ancient white stones of the monastery. They walked steadily and in the diligent mode of pilgrims. Joss listened to the cry of the gulls and smelled the salt in the wind, which seemed itself quiet and reticent to break the mute accord of the two men. Yet into the silence the Elder was speaking and Joss wondered when speech had begun, though he was hearing all along as they walked.

"To think is an act of suspense," said the Elder. "If you know everything beforehand, there's no attention and no discovery, certainly nothing happens."

And then, before Joss could interject, though he was by no means interested in doing so, the Elder explained that speech was a kind of recapitulation of the many actions of the universe. Everything from planets to ferns to Socrates was a kind of action, and speech was the means by which one protected or preserved the creation from vanity. By speech men achieved solidarity in the acceptance of the universe.

Joss thought about all the millions upon millions of words that man, woman, and child must have croaked out over the millennia. How much of it was curse or banal or tired, and some tiny spark of it beautiful and honed, and maybe even less coming close to love, though all might try for it in their own way. He forgot his stubborn refusal to speak and objected that it was hardly that.

The Elder admitted that it was a struggle to say amen, then launched into more metaphysics.

"So it is not understood that flesh is in the word, that language comes first, from the plenitude we call silence. We are born already in motion, a feather upon the breath, just as when we speak we are already spoken to, we would never speak otherwise."

Joss suddenly recalled a conversation he once had with Hooboo, but said nothing.

"Even our curses and the gaggle of loathsome horrors that spills from our lips is but a dark gesture of ineffective flight for the flight is still the gift of breath that is neither outside, nor inside, because beyond all such categories."

Evidently the Elder was ridiculously under the impression that speech was inherently liturgical. All the while they were steadily ascending a narrow trail towards the gleaming white buildings at the top of the hill. When the Elder spoke again, the view of the monastery prompted different thoughts, the impetus remaining unknown to Joss.

"Dullness afflicts them," he said. "They do not realize that awareness of the unique is the condition of love."

And here, Joss lurched upon the rocky trail, and the Elder reached out to steady him. He irrationally felt as if his heart was suddenly exposed.

"Well, lad," said the Elder, "to be upon the path is already the Way of Love."

And for a moment, Joss was not walking with an old man, but a vigorous youth with wild, flowing hair, but it was a brief flicker.

The Elder smiled and whispered, "Sophia is the memory of God."

The ardor of his heart

The Macedonian slave boy begged off secretarial duties again. He's gotten used to the eagle. It's the visions, even second hand, that try him. I did make an effort to warn the youth. You're not simply near the fire with Him. He's the very flame. Well, that creature that came in with the storm may be finer stuff than I imagined. I rather think it's an angel, the way he weathers the approach of the killer of death. Yesterday, the Lord of Times allowed me to understand something more of what we had experienced.

So, what I was remembering was painful to me — my brother James, and Cephas, and I on the night of his agony. We were the close comrades, the chosen friends, you see. It was like the sleepless vigil before Yom Kippur when the high priest prepares to stand before the Unspeakable Holy, to bring with him all the ragged times of the people, to allow us to approach in his being what ought to be our doom. We were meant to share the hours, to encourage. Of course, we were less than useless. It was more than political fears, the mercurial temper of the populace come from all parts for the Passover. It's hard to explain, but there was a palpable oppression in that garden, darkness that seemed to weigh more than the anguish of all the earth. We just couldn't endure it. The body gave out. We slept with the semblance of death.

How he lived through that night . . . I'll tell you this. The beginnings of my visions were there, in the dreams imprinted by the ardor of his heart.

Philological lesson

When they entered the monastery, Joss was surprised. Not a single monk appeared to greet them or ask their purpose. It was like visiting a museum during closed hours. The Elder took no notice or seemed to believe everything was as it should be. Instead of explaining, the old man began to instruct him about different notions of jealousy in various languages. For instance, the Russian *revnost* has the character of power, even tension, but not the negative emotions of fear, hate, or envy. He then mentioned the Old Slavic derivatives of *r'v-en-i-ie* and *r'v-a-n'*, which were associated with *lucta,* battle. Consequently, *revnost',* jealousy, is evidently the same as *rvenie,* zeal. From here, the Elder adverted to the Sanskrit *ar-v-an,* running headlong, hurrying, and *aurva,* rapid, on horseback; which was correlated with the Greek *oreFonto,* they hurried, *o-rou-ei,* to hurry, to rush; and with the Latin *ru-i-t;* with the Old Saxon *aru* and the Old Nordic *örr,* rapid, ready, on horseback.

The list was obscure, though one did perceive that for the Elder, the words were almost an afterthought or better, that way of transmitting a prior act so that it would not be in vain. Jealousy was first the rape of the Sabine women or Lancelot rescuing Guinevere from the fires before it was manifest in a word.

The Elder paused then and earnestly informed Joss that the first act is done alone. Before the act, there is no word to become common property, a shared knowledge, so that the greatest imaginable pressure is concentrated in the singular person who is invoked by name. The act does not yet exist. The one who is summoned by name is called to perceive the act's inescapable necessity and must then exercise every wisdom, endure enemies, opposition, and frivolities of fortune in order to achieve the unknown act. If the mission were to fail, the word would never come to be.

"And what if your mission included all the names?" he asked with pointed intensity.

Joss's head began to pound and he stopped listening. He could only think of Claire.

Unexplained

What we may have talked of is long forgotten. Only your azure eyes, the sweep of your hair, the white sweater, all that, and the feeling of yearning that could never be quenched, so raw and sad, we acknowledged desire by saying nothing of it. And also, the feeling that any action, the common thing, would desecrate, something fallen, something dunce getting in the way, turning passion into vulgarity. To love by refusing to join flesh, how could one explain that?

Before all oreogenesis

> In the prepared high-room
>   he implements inside time and late in time under forms
> indelibly
>   marked by locale and incidence, deliberations made
>   out of time, before all oreogenesis
>
>   on this hill
>   at a time's turn
>   not on any hill
>   but on this hill.
>
> -- David Jones, *The Anathemata*

The bishop of Ruritania

Having climbed to the top of the hill and then having entered the monastery with such exceptional stealth, they now began a descent down. The old man looked back at Joss again with a doubtful expression, as if he still did not quite believe that the young man was following. The Elder brought his finger to his lips to encourage silence and took a few paces down the winding stairs. Joss silently chastised himself in the third person for being such a dope and used the formal Josiah in doing so, always a sign of exasperation. He was cold and tired and could not quite understand how he had assented to go with the mad fellow.

There had been a moment of solemn, almost innocent appeal that he had not the nerve to refuse, but now that he was shivering and quietly descending with his dubious guide into the shabby, much forgotten bowels of the monastery, he cursed himself for a fool. After they had been at this for some time, the Elder allowed himself a quickly repressed smile. A little later, when they had come to a narrow, even passage, the old man stopped and laughed outright.

"It's just this way," he said, waving to Joss with a gleeful light in his eyes.

Prior to his encounter with the heraldic image of the Beloved, Parzifal had failed to ask the question. Confronted with the equally provocative and enigmatic rites of the Fisher-king, his courage failed him. The chivalric warrior who had yet to meet his match in battle was afraid to embarrass himself by admitting to the company of the Grail that he had no idea what was going on. As he had naively held to his mother's final entreaty to hail everyone like an ignorant, well-meaning yokel, he then followed Gurnemanz's advice and tactfully remained silent. But he is guilty, as Cundrie and Segune avow, though Arthur and his Court can hardly allow it.

"Look here," said Wherryweather, feeling ashamed and stubborn all at once. "Don't you think you had better tell me what this is all about?"

"I'd given up thinking anyone would come. Every year I sent invitations and every year, no one came."

"You sent the invitations?"

"Of course. I am the bishop of Ruritania."

The crack in the floor

Joss began thinking very hard as to whether he was likely to ever be heard from again.

"It's only just a little further now," said his guide, resuming his steady pace.

With a shrug, Joss matched his speed. They had followed such a circuitous path, he was sure to be lost striking out on his own. They continued on for a while, discovering even more passages and twisted turns than seemed credible from the outside. Then the steps of the Elder slowed and grew increasingly reticent, until they stood uncertainly in a prolonged pause at the threshold of a small cell.

Joss stared into its blank space hoping to find some clue to its meaning for the prelate. It appeared no different from a dozen other similarly empty abodes that they had just passed. Slowly, the Elder entered the cell. Like a child afraid of the dark cellar because manifestly that is where the monsters reside, the old man cautiously surveyed the very dull room. At first, Joss could not understand what he was about. Then he became aware that the Elder was concentrating on a very thin fissure in the floor of the cell. The crack in the floor seemed banal and certainly innocuous, yet the very trepidation of the Elder lent it an almost embarrassing fascination.

A slight chill emanated from the crevice. A faint odor hardly pungent or disagreeable nevertheless produced a feeling of nausea in Joss that slowly built in power until he fell prostrate upon all fours. To his shock, the crack appeared to have opened to the width of a small ditch. He looked down into the slope of the declivity, his eyes swimming in darkness.

An impish smile played across the old man's face. The Elder began again his pedantic recitation of etymologies. He told Joss that in Hebrew zeal and jealousy are expressed by the same root word, *qine'ah*, derived from the Semitic root, *qn'*. He added to this, as if he were bestowing information of great importance, that in Arabic, it has the sense of becoming very red and that in the Syrian it meant to be of a dark color. All this was evidently intended to build to a crescendo. The Elder was now speaking very forcefully, telling Joss about a rare Hebrew word. Something about how the Seraphim came from the obscure heights, flew from the interior realm, came from the glory of divine vision bearing the coal that was pressed upon the unclean lips of the prophet, Isaiah.

And then this word, this lexicographer's treasure, was stored and kept ready for a seemingly homely and passing thing. It was the lit fire, a coal fire, on the shore, where speech made declarations between the fisherman and his Lord when Peter was welcomed after the weakness of betrayal.

"The same fire, you see?" said the old man with sudden urgency. But Joss did not see. And then there was only the cold.

Chapter Four

Prince Raveh's War

This foe is dark

Now Mordred took counsel. He spoke with Kandran Valmack, and the Lord Bruhl of the Qa-Rendazi. Kandran Valmack gathered his wits. A head taller than the others, he bowed his gaunt face, whispered careful words.

"This foe is dark. He aims for something we cannot decipher. Slowly, we must proceed. Let us wait for our spies, wait for clarity."

These words touched on discomfort, the uncertainty Mordred had not yet allowed to come into focus. Then the ghoul chieftain threw out his arm against the sky, the sun low and burnished as a temple lamp, incarnadine like burning blood. Lord Bruhl pointed down to the barren flatlands dotted with the fires of his riders decamped upon the plains of Tremenar.

"The old ways are best," he said. "Always we have surprised our enemies, discovered them fearful of the death we bring, crushed them, run their bones into ground. Your kind is weak, trembles, blinks before their doom. Do not shelter the timid in clever plans. Victory favors the bold. We shall ride the wind."

The Arturi and the magical boar

To Tamberlin came the folk, both great and small. The hunt drew them. It was spoken of across many hundreds because of the rumor of the white hart. This was understood to be an omen of significance, though it was not agreed what it might foretell. The closer to the humble earth one got, the more it was regarded with awe and fear at once reverent and hopeful. Among the wealthy nobles there was outward skepticism, even light-hearted laughter. In truth, not a few of the young men secretly harbored and were surprised by a surge of desire for glory. They hid their ambition by speaking as if the whole thing were a lark cooked up to enjoin festivity, taken seriously only by the simple folk quaintly attached to their ancient superstition. Regardless of varying disposition, Prince Raveh was attentive and hospitable to everyone. For the moment, his penchant for sadness that often dragged him towards lassitude no longer beset him. His chamberlain and many servants saw to the needs and comfort of the arriving guests. Beorn smiled and laughed with genuine, disarming ease.

The night before the hunt a feast was given, sumptuous, and abundant with the boar entire and pheasant, there was wild caught salmon from the prince's streams packed in ice and brought through the mountains, there were oysters with the occasional rare pearl placed in its accustomed and natural setting as surprise, so watch out, not to mention exquisite deserts. Beorn employed a pastry chef that was the envy of kings. In addition, the best wines from the prince's well-stocked cellar flowed like rivers to the sea. Camaraderie was sufficiently sincere that all fell into a sleepy content. It was then, in keeping with tradition that a song was called for. And here, there was a stirring and at the back of the crowd near the entrance to the main hall a bard arose and in his hands he held a great, strange lyre. Something determined in his manner made the heart leap.

Sky was there. Benedicta and the others thought it would be good for her. And now she was glad she'd overcome initial misgivings to be summoned to Raveh's country estate. The girl rushed forward to hear the bard. Before the fire of the great hearth, he turned to face them and they all momentarily held their breath, for his gaze was defiant, nearly savage, held by some mystic fury that only slowly faded. It wasn't quite clear what was behind it, though from the first, his fingers plied the fair strings and the music softly played upon them until there was nothing but courtesy.

The bard told the old tale of the Arturi and the vast hunt for the magical boar, Twrch Trwyth, which stretched from Ireland to Cornwall. He sang of the hundred and twenty oath-taking riders, and of the proud, silent lords, and of those who shout and laugh. And all the time that he played, the folk said it was surely an old one, a true vates that had come among them.

Prince Raveh studied the bard, remembering his father Arco and his father's great friend. He was surprised, but sure of his surmise, yet said nothing since evidently the singer had his own reasons. The bard did not stay, but parted them like the Red Sea, peering to right and left as if he would glimpse a particular one, but nowhere did he see the Witch of Kyr.

"If only the Elder had come," said Sky.

"Did you not see him, then?" said Beorn. "I tell you he was here."

On the morn

In the morning, when they were still feeling the wine, the air was cool and slightly damp throwing a veil of light mist over the entire woods. Boys were holding their hands up to their faces and blowing to warm themselves. Huntsmen were seeing to the dogs, the hounds lively and oblivious to the cold, their eyes glancing from their masters and then towards the thick tree line, the energy in their limbs and tails ready to be sprung. The chief huntsman glanced unconsciously at the little brass bugle tied to a lanyard about his neck. He was talking judiciously to Lord Raveh and at the same time surveying the horizon like a general measuring the forces of a far off enemy. Gentlemen sat their mounts in small groups. Some spoke in jovial tones, whilst others cast a different manner, blasé or serious as the moment found them.

Some distance away from the prince, but near enough to be heard, Phylida Angstrom was perched on a sprightly chestnut mare. She was speaking in a hushed, but quickened voice to Sky Odyssey. Sky felt an impulse to bolt that her mount resisted. The horse knew the emotion fell short of command. The suspirious blur of words continued their assault, less meaningful then the restless barking of the hounds. Phylida was not saying anything, Sky concluded, and not for the first time it seemed to her Phylida was not a genuine woman, but a fascinating, peculiar artifact who for the occasion was sharply dressed in a midnight blue hunting jacket, lavender kid gloves and matching jodhpurs. She kept turning her porcelain doll's face, even as she spoke with animated intensity to Sky disjointed phrases and observations posed as intimate confession. Then at last the obvious explained all and Sky could barely suppress a laugh when she realized the point of the whole performance. The girl kept looking round to see if the prince had noticed them.

Abruptly, a new rider appeared. Now Sky blushed and was surprised. Deco was most agreeable. He gestured in a westerly direction and indicated the general location of the country estate where he was staying with some friends. She would be most welcome to visit, or at least, if she wished to investigate the local beauties of the region, he could act as guide; it might be pleasant.

"And so you are an enthusiast of the hunt?" asked Phylida.

Irritation flooded Deco's face. "One is obliged to come to these outings," he said, and then with a curt bow of his head, rode back towards a party of young men.

A light of ill omen

Red Jamie was riding with Captain Browers, one of the prince's cavalry men. The Captain was what the ancient huntsman called a good stick. He was kind to his horse, which was always a good sign. Beneath his cordial efficiency, Browers retained a trace of the sergeant who rose from the ranks by dint of courage and good humor. He was exactly the sort Red Jamie got on with: hearty, Stoic, not given to silly chatting. Still, the huntsman would have liked to say something. Red Jamie would have told him the hounds were eager, but not quite right. He would have advised how the wound in his hip, acquired when his father first took him on a wild boar hunt, always ached more cruelly in a certain light of ill omen. But he did not know the man and so allowed himself to enter the companionable silence.

It was a strange thing to be chasing the white hart. No man living had ever seen it. Vaguely he recalled his great grandfather speak of the creature which held mystic significance for the folk. He was yet tied to his mama's apron strings and would wander into the corner set aside for the elder. A boyish wonder arose, lived in the lilt of the old man's voice as he told to the bairn the tale. Sitting beside the elder, Jamie could almost see it, a fugitive glimpse of celestial light, the creature suddenly flashing into a clearing and staring with serene, wise eyes into the face of the hunter and how the hunter had instantly thrown aside his weapon, tears streaming down his cheeks. But it was over in a long second — and then the sky darkened and something fierce followed. Of this, his great grandfather would not speak.

Away is near

At first, there was a rush of excitement. No one yet saw the white hart, but a feeling of anticipation took hold of them all. They rode with zeal, ready with sharp eyes to come upon the hunted. Then fragmentation, the party broke up into little pockets. Some went north and some went south, others took to east and west, each certain of choosing right. Raveh and his chief huntsman kept their cool. They waited and watched the best dogs. Suddenly, these were running with abandon and all were off, a feeling of happy battle dancing in their veins. The dogs got ahead of them. In their eagerness, zeal brought them to sorrows. The wind sent their message; unnerving the wild and mournful cries of the hounds, so richly full like human anguish.

It was shocking, the way a dream is interrupted into abrupt waking and the cold shakes. Phylida paled and fidgeted. Her sprightly chestnut mare wavered, tracing a scattered, fearful path. The girl tried to make a brave show of it, but her smile was wafer thin when she suggested a distant thicket far from the crying hunt. Many of the young men, to be fair, suddenly grew ashen. They might be glad of a reason to seek that thicket, but pride kept them in place.

"Come, come away," pleaded Phylida.

Perhaps some pity for her arose in Sky, though her eyes burned with defiance of the fear carried by the wind. Then she spurred her hunter and they made for the trees.

"It was strange," thought the prince, that the two girls should have followed so avidly precisely the path to the canine keening. The one seemed to plead for mercy, and then the other took the lead.

The Viae

The Viae is what they called the transit line. In its heyday, a system of interconnected tunnels and rails above ground and below, the Viae was a marvel of engineering skill that allowed various devices from the small bullet shuttle to cargo trains and cruisers to convey goods, passengers, and troops to the farthest reaches of the City's dominion. And still, near the City the line was mainly in good repair, though further out service was sporadic and apt to breakdown. The more ambitious lines had long since sunk into desuetude so that only the very aged could recall a time when the names of defunct stations represented a thriving destination of the realm.

Between the near and the far was a middle distance that remained subject to contest. There, the enemy might resort to sabotage or engage in direct conflict. In the week after Saturnalia, there was a particularly savage attack upon an express train transporting civilians that included women and children. The outrage occurred along a spur that petered out a short distance from the ancient ruins of the abandoned city of Kos. The nature of the crime captured the imagination of the City. Public figures, journalists, teachers, matrons, artists, the entire bosom of civic feeling was awash in righteous anger. So while in actual numbers the victims were less than a dozen, the cry for vengeance was unusually vigorous.

The Guardian promised a powerful response, even if that unfortunate party might perhaps have foolishly traveled past the area deemed safely prudential. Indeed, Malchidion sent a most renowned fighting force, the Sixth Legio. That valiant legion carried the banner of the scarlet griffin, its loyalty and courage could scarcely be questioned.

As the line had become open to repeated incursion and rumor, the sixth approached Kos from an angle traversing territory mainly rural, untouched by the Viae. A few scattered barbarians, hardly more than a gang, barked at them from a distance. Later in the evening, however, a deep sepulchral rumble mixed with a high pitched screeching as if a dozen trains were simultaneously braking echoed throughout the terrain. The foot soldiers looked at one another with unspoken dismay, whilst the horses of the cavalry gave white eyes to the night, rose up in fear to warn those marching relentlessly forward.

Quiet removal

The barbarians relied upon a strategy of numbers. They could overwhelm a lonely outpost, but their tactics were rudimentary. In battle anywhere near equal forces, the City was sure to triumph. The enemy might charge in waves of zealous warriors, yet doom awaited them. They would be baffled by structure and method. Like the Mameluke knights' hopeless display of bravery before

Napoleon's more modern army, they would end floating down the Nile, their plumage and gorgeous brocade swelled out like drowned petals of exotic flowers.

Of course, if there were Qa-Rendazi, that was a different matter. So far, if they were involved, they had yet to tip their hand. This expectation was borne out by the first dispatches of the Sixth which were nearly punctuated with the faint whiff of boredom. Further posts acknowledged some degree of professional resistance. The efficient and regular report of progress slowed, and then became increasingly intermittent. The tardy dispatches were puzzled, then mildly troubled, frankly desperate in their last, fragmented forms. After prolonged silence, a scouting party was sent out in advance of a relief expedition. Those who returned did so with somber visage and ashes in their hair.

The Sixth had all but disappeared. A few survivors were discovered wandering in woods or hiding in the dark ruins of Kos. All questions were met with confused shrieks and cries. The City recalled the reinforcements. A report was circulated that the Sixth Legio, having satisfactorily dealt with the savage nuisance, was now engaged in routine maintenance of the frontier. The miscreant spur was quietly removed from line operations.

The prince acts

Weeks after the confused hunt for the white hart, Raveh received a letter from an old comrade whose brother had been in the Sixth. The news reports of the deployment of the Legio on the frontier were false, he said. No one had word of them. The prince made inquiries. Trusted men returned with disturbing, baffled reports. Raveh began to contemplate an action. It was, naturally, completely impossible. That was the opinion of his old tutor, nudging him, in his quiet way, to listen to the Senators. What were they, really, but puppets of the Guardian? And then there was Shadrael, the oracle. He had a soft spot for her, beautiful and quirky. But she brings sighs, that one.

Restless, he put on his cloak and went out upon the north facing balcony. From there, he could see the marble columns, the arcade of the old palace, and the broad stone terraces that ended in the outer walls. Sentries, bored, dutiful, wishing for ale, kept watch upon the paths that led to the City. Barely in sight was the edge of the portico that sheltered the ancient bronze doors of Chronos-Thoth that marked the end of public space and the dark entrance into the realm of the Chora Makra. A myth, of course. The Chora Makra was everything beyond the City, though the Elder quipped that it *was* the City. Further along, on the side where the sun cast shadows upon their recumbent forms, the giant Shiriloth rested, awaiting the words of their masters.

The prince suddenly remembered for no reason that he could discern a conversation with Blackwell. Blackwell had asserted that there was a fellow who had made a career of painting dancing bears. Beorn considered this a charming, if fanciful jest, until one day, in a wing of his mama's third best house, he found himself staring at a long line of ursine eurythmics. The discovery had filled him with laughter, at life's bounty and caprice, but mostly, to sometimes be surprised in a small thing that is playful, like a sweet dream of childhood. But this brief repose did not last. How rarely did he laugh. The prince felt himself that a fragile peace was ending. Or perhaps better, a contained violence that passed for peace was gathering into a storm that would carry them all away. He smiled grimly. Even in his youth, he had known it would end this way.

And so, Lord Raveh summoned his riders. He called forth the foot soldiers, too, each from his village and from the counties of his land. They were good men, hard in fighting. The cavalry included men of the guard who had fought in numerous border wars, knew the tactics of the barbarians well. And then Beorn rode for Kos.

A useful lie

The aims of the Qa-Rendazi were never clear. To pillage, rapine, a lust for destruction, all that was common. Beorn, and his father before him, did not believe the enemy was so easily comprehended. They did act like that sometimes. And yet often they would bypass easy targets, leave supine wealth alone. Other times, they menaced tiny villages, places with no possible strategic or economic value. The desolation left behind made hardened soldiers cry. And for years they might disappear altogether before descending from the mountains or screaming like a herd of demons from the desert or embarking from ghost ships sailing the wide seas with the uncanny unison of a horde of locusts. *Something else is behind it. The easy tale, the one the Guardian tells the citizens, is a useful lie.*

The enemy past

Lord Raveh read over again the transcribed reports taken from the survivors of the Sixth Legio. He had already concluded that no clear sense would come of it, but something compelled him to try and find a thread of meaning in the disparate madness. What they asserted, collectively, was a brutal, aching revenge. "It is your own, the very past takes arms against you." This was the dire, mystifying proclamation of a survivor. Raveh stopped at a field hospital. There was a patient he wanted to see. The soldier often could not be torn from compact, fetal retreat. He moaned and cried out at the slightest touch. Yet on occasion he would stretch himself and speak lucidly without any apparent awareness of his alternate condition. In those instances, the soldier gave the most thorough and detailed observations.

"Sergeant Wolley," he said, "had first encountered the enemy on Tuesday, a fortnight after Saturnalia in what appeared the current year."

This evidently was his own appellation, though recalled as a for-mer title with little to do with the man who now spoke. The soldier asserted the enemy was not the expected rebels. They were only a show, behind which there were uncountable shadows, hordes dressed in the regalia of many centuries. "Yet that is not the worst of it," said the man who was Sergeant Wolley, puffing with a kind of bitter non-chalance on the proffered cigarette. When he began to fade into silence, the orderly told Raveh that when pressed, Sergeant Wolley normally resumed his protective bodily knot, but sometimes he would stare straight ahead peering intently at invisible scenes. As if in answer to this third person report, the soldier began to speak.

"Can you not see yourself?" he admonished. "All that's just appearance — what we fought; you feel it, don't you understand? Everyone, all their times come at you, not just the soldiers, everyone. Wives, parents, slaves, lovers, children, even the beasts. All their hopes, everything. Cruel, cruel, cruel, the death."

The savage darkness

So much of war is waiting and monotony. The men were playing cards, whittling, staring into their telereaders, perusing old letters when the merchant trader came and asked to pass through the line. He might have been a spy, but Raveh did not think so. He spoke with just that combination of resignation and dry wit that the prince associated with virile realism. The trader appeared sincere, though that there were a people who did not have sacred groves or who refused to acknowledge simple verities like the distinction of the human sexes seemed insane. That any society should slip so far from human feeling was a barbarism too lonely, too uncivil to contemplate.

And yet, of course, there must be such. While the prince was talking to the trader, a furtive thought began to whisper, badgering, elusive. The prince cast his gaze back in memory through the oblong space of his villa window, down upon the rooftops where people were eating, conversing, engaging in amatory talk, arguing sports and politics. Further down, the houses narrowed, the wash hung haphazardly, the rough gossip of peasant wives, and games of children. And then he thought of the enemy in darkness, without warning or apparent strategy, to leave a string of towns and villages desolate, burning, killed to the last man, woman, and child, neither aged nor sick spared, down to the least of their beasts. For that was how they came. He thought for a cold moment of the Elder and their mutual friend, so kind and generous, now a recluse at Casa Balthasar. What savage darkness had unbraced the affable faculties of mind? Brother Timothy had encountered something too terrible for the rational intellect to contemplate. Was it something in us, after all?

Random, ruthless, like an ominous winter flood crashing down from the mountains, there were those who said it was holy, that it was good to exterminate one's enemies.

Chronos is ill

Day 9? There is something wrong. Chronos is ill. We are no longer certain of the time. After the last brief skirmish, everyone was quiet. I was quiet, too. We won rather easily. The enemy made a pretense of attack, but it was not aimed at death blows. At first, we suspected a feint, some diversion, though nothing followed. Later, I wondered if it were some sort of warfare by contagion. The men began to suffer incredibly vivid memories, past events of varying nature. Some were of childhood, others more recent. Some were pleasant, others decidedly not. They are so real, holding that quality of the present that one cannot dismiss them as a mere shadow. When you come out of it, the body falls into a stupor that can persist for days.

Banal horror

Beorn never spoke of his mother, the slow decline into dementia, the steady flattening of life to the endurance of small, daily tasks that might quickly escalate into accusations and anger, an existence without savor or hope. Near the end, an apothecary had suggested a certain dram. Lord Raveh threw him out with a groan.

Beorn often wondered about the Elder and his friends who seemed to believe in the triumph of kindness. The Nazarene irked the authorities by forgiving sins. Raveh was never clear if this was because it was an arrogation of priestly privilege or outright blasphemy. And, of course, there were the healings which were often equated with the removal of sin. It was hard to construe, and clearly, there were some who suffered maladies apart from any specific outrage of divine order. All that religious handwringing; the prince knew you could reach a point where guilt or innocence was somehow beside the point. There was a level of suffering, perversely inane, that cared nothing for custom or moral code. In that hell, decent men became quiet.

That shattering, fragmentation of person left no room for dignity. There was no glory, nothing that could be defeated by arms or any other human means — monstrous, that relentlessly banal horror when the messiah did not appear.

Army of desolation

First, there was stealth, the subtle whispering of steps, and then with a roar, they came. The watchmen had not been lax, but the army of desolation surprised them anyways. Qa-Rendazi warriors dropped from the tall trees on the outskirts of the camp, an undulating war cry descending from above, and other militia rose from hidden trenches brandishing iron and steel. Their horses appeared, smelling of sulphur and wrapped in gray smoke. The charge seemed random, then not; it was a pincer movement, the closing wave falling upon them from the forest adjacent the ruined stones of Kos.

The enemy arrived so quickly, the sentinels were silenced before alarm could be given. Raveh came running from his tent. The cohort formed, a rough phalanx met the enemy. Beorn commanded the cavalry. Captain Browers joined his liege lord. They gathered a core and moved with mad abandon. Death came by missile and arrow. In near quarters, the saber thrust gathered blood from comrade and foe alike. Pikes and spear thrust harried the horsemen, but the force of movement won the moment. In the end, they survived. Disconsolate reward, for how could one rightly defend against so subtle and pervasive an aggression? Then in the night a mist arose and with it the ghostly cries of the long dead added to the lament of the newly slaughtered.

The tearing of the world-wall

Day 15 (perhaps). I know not for whom I write this. The City will not acknowledge our suffering. I alone have gathered the folk of my land, because I thought it right and good to maintain loyalty. There is a scourge about this place. I discovered not a few of my soldiers drawing a dark whirl in charcoal upon a blank wall in the ruins. One of them is a ferrier by trade, another a doughty farm lad from the village of Cam where my old nanny was born. When I asked them what it was, they said "it were the tearing of the world-wall." Further inquiry revealed the most curious metaphysical imaginings by men unused to speculation. It was their opinion that we did not merely face Qa-Rendazi and their barbarian allies or even an army of the undead, but some monstrous rending of the flesh-fabric of time.

General Tsarik

A Cossack with a grizzled beard peered about the room the way a dog does who finds himself unexpectedly in the forbidden parlor. To mask his embarrassment, he ostentatiously shook the snow from his coat and studied the prince with brazen curiosity. Then the trudging sound of massive legs like logs split off from a tall pine followed by ponderous breaths as rackety steps were mounted. The Cossack bowed deeply at the officer who entered. The stern old general made his way to the lone chair by the fire. All this time, Raveh lay on the divan with his book in his lap. He didn't bother to get up because it manifestly couldn't be happening. He was in a hunting lodge where Arco used to take him as a boy. More to the point, General Tsarik had been dead three generations before his father was born. Tsarik lowered his heavy body into the chair and without looking at Raveh stared into the flames.

"Elnaria is a great expanse," he began. "You think it does not know how to drink up blood? The folk have plenty to give."

Raveh was neither surprised, nor interested in the ancient warrior's cold-bloodedness. Still Tsarik did not so much as glance at the prince.

"You think I give a fig what that pompous Guardian does? I would gladly retire to my estates in the north, be a provincial governor far from the City. But come now, I tell you this has happened many times. The enemy pounces, but to no end. It is an episode. Soon, they will vanish. The plague is terrible, but the survivors go on and one day the bitter wound lacerates no longer."

Lord Raveh found himself looking out the open doorway at the sky which was a soft blue-violet pierced by the first glimmering stars. He almost recalled that sky and those stars caught in the net of youthful eyes still touched by the residue of an original wonder. When he attended again to the general, he discovered the remaining thread of an on-going oration.

"It is good to confront the enemy. The warrior must perish so that the people will know they are loved and protected. Without honor, the folk are doomed to life without beauty."

The prince felt he agreed almost despite himself. He thought about making an essay at speaking to the old ghost, but must have dozed off. When he awoke, the general was in the midst of a different rumination.

"I tell you the way most folk tell the story is completely wrong. They act as if it is part of a simple story. A shrewd, mystical peasant has a good run. He's kind and the folk love him, so the rulers must despise him and desire his death. He rides into Jerusalem and is greeted with Hosannas. There are two things to consider. First, nearly always before, when they sought to make him king, he ran from them. He healed and told them to be silent. But not then. He raised the stinking corpse of his friend just outside the City at the holiest time of the year when many have come from afar. You couldn't keep that quiet. And then he purposely enacts a prophecy by riding into the city on an ass with foal. Now he clearly is claiming to be king. Everyone knew it. It wasn't a pathetic mistake. And he is said to have had power. He tells his faithful, unhelpful steward to put away the sword. He can call down legions of angelic warriors. He could have taken Rome, built a lasting empire. Say he is deluded; he believed it well enough. But he doesn't call them. He's seeking exactly the retribution his enemies have planned. He's refusing the victory. Why?"

Again Beorn drifted into a recurring dream, the oblique sense of having wandered outside the frame where he floated in a cold darkness before a panorama of gilded pictures, each convinced of its own natural integrity and lasting significance.

The prince recollects

Chrysippus was pious in his own, skeptical way. Xenophanes, he said, had noticed that men revere gods after their own likeness. Thus, the Ethiopian worships a god snub-nosed and black, whilst the Thracian divinities are all red-haired and have grey eyes. He wondered if the beasts had hands, would they fashion similarly, making unto themselves a grandiose mirror?

Young Beorn had answered quickly, "It is certain for cats."

In the summers, he would spend time with the peoples of the steppes. Arco wanted him to learn their ways, especially falconry and the art of horsemanship. The house had its own equestrian master, of course. Among Beorn's tutors there was one for fencing, another for Latin and Greek, a third for dancing and court etiquette. Yet the riders carried the wind. Their chieftain, Mahai, was like a second father to him. Years later, Beorn came down from alpine solitude to discover the tents of the peoples dotting the plain. A young man rode up to him, and then jumped down to embrace him when he was known. It was Mahai's grandson who remembered the youth that was a favorite of the old chieftain.

His parents had been away, as they often were. Chrysippus was available for advice, and various other persons, an avuncular diplomat for example, also served as the depository of residual authority. All the same, in practice Beorn was left to wander at whim. He became knowledgeable regarding many works of art in certain rarely visited rooms that the family hardly even knew existed. The stable hands, the scullery maids, everyone knew him for his quiet, pensive nature. Yet he became strangely emotional when he returned one day from a long walk to discover a set of his mother's gloves casually tossed upon a small table. He heard his parents talking in the intimate tone of a couple before he saw them. It was strange, but just that tone, not the words, is what he remembered. It conveyed in a way not even made palpable by their absence the separate world inhabited by Arco the Lord Raveh and his Lady, as if they emerged from a magic realm in order to communicate with those outside.

"Oh, Beorn," laughed his mother when she saw him. "Come see what I have found for my sweet boy."

It was a small silver pin of an airship. The captain had given it to her because she was so beautiful.

Night visit

In the long night in which Beorn remembered these things, there was a stirring, a rustling in the ranks. A bold one came near, not skulking and making his way like a burrower afraid to go far from ground. The cloak was pulled back to reveal a familiar face. It was the one he first saw explaining to his father some feature of the inadequacy of sets to describe reality. Arco was keen to discuss such things. And when Soren Blake glanced over at the prince's son, he said, "the child forgets more than you or I shall ever know." And now here he was, not a day older, though Raveh had grown to match his years . . .

"Remember that Night is first," he said. "It is the Womb of years."

Strange, but Raveh did not find it out of place that Soren Blake should come to him and say those words. "At Tamberlin, you came to hall singing of quests and the love of the hunt. I alone knew you," he said.

"You are thinking," said the vates, "that some stratagem of guile is needed to defeat the enemy. You would cast yourself as Jacob playing at Esau to deceive a blind father. Such cunning is misplaced — just as few understand the import that the Kingdom of Heaven is taken by force."

Then perhaps a question or two occurred to the prince when the vates smiled silently and moved on.

Spinning song

The woman who sat before the spinning wheel was neither young, nor old. She hummed a tune she'd learned from another, a maiden aunt. It was something kept by families and passed on, a song of waiting and abiding. It passed the time. At her feet the babe lay warming by the fire. The ancient deerhound too frail to hunt lifted its head now and again to see that all was well. The one who entered always carried with her the north wind. At the brisk air, the deerhound barked alert, but could summon no more than that. Lady Winterbourne patted the head of the dog and glanced about the humble cottage as if she expected to find another.

"He isn't here. He went out," said the woman without looking up from her work.

"Yes, I know," said Lady Winterbourne. "I saw him crossing the fields on my way over. I thought perhaps your daughter . . . ."

"Caitlin is with the mother abbess. She is seeking the hallow ways."

"It is a perilous path," said Lady Winterbourne.

She was quiet then and the woman resumed her song. Lady Winterbourne bent over the babe and made a little sign of blessing. She left a tiny flask of valuable perfume and a pouch full of coins upon the table still bearing the remnants of the husband's meal. Turning at the door, she waved farewell.

"I, too, know that melody," she said.

Hidden realm

Rosy fingered dawn announced the new day. Soren Blake came for him riding upon a thin, but spirited horse that gave the impression of a sketch by El Greco.

"I only drew him this morning," laughed Soren. Prince Raveh's own warhorse was waiting. "Come, we must travel through the sea-wood of Broceliande. I would yet show you the battle that awaits."

They did not stop to break fast. Quickly, Beorn joined the journey. He still nursed a vague hope that some tactic of victory might be discovered. The bard's magic must have been upon them. Lord Raveh's men were sharpening their blades and cleaning their kits, quiet in the early morn. No eye turned to remark their passing, nor voice rose in query or salute.

Broceliande is the water forest of dreams. They crossed a bridge obscured by milky fog. The other side was unmapped country. Wherever they went, the sound of running ghosts stirred the air. In the midst of tall timber; coming in and out of the mist a company of wolves. The horses pricked their ears at that, the white shine came into their eyes, yet such noble beasts would not be mastered by fear. They kept the path preferred by their kind riders hoping for the best.

Soren and the prince rode on, the miles stretching into oblivion, and still no end in sight. Lord Raveh was resolute in silence. He would not say they had come a great way for nothing. As for the bard, he too kept his peace. They might have died, were it not felt already near redundant. And then they came to long, low fields bathed in dove gray light. Each thought, "I have been here before." At last, a shy, little brook babbled like a child, too innocent to be grieved.

"What was it you wanted to show me?" said the prince.

"I have been showing you all along," said Soren Blake. "Everywhere we have ridden is the inscape of your heart."

The protected pavilion

They stopped at the spring to refresh themselves. The riders dismounted and shook weary limbs. The cold water was elixir to fatigue. Both men felt their minds sharpen, their hearts spark with joy. Their horses, too, drank deeply with delight. And then their eyes seemed to be opened with new vision. Nearby, across the water, bright tents and gleaming banners set forth the movable feast of some resplendent monarch. On the far side of the waters, a young man met them riding a white colt. The youth was armored in fabulous light. His hauberk was golden like the sun, his spurs radiant comets against a sable field of night. He wore no visor. His face was fresh and bold and guileless.

When Soren saw him, he sang a song of the vates Claudel. "My God, a young man, born of woman, is more pleasing to you than a young bull. I stood before you a wrestler — not believing myself feeble, but that you were the stronger. You have called me by my name as one who knows it truly, you have chosen me among all those of my generation."

Lord Raveh was surprised to find the grounds unguarded. The knight of splendor welcomed them in the silence of his gracious countenance. Then the beautiful child led them to the pavilion, the herald of good news led them without a word, and they entered into the presence of the king.

"Ah, you have arrived," said Arthur.

The Healing Cup

The king waited upon them like Father Christmas, the board filled with festal delights. To the prince's unasked question, Arthur answered that the pavilion could not be breached either by the cares of the day or by the grief of night.

"There is no need of armies," he said. "Only the child and the friends of the innocent come here."

Then, for a time, Arthur spoke avidly with Raveh. They shared the bond of cavalrymen, knew the rigors of the kingdom's defense. When Arthur turned to include the vates, he surprised the prince by calling his old friend "Taliessin." Arthur spoke for the benefit of the soldier words known to the bard. He explained that those who told the story in such fashion that the questing of his knights was little more than canvas for imperial ambition or individual glory, worse, mere entertainment for a Court grown dull revealed by such telling their utter ignorance.

"Taliessin understands. The king is aboriginal priest, and this realm is the temple of the universe," he said with the voice of liturgy both wondrous and grave. "The seeking of my knights is the search for the healing cup, the beauty that makes all things new."

Then Arthur looked with gamesome eyes upon his guests, glad of their presence. Many folk appeared upon the green field. There were the Fay adorned in gossamer and lights that trailed behind them like a splendorous train. Human folk, too, all gracious and kind; of these, the old were not aged, but wise. Their limbs were lithe as any youth, but the eyes gave them away, far seeing. The children, too, were pleasing and full of fun, yet free from any crying fear or selfish need. They came riding fierce saber-toothed cats, and flying down from the heights upon the backs of hydracanth, those aerial dragons that love the sea.

Then daring tumblers from Mirador arrived throwing sparkling, many-colored glowsticks, which formed patterns in the sky more ornate than the aspirations of the most baroque illu-minated kaleidoscope. The gambols and games played were both spontaneous and musical, flowing with a kind of artful poise so that the movements carried the momentum of thrilling grace, an aesthetic performance aimed at communal joys and ludic integrity.

The finale was dance and choral praise for love's kingdom. The Moombadune from the long Court of Valimar lay down their cloaks and sang the epithalamion of the most high king and his sophianic bride. When they had finished, everyone was quiet with awe and content. There was something yet their host wished to say. He took into his manly hands the chalice upon which was etched in silver the tree that bore the luminous fruit, turning it delicately so that the reflected light fell upon them.

"There is in those Greeks, in those wonderful poets and sages, something too reticent, my friends. Nothing in excess, nothing too profound, nothing too far-fetched; they take temperance too far. Better to listen more deeply to that yearning buried deep, that gift that binds you."

And what he meant by this, you may discover, but listen. That kingly man clapped Beorn upon the back. He knew the ways of courtesy and what manner in which to acknowledge a noble spirit. To Taliessin, he gave these words.

"The realm that slips beyond one, touched and forgotten, even in dreams, hearkens by the long ships, those galleons of eternity that break the waves of the empyrean. The Sha-rule know them, those dark maidens. You may yet hope for more."

The figure of Arthur

The vates David Jones has remarked upon the thickly woven strands of historical accretion that fortuitously shaped the myth of Arthur. Artorius, Romano-Breton dux of a heavily armed, mobile cavalry of the late fourth century begins a journey through misty legend into the fabric of myth. A potent strand of Welsh stories feeds the Celtic stream, but to this is added heroic tales from France, Germany, and the English literary tradition that includes Geoffrey, Wace, Layamon, Chaucer, Malory, of course, all the way up through Spenser, Tennyson, Morris and the Pre-Raphaelites, not forgetting a more recent poet, Charles Williams. Impossible to shear off sorcerers and magic cauldrons from the medieval romances where the Grail emerges as both the inheritor and clarifying prism of the many colored robe, though some suppose the mix of sources a mélange held lightly by the mythic signifier. Yet here he stands, speaking of his knights and his troubles, King Arthur, lord of Albion.

Those who would dismiss him as mere fiction cannot explain why Arthur should have arisen in the first place. A dozen theories related to economy or political expediency cannot answer for him and only a fool would be satisfied by such genetic scrutiny. The truth of Arthur is that he is the name of an action. The cryptic reserve about the location of the grave of the regal bearer of that act is more than residue of pathetic hopes nurtured by a beaten folk; it is indication that the origin of his identity resides formally beyond time, though he feeds those who participate in his identity through historical acts. And the wise vates harbor more knowledge than this, of the naming mystery of all being which can only be approached in humility.

Those who refuse the receptivity of innocence rashly conclude that their own identities are lucidly comprehended by an index of social function and idiosyncratic assertions of naked will with regards to gender or sometimes even species. Others suppose everything can be adjudicated without the need for wisdom or interpretation. Rather, they think to quantify and fix the plenitude of person, perhaps with DNA mapping. In short, they clothe themselves in presumption, unable to enter the pavilion of childhood.

The third best house

The king was silent a while, his festive gaiety put aside for Lenten thoughts.

"I have been thinking of late of joinings out of season, the illicit fruit of my sorceress sister and I, for Mordred still haunts the land. Our sins seep into the ground with our gleaming tears."

"He weeps for the land who dreams his bitter dreams," said Soren.

Arthur himself showed them the path, long and arduous, at the end of it, the tower.

"The keeper of that far fortress is wise, but hidden in her ways," answered Arthur, perhaps changing the subject. "I have always found her counsel worthy to those able to kill their cherished lies."

Lord Raveh and the bard found their horses refreshed and waiting, eager to run. Strange stars marked the canopy of a sheltering, unknown sky. The land was innocent of men. A snowy owl flew undisturbed through a seamless veil of quiet. When they reached enduring fields of cold tundra, a herd of reindeer galloped past them without fear of hunters. Soon enough, recovered strength waned into effort and concern. Uncounted miles and there was nowhere to rest. At last, they simply stopped to sleep, leaning against the horses for warmth.

In the morning, they shared provisions gifted by Arthur, dark bread, venison, a pair of small, sweet oranges. The boon was only good for men. The horses grazed meagerly on frozen grass. Then ice and strange fires took over. An elephant seal popped his head up from frigid waters to wonder at their passage, its whiskered face more curious than pensive, though he barked a lot. Now they headed towards an adamantine edifice of stone unknown to other worlds, its color amethyst, violet, brooding in silver and black amidst the clouds. They were fortunate to have been placed upon the proper way. There were dozens of paths to misadventure, all of them doom to mortal life.

At the foot of the tower they discovered a small grotto with a limpid pool. It must have sprung from roots deep underground, for while clear and cool, the water was temperate and pleasant to touch. There the friends stooped to drink. The horses, too, were not shy to slake long thirst. After drinking, a new wonder came to the vates and Lord Raveh. An image began to form in the water that Beorn recognized as the tiny annex to the second best library in the third best house. His father had built the attached deck with a fine view of descending hills that often hid themselves in a shroud of mist. There was the table where he himself had left the apple now dessicated to mark the chart. And there was Sky looking down onto the land with the distant thread of river glinting in the sun.

"A fine little world," he said, "but there's a shimmer about the place and the fabric of aeons grows thin. Arco forbade my entry."

Soren shot him a bemused look.

"I do not know if he believed in the firmness of my obedience or not," added the prince.

"Your father knew himself in his son," said Soren. Then gently, in a soft whisper, he urged the girl hoping to reach her.

"Listen closely, Sparrow. The light you see is an eggshell that carries through opaque membranes distant voices, our memories ancient and new."

The tower

When Lady Winterbourne journeyed to the tower, the passage always came at a cost. The lonely barrens she had mastered long ago, but one could never prepare for the wandering souls. They might be anyone, yet each carried need. Wretched creatures, they bore the past like tattered rags, hardly aware the times clung to them and tattled everything. It was an ordeal to encounter them, vaporous, confused, and screeching out weary demands that made no sense. She did what she could, spoke words that neither condoned wrongdoing, nor denied compassion. It was a relief to discover the region of fire and ice where solitude was only broken by the innocent beasts.

The tower itself raised high above the wall of mountains that held their backs to the sea. Depending on the air and time of day, it might appear black or purple or softened to a shade of violet. The Sha-rule called it forth in the time before times. It was her habit to thickly veil her face before ascending. The place was strange, brought forth elements of her visage difficult to predict and requiring care, lest the unwary be harmed by too much light.

Strife is all

The keeper of that tower spoke in such a beautiful manner, her voice was musical, and earthy in timber, yet sinuous with the secrets of water. The prince and Soren wondered at her and they reproached her veil, that thick garment the Orthodox call a homophorion. She sensed their thoughts and laughed softly.

"But I might be quite unusual, from a far country where things are different. I might have tusks like a boar and the golden eyes of a leopard."

Out of courtesy, she let them wonder. She poured them each a small goblet of brandy that warmed like cherry fire. The Sha-rule say that never yet in that land had anyone seen the true face of another.

"For always in battle we find each to grapple, to wound, even in our kisses. The strife is all," she said.

Beorn bowed to this. It was the way of things. But Soren Blake would not. Something in him raged against it.

"Gentle lady," he said, with what humor let another tell, "I cannot accept it."

Then that daughter of Mystery smiled. She went to the casement and opened the high window. The three looked out in silence. Bronze sails glinted in the gray-green sea like the wings of dragon-flies dipped in sepia suns.

The point of it

Lord Raveh was frank with Soren Blake. He felt their friendship could withstand honesty.

"One of your poets, what does he say, 'mankind cannot bear much reality'? I tell you human life is too ugly for anyone who thinks about it to rest content. This is the cause of the being of the gods."

The vates knew well that grim resistance. He answered softly. "It is ever the temptation of we who struggle to imagine beauty disappointing in the end. We court disenchantment to fend off pain."

Irony, strange magic, who can say, but Raveh did not remember the journey back from the tower. They had looked out upon the sea of dreams, and next he knew, he was riding into camp with the vates. Brief sadness rested in Soren Blake's eyes, but then his voice carried thunder.

"To vanquish your enemies, to kill the vile ones corrupted by evil, that is the limit of your victories."

Beorn shrugged. "Isn't that enough?"

"Love aims at more. Endurance is the martyrdom of the infinite."

Beorn expressed in his good-natured way the rather nebulous result of their endeavor. "What was the point of it?" he asked.

"The point of it? For you to learn love's ways, to become one with love — which you have not yet done."

The shade of Kos

The battles that Lord Raveh prosecuted slowly drained his forces. The pell-mell of the barbarians was still open to disciplined response. Raveh's militia could handle them. Yet unease continued to build, because during martial conflict and afterwards, one had the sense of reserve in the enemy. The Qa-Rendazi for reasons of their own simply waited to unleash a crushing blow. Hardy veterans began to show nerves, making elementary mistakes and screaming at their comrades. Then the country folk revealed the persistence of old ways. Even when the City and the lowlands became wealthy and learned new concepts, ideas that often poked fun at country backwardness, the highland pride refused to be abused. It was the honor of the vexillarius to represent these fierce ways.

Thus, in the Legio, the standard bearer alone wore the cloak of the presiding beast. The lion, the wolf, and the bear provided pelts to signify the living tradition of the spirit warrior that once fought for tribal victories. Now Raveh's men began to dress in the cloak of ancient, protecting beasts. The prince did not contradict them and for a while, it worked. The enemy was either surprised or perhaps gained greater respect for warriors with valor close to their own, though the advantage was brief. New forces appeared in the train of the Qa-Rendazi. Werewolves, the spiked Gingalash, the worm riders of Morwen sent fire into the ranks.

Only the counter-magic of Taliessin answered to this malevolent scrimmage. Songs of mystic strength invoked a shield that kept back the newly brought enemy. Beorn would never have reckoned the nature of the gift; how natives of a remote isle on earth gave praise to God in Gaelic tongue. The power of those Psalms echoed across dimensions, passed through the bard as protection. Nevertheless, several of the best horses and riders were lost. Black Thomas who never blanched before pikemen or distant archers, the mad, wild Marcus Tirinoth, master of stealth and speed, died beneath his leopard skin, and Captain Browers.

After that battle, the men retreated behind the ruins of Kos. They were weary of fighting. The enemy was eerily cruel and relentless, calling out at sunset the names of their dead. Even after the militia had torn away all identifying markers to resist further humiliation, some evil necromancy triumphed. Hideous, guttural noises were followed by a sneering recitation of those lost from their ranks. It was a vile, unnerving game.

On this night, Prince Raveh stood upon the wall and dared violence to find him. He cried out, vainly seeking in the darkness any sign of wisdom or decency in his foe. A glimpse of moonlight glinting across a battered helmet drew him to the faintest outline of a warrior standing insolent and unprotected on the darkened plain. Without seeing more, Beorn grasped that some captain of the others had come to answer. He raised his voice and spoke remonstrance.

"Leave our fallen in peace or at least do not mock them who died bravely. Or have you forgotten all traces of honor in whatever vile place your spirit calls home?"

The shadowy enemy offered no retort and appeared to remain unmoved, though the aftermath of subsequent battles proved dark silence.

Memory enchanted

A fragment of time approached softly, strange emissary from a stranger kingdom. A little boy was playing at the edge of an artificial pond that decorated the estate of a friend of his father's. The boy was perhaps nine or ten years of age and dressed in the manner of a nobleman's son. Very carefully, the boy arranged tiny figures aboard the deck of a model ship as he prepared to launch upon the vast sea. Lord Raveh remembered with a start. "Yes, I was this boy." A long corridor punctuated by statues of satyrs, orators, and whimsical nymphs led to some steps that ended in a roof that also served as floor for an outdoor patio. Arco was sitting by the table where the dappled sunlight partially hid his profile. Beorn could hear the shadowed voices of his father and his friend talking about the odd sorts of things adults find of interest.

Next, he saw Soren Blake approach the little boy. He's going to ask me about Pharaoh's chariots and if I enjoy tales about talking beasts. Then he's going to express skepticism about whether ships without carved prows are capable of intelligence. And last he will tell me something very important that I am not to forget, though I did forget, because I can't recall the words. Arco, my father who is yet Lord Raveh, and Timothy are waiting for him.

The autumn champagne

To spin this thread, there must be the sun burnished and low, crouching like a fiery pumpkin over the shoulders of mangrove trees, the waters flecked with gold above shimmering tea darkness, menacing and serene.

To spin this thread, there must be fine houses, large edifices with cold cellars and slumbering wine, with men surrounded by tobacco smoke talking of horses, with women chatting, their savage claws masked by delicate paper fans amidst satin flowing like butterfly wings.

To spin this thread there must be memories grown sweet with age, hidden love concealed amidst care and scramble suddenly obvious, adorable, untouchable.

To spin this thread, poignant with the beauty of fragile time, you must imbibe deeply the autumn champagne.

The gray hordes

Then surprising help came. Cohorts from the Third and Eighth Legio arrived as reinforcements. Word of Raveh's bravery had reached them. Their generals knew the City had quarantined the truth about the Sixth. The numbers of cavalry and foot soldiers swelled. Raveh's militia renewed its courage. Battle tested their hopes. It seemed impossible. Wave upon wave of the enemy line charged. The cohorts met them with grim determination until the barbarian forces began to lessen and then stopped. Only the Qa-Rendazi remained, yet that was enough. Beorn spoke with the leaders of the cohort divisions. The numbers of the enemy appeared to mirror the influx of defending soldiers. Where they came from remained both daunting and perplexing.

And then, during a lull, an answer suggested itself. In the north, where the trenches squirreled and twisted for miles and the barren plains offered no resistance to projectile or prying eye, the men would hunker down in their damp, wretched dens, playing cards beneath a guttering lamp, whilst waiting for mysterious, seemingly pointless orders for the next furtive charge above the veined maze of dirt and cement scarred with spikes of barbed wire. But here, where trees and streams and meadows rebuked them, the heedless enemy carried forth in the stark light of day. At the back of the front line, astride a pale horse, the leader of those gray hordes, a general on a ghostly stallion stood tall in the saddle, his straight back and haughty glance admitting no concession that his battalion was a savage rabble. Without thought or hope for respite, the relentless foe dressed in motley garb, the rag and bone of a thousand armies from a thousand wars, waited with ominous patience.

And here was the humorless, grotesque, bitter flower of all that strife. The best of them, the most courageous, the most loyal, the ones who loved the city and willingly gave their blood were destined to join themselves to betrayal, to become the monstrous night — for Beorn knew that rider and knew the horse, both slain in a charge many winters ago: Arco and the noble Star Dancer.

Bittersweet

A bugle cried out in the fog. The last dance in that idiosyncratic killing was upon them. Taliessin had departed for reasons of his own. The legions fought with desperation and ferocity. The malady of memory persisted. Submerged passions and pain they had thought grown callous and scarred over had come to them with uncanny immediacy. Some were stung into a catatonic state, unwilling or unable to remedy the needs of the moment against the times come suddenly back to life. And others drew umbrage from the meanness of it, sought to slaughter in rage anything that moved. There were tactical advances and retreat that made local sense, but no one could apprehend the meaning of that war. Afterwards, it was impossible to explain. You could not write up that action, and so it cannot be told here. One final mystery crowned the entire episode with the signature of its strangeness. Before the disappearance of the enemy, for it was more a vanishing then despairing or strategic retreat, a sense of witness, a Presence came amidst their hatreds and stopped them cold, what it wanted, no one could say.

Then Beorn, Lord Raveh, raised himself up high in his saddle. The line had held. The prince felt the bellows heaving in the chest of great Battleheart. The steed was near to bursting, another run would have brought him to his end. Across the blood-caked field the carnage was vast, incredible that so many had ever been born, and all doomed to lie in that obscene repose. Prince Raveh slid from the horse and threw his arms about him, weeping. He stopped himself short with a bitter laugh and gestured towards the panorama of the dead.

"All these," he said, "descend into unknown chambers, sleep for a turn, and then come back for a reckoning. Our very victories are ever prelude to that humiliating grave."

The prince patted the neck of his warrior-friend. The horse, far spent, slightly twitched its ears and flared its nostrils, but could not even raise its head as was his wont to acknowledge the liege-companion.

Intervention

The men were silent, shook to the core. Something outrageous, beyond known categories had intervened. But even so, eventually, one must go on. They built fires and gathered around.

"Add a little more forage," one said.

"It's crisp, just like when I was young in the mountains with oma and opa," said another.

No one mentioned the overwhelming because it had no name and they could not accept the being of anything so inexpressible. Beorn clapped the back of a grizzled veteran. They shared a flask.

"I won't ask you to say anything," said Lord Raveh. "It seemed to me," he added, "that the point of attack altered. The enemy turned and fought along our side. Their arrows floated above our heads and struck . . . elsewhere."

The old soldier quenched his dry throat. "I suppose the lion and the boar make common cause when it suits them," he said. "Only what manner of enemy unites the likes of them and us I don't want to know, prince."

The white hart

Those who deplore war, who treat young men dreaming of heroic deeds as naïve fools indulge an easy moral superiority. Prince Raveh wanted to tell them that men were nearly always foolish anyways. Women, too. But the cycle was bleak, careful, unadventurous, given to mercenary wisdom and obsessive fears, always scheming and forestalling that terrible moment when resources and planning would mean nothing at all.

He was suddenly reminded of that day in Tamberlin. It had felt eerie from the beginning. So much anticipation for the hunt and rumor of the unspotted creature, everyone was excited, but there was something else they wouldn't admit. He was well acquainted with that emotion. The very light was pregnant with it. Awe, terror, fearful longing. When he saw Sky riding down towards the hounds wild to remark the numinous, Raveh's mount felt it too. The beasts reason in their own way and they often recognize more lucidly than men the frisson of the holy. He'd checked his hunter, wary of the uncanny danger in the white hart. And so when Sky gave full reign to her horse that madly charged, he knew she was one of the unacknowledged tribe.

By the time they finally arrived, her pretty companion was pale and shaking as much as her poor horse. What happened remained as enigmatic as the girl's smile. Sky emerged from a thicket and acknowledged their regard with mute amiability, acted as if nothing had occurred. Everyone made a joke of it to dispel the uncomfortable ambiguity. And that was the end. The frazzled threads of the hunt gathered in order to disburse without memory or festal triumph.

What he could never tell the pious citizens who deplored the savagery of it all, and they were right about that, was a bond you simply couldn't properly explain, not unless you'd joined yourself to others, put yourself at risk, and faced the death. Rallying amidst the chaos of battle, a vertiginous wall rose up like a sheer cliff, vortice of abyssal night, something to invite horror. Yet if the pitch was just right, a kind of grace might descend and instead, joy would surge in one's veins.

Shy silence guarded that brotherhood, the valkyric sisterhood, that sharp emotion that was pain and glory and generous abandon all at once. It was a sort of prayer. So he said nothing and the soldiers made crude jokes and laughed and enjoyed the gawking admiration of the folk never destined to wear a warrior's cloak.

At Votern

Pleased, but uneasy with victory, well, at least with the avoidance of defeat, Lord Raveh mourned lost friends. The men quickly turned from the ferocity of combat and the near prospect of death to an almost gamesome lightness he knew well, as if a boyish heart were let out to recess from the fierce work at hand. They had come to the town of Votern which lies southerly, but near the banks of the river Oise. The people of Votern raised a hurrah for the army, but Lord Raveh knew that some retained a cautious eye upon the soldiers for war unleashes passions dangerous and hard to contain. When it became clear that the warriors had money and a desire to eat and spend, the welcome became considerably warmer.

It was Beorn's way to keep aloof from such pleasures and the men respected him, yet did not draw him near to heart. So it was that as the evening grew long and Lord Raveh had stabled his horse for the night, the prince wandered away from the town on foot with a desire to listen to the river and be alone with his thoughts. The prince happened upon a rustic cabin that he would have taken for a ruin but for a little tendril of smoke whispering forth from its chimney. And even then, he would have walked on, but the door swung open and an old woman stood in the doorway. From within, a kerosene lamp cast upon her a pale nimbus of light.

"So, brother Beorn," she said, "have you yet learned the lesson or do you still doubt the way?"

And he knew that despite the old woman, it was Shadrael who called to him.

"There is no lesson but sacrifice," he said.

"That is no lesson at all," said the old woman. "Come in. You do not know the meaning of the word. Acquainted with sorrow, soldiers are always ready to bargain. It is the child that refuses."

Raveh sighed and peered into the familiar eyes in the aged face. "What do you want from me?" he said at last.

The crone went to the table and took the lamp swinging it about until she came to a battered trunk lying in a corner of cobwebs.

"An old woman cannot be flattered. She is skin and bone, yet life clings and she has nothing but shadows and memory to sell. It is a famished existence."

Raveh was searching for an answer when the woman pulled a key from the pocket of her apron and opened the trunk. She drew out a gown of gossamer and peach, golden with time's equivocal face.

"Here is something to offer," said the old woman. "You might gift this to the maiden. You know the one."

Chapter Five

Dance of the Heart

Street scene

The long boulevard of shops is filled with folk. There, near the boutique that sells Belgian chocolates and other sweet-meats, the university rector may be seen in his pale blue gown trimmed with ermine. His four-cornered biretta matches the gown, at the belt is a small maroon purse with golden tassel. There are elegant tins of caramel cashews and sea salt that he favors in that shoppe. Near him, incongruous, a taller man dressed in mourning, his long sleeved black robe and separate hood drapes well over the hidden face. If he fancies a mint or scrumptious dainty, it is veiled in the tragic prose of his habiliments.

Then, down the center of the street, everyone gives way. The dream carter comes, his face equally masked, though covered by the probiscus of a long-beaked swallow. His lime green trunk hose ends in a doublet of gray with a dowdy cape wren brown. The

carter raises his arms, holds them forth before him, levitating perhaps a yard above his head is his especial charge. It seems a dull
little casket, but then it will suddenly glimmer or groan with a
shuddering that makes everyone look away. "Ouru-ouru- ouru-ri,"
he cries out before him.

This is the dream, it comes for someone meaning something,
though few can say what, destined to cross the milky stars, it may
seep into the drowse of humble or great, the writing on the label
is too small to read. No one touches him; it is a sacred task, and ill
luck to the fool that endangers the fragile skin that carries oneiric
wine.

Where the bodies were

The Mumbo-Junkies were at it again. The latest performance was
announced for The Drowned Mermaid, a local café. They weren't
happy unless protest was involved. The notion of good poetry
was already guilty of hierarchy and a host of bourgeois sins. If
truant vegetables and rancid meat was thrown at them, so much
the better, they considered it a badge of honor.

"Hurry, Deco. Jacques is going to be there. That thief,
Duchamp, as well," said Emile. (Duchamp owed him money.)
"You know it's going to be *scandalous.*"

Emile spoke in enticing mock horror, but Deco could not ac-
commodate his friend. He was taking his pal to see someone in the
spook zone. She had a notion they might tell her something she
wished to remember. Deco wanted to tell Sky there were plenty of

worlds where people paid to forget. He met her at the fountain in front of the Hotel Grand. It was the second time he had seen her since the misadventure of the hunt at Tamberlin. The first time, the time she asked for his help, Deco had run into her as she was on the way to an Anshari gathering of some sort. She'd seemed subtly changed, more certain of herself, but also eager for answers. Now, he wondered how much that was an accident of the moment. The Elder was still missing. Sky was determined, yes, but the edge on her nerves was back.

They walked a roundabout path looking for the house to match the listed address which was obscure, one of those numbers with a half at the end of it. When at last they found it, a tiny apartment that teetered like a birdcage on top of a stack of more substantial buildings, the fella waiting for them was someone they had met at that party of Madame Dahlia's where Deco first discovered Sky.

The apartment was a standard distribution site, not too bright or clean, but hidden in liminal shadows still close enough to public space. Pennyfeather glanced over at them with a nearly bored air — she with a borrowed man's fedora shadowing her lovely face, he making an effort to portray bold non-chalance when they were both the usual mixture of innocent curiosity and slightly guilty awareness of the clandestine.

Even the most intrepid clerks were wary of certain quarries. There were old stories told about a sketchy itinerary, suspect vaults, inauspicious openings onto forgotten alcoves, a notorious third turn on the thirty-eighth longitudinal corridor, an aspect sometimes available and often not. Ambiguity haunted the paths that led to such places from which even a veteran clerk might disappear never to return. Pennyfeather had charted many of these "spooky strings" and taken note of variables. For instance, a blood moon would presage the sudden appearance of certain archives, though make haste. Stay more than five minutes and one could be entailed for months or sometimes even years, what was left of you, that is.

Few suspected Pennyfeather the sort to have dared enough to accumulate this specialized knowledge. Yet the genius of the clerk was still rarer, for he had a knack, there was hardly another way to put it, an occult feel for where the bodies were. And so, he knew which vault was likely to yield information on medieval Uzbeki peasants and what shelves of the registry detailed the quotidian minutiae of early 21st century suburban New Jersey housewives, if one should be perverse enough to require such information. Mnemo-cylinders, of course, you could make a pretty penny on those, provided you weren't caught. Hung, drawn, and quartered was generally an effective deterrent.

Even he, however, was stymied by this particular quest. Pennyfeather had, under pretext of academic research, made inquiries that called upon the interests cultivated by the necro-hypnotic branch, a group reclusive and creepy enough to ward off almost all outside contacts. Their response was so enigmatic as to constitute either a refusal or incapacity to communicate with anyone lacking familiarity with specialized code. In the end, he'd resorted to his usual seat-of-the-pants intuitions after all. He wasn't sure he'd happened on the right stuff, but it was a good guess.

"You understand, these logs are transcribed from the archives?" he asked with a gloss of professional honesty. "The real ones have a watermark."

"And what reason do we have to trust this isn't a complete fabrication?" asked Deco.

Pennyfeather shrugged. "None whatsoever. How could there be proof for this sort of work? In the end, it's a matter of plausibility. When you read the data, does it convince?"

"And does it? For you?" asked Sky.

The clerk did not answer, but shoved the package wrapped in brown paper over to the girl.

"See for yourself, amie. Judgment is such a personal act."

Affirmed inerrancy

All the records stipulated historical accuracy. The office of the Guardian affirmed inerrancy. Each individual was summed. They were not less, nor more. The assessment could not be altered. Once an act is performed, a word spoken, it is for always, echoes unto eternity. The priestly class might promise provisional forgiveness, but outside the negation of oblivion the hope for escape from the ineradicable, the unsightly remained a purely irrational aspiration. And thus, despite the portentousness of the claim, a squalid, ironic boredom rested upon all the names. Even the hand of the scribes mimicked in the unofficial transcripts seemed to express a barely suppressed yawn before the tawdry dullness of unexceptional perversity.

Pennyfeather had gathered for Sky a quartet of names. They might be wrong, but he felt all possible and one or two likely. It was a masculine crime, but he'd included a woman on the off-chance. That type was less gripped by the nearly mindless mechanism of habit. Instead of perverted sexuality, a womanly zest for malice; he threw it in because his aesthetic sense wanted to balance out the index of hideous monotony.

Followed

Sky clutched those documents with a feeling of dread, yet also, guilt; even, in ways she did not wish to explore, excitement. She glanced over at Deco who still had that boyish expression of bravado. Sky hated hysterical women. She was certain that somewhere in her past, there was reason for this. Nonetheless, she had to resist an urge to slap his silly face. And then, to make matters worse, she began to suspect that someone was following them.

At first, Sky passed it off as neurotic projection. She had these papers and felt that everyone knew, like a lad skulking about with a naughty magazine. Only after they'd moved out of the fringes of the spook's netherworld, she continued to sense a persistent someone. Sky didn't want to crane her neck backwards to confirm her suspicions and she was too embarrassed to say anything. Paranoia was ridiculous and Deco was enjoying the lark as if he were Errol Flynn cast in a swashbuckling cinema. Then, whether through panic or ill luck, she tripped. In getting to her feet, Sky caught a glimpse in the distance, but not too distant, someone, a man, perhaps. For some reason, she couldn't bring him into clarity. *He's following us*, she thought.

Sky began to walk quickly and Deco nearly had to run to catch up.

"What is it?" he said.

"Nothing," said Sky, fighting back tears.

And now, Deco was on the alert. "Can't see anything," he said at last.

"No, me neither," said Sky bravely.

"You know, when I was a child, I used to get seizures. Just would swoon out. The doctor's couldn't say why. I always had a feeling, just before, that someone was following me."

"Oh, Deco. How awful!"

"It's alright. Hasn't happened in years, but to be honest, I still have days when I suddenly think of it and start to get the shivers."

They walked a bit farther, feeling like children whose grown up adventure suddenly isn't fun anymore. False banter quickly gave way to discussion of who to consult. The Elder having seen fit to disappear, in the end they decided upon the priest.

The knowledge of good and evil

"Didn't he tell you?" Father Bunn gazed at them with his innocent, guileless eyes. There was a pause. "Maybe he doesn't know. The Archives are not like microfilm gathering dust in the library. They don't degrade over time, nor do they exist as simple records of information."

"But these aren't even the originals!" objected Deco.

"All the documents are of similar nature. A copy is just as likely to do the trick."

"What do you mean trick?" asked Sky, her face a peculiar shade of trepidation.

"No treats, I'm afraid," said the priest, his expression quite grave. "All the files are binding spells. You can read up on anyone you like, but not without incurring the cost. You're connected now to anyone you've looked up. Their destiny and yours are linked. Further, they know about it at some level, often below conscious awareness. Still, there are ways, if one is not too scrupulous, to dredge that up. They know about you. It's the price of knowledge. Someone should have said. It's in the code for universal readers."

The lost girl saves the day

Sky was amazed at the priest's words. She quarreled with Deco who was inclined to take it all as an elaborate jest.

"Surely you can see he wasn't joking?" she said.

"He's having one over on you," insisted the scion of mercantile wealth. "It stands to reason. You don't risk Nero's regard when you read about the mad tyrant."

And this all made good sense, only Father Bunn had never before displayed malicious wit.

"I think he means it," she said again.

Deco decided to end the night. The fella wasn't any fun when she got like that. And so she was alone, stewing on it: *Did knowing about someone, anyone, bring a vital connection? Libraries are dangerous*, she thought. *If folks knew, hardly anyone would read a book.* And then she considered how few actually made use of libraries and had the bitter thought, *hardly anyone does.*

The darkness of the narrow street was innocent enough, but she doubted its sincerity. What came next was walking, the usual thing, one foot after another. She did this for awhile, until she began to imagine soft footfall mocking her by matching every step with delicate mimicry. Now that Deco had left, Sky didn't care about making an impression. She could stop and look around however much she liked. And truly, there was nothing to see. Then she would do the walking action some more, she was quite used to it. Only, still, that soft, almost crepuscular intimation, a sound so subtly trying not to be a sound; Sky turned quickly. An outside observer would swear she had Tourette's or something. For a brief, fantastic moment, she thought she saw him, still caught in phantasmagoric haze, but a man, lithe, pale visage, the older optics would have said the rays from his eyes, sending forth mordant, nearly ironic appraisal. And then there was the ordinary darkness, the trick of night, to make you think the borders of things had grown less certain.

A little while longer and she happened upon an old cobblestone square. Maybe things were better. It had been ten minutes and the quiet was of the usual kind. There was a fountain, dried up or turned off. A street lamp cast its shadow across the quad, which was unremarkable, except that when you looked hard, there might be too much shadow. Sky hurried. At the end of the square, she peered back. There was no one following, but the excess shadows remained. Sometimes they looked like sinewy smoke with no defined shape, but then they would suddenly gather and begin to suggest four distinct figures of varying height and body type.

Sky began to really run. She cut through an alley, a short capillary that led onto a boulevard. The shadows had transformed yet again. Still four, but assuming the form of lupine beasts with wolfish eyes that flared blood red in the night, there was no one there to hear her scream. And then! Then there was someone sprung up almost out of the night air it seemed, a woman standing before her with a determined, yet almost mocking expression on her face. The woman opened an object that appeared quite a lot like an umbrella, but when she spun it about in a rapid circle like a prayer wheel, it gave off a shimmer of stunning light.

As she did this, the woman cried out or perhaps sang an undulating command. It was an impressive sound, whatever it was. The result of this opportune behavior was that the shadows that had been closing in on poor Sky vanished.

Sky was so stunned and relieved, she said nothing when the woman turned and smiled. Her deliverer was dressed well, but not ostentatiously. Her face was rather severe, but good bones. *She's almost familiar*, Sky thought, and suddenly, "Oh, it's you!"

Lady Winterbourne shrugged. "My man won't recognize this aspect. For him, I am always the lost girl."

The plenitude is full but never finished

A sitting room in a Regency Park townhouse is a very fine place to recover from an attack of demonic shadows. Lady Winterbourne was a gracious hostess. Sky suspected the tea had been fortified with an ingredient that normally resided in a crystal decanter. The biscuits were delicate with a dark chocolate center and a hint of orange flavor. They sat for a long time together talking of little things, as if they both wished to prolong the company without the intrusion of more serious matters. Yet Sky could not help asking questions. She was so curious. On the subject of her varied appearance, Lady Winterbourne said, "The plenitude is full, but never finished. I was like this the first time we met. Something must have happened — that this window is now open to you."

Sky had a feeling she knew what had happened, but remained silent on that point. Tamberlin was hard to explain. It did prompt Sky to wonder aloud why one should see through one window and not another, to which Lady Winterbourne could only say "the Wise chooses the timely aspect, my dear." And when Sky asked who or what is the Wise, her friend, she thought of her that way, said "*we are*, in a fashion, but that is the gift of Spirit" which was not much better, but as far as Lady Winterbourne was prepared to explain.

After this, they played a game of scrabble, only the *Q* seemed to have gone missing.

"It's the magic mouse," said Lady Winterbourne. "She takes things like that when they catch her fancy."

Accuracy

"There is danger in touching. The ancient feeling for the pure and the impure, it isn't just some superstition, an atavistic failure to perceive accurately. Touching is crossing over. The eyes touch, too. A man who can behold a woman's beauty without coveting" and here, the speaker cast her eyes down and nearly blushed at some memory, "that is the courtesy of the eyes."

As Lady Winterbourne was talking, Sky had the feeling she had heard this voice before, only then she did not have vision to connect the voices with a face. And then she began to think about Father Bunn, and what he said.

"There's all sorts of ways to make contact, aren't there?" she said.

"Aristotle and Aquinas, too," said Lady Winterbourne, "assert that the keenest intellects are those most sensitive to touch. The sharpest mind discerns the slightest mediation of spirit in the handling of the flesh. Thus, in a crowd, jostled by a multitude of bodies, the Anointed turned about and asked, 'who touched me?' The desire of the one in pain cut through the noise of the many."

Masters of stillness

Sky told Lady Winterborne about the end of the Etheric affair. It was still a source of great perplexity. "I don't know why I couldn't speak of it," she said, feeling ashamed.

"We bear some burdens for ourselves, whether we would or no," said Lady Winterbourne. "And some are for the others. My man once said that the world was an ordeal for everyone, and that whenever he saw a soul that was struggling or heard people whispering about someone who had cracked up because they couldn't cope, he said compassion was only justice, because that person endured that trial on his behalf, so that he did not have to."

When she said "my man" her features softened and the eyes flashed with a glimmer of her younger self. "He knew lots of artists and some folk who tried to think more deeply about their lives. It cost them, you see, because folks understand that wee little people and giants have trouble fitting into suits and sitting down in ordinary furniture, but when the spirit is odd shaped, they just roll their eyes at the discomfort of the soul; only these odd ones are closer to what we are called to be."

Sky sipped the warm tea and tried to imagine the shape of her soul.

And then Lady Winterbourne said, "In the ancient days, men and women practiced slowness in order to understand. And then we tried the other way, zooming past one another with our foot on the accelerator, unaware that the circle was getting smaller, and time was racing in an ever tightening gyre. But the Vendakar, they are the masters of stillness, which is the shortest distance between eternities."

Sky averred that she could never learn stillness.

"Shaa, my dear. My man is also impatient. It is one of the hardest lessons for us to learn. We want to do everything ourselves, and yesterday, no?"

Her laughing eyes made Sky smile.

"I will tell you what you shall hardly believe. Probably you will not believe . . . " Lady Winterbourne stopped then and returned an impish smile that was perfectly natural, so that you did not accept the sober face that she so often presented to the world. *You are playing at that,* thought Sky. "Alright," said her friend. "I tell you anyway. A whole life can be preparation. You might wait and wait, and never find your way onto the stage in order to stammer and flub your lines, though you've practiced that part often enough."

"How awfully sad making," said Sky.

"But your waiting might be exactly what is asked of you, hard as it may seem."

"I don't understand," said Sky, who suddenly felt as if she might cry.

"Do not fear that the loveliness you long for shall remain forever unexpressed." Now Lady Winterbourne appeared on the verge of emotion, but she quickly recovered herself. "Each part is essential to all the others. Only together can we truly be free," she said.

Parables of the flesh

"I will tell you something else. It is related to this. The healings of the Anointed are parables of the flesh. It was important for the needy to know that love attends to every small thing. We are made for joy. Yet some think only of health, as if the thriving of the body alone were life." This was so funny that Lady Winterbourne laughed. "*And when these poor clothes are incapable of withstanding the glory of love* . . . I tell you, the way of love is hard. Love is the bearing of wounds. Blessed are those who mourn."

"Yes, but no one wants grief," said Sky.

"Sin is armor against pain. So often, the gift of love is patient of our sorrows, of lameness, and the sickness unto death. Those who cannot hear this think not to follow the beloved; the Cross is always for someone else."

Incomprehensible kindness

"The eyes of heaven, my dear, are so much more tender than we have imagined. When we get to the end of our patience, we are ready to settle for some ordinary imposition of power to bring our anguish to an end. And of course, we cannot perceive grace most of the time. It seems to us like it just isn't there, so we conclude that it must not be. I mean, we assume it cannot be with our wicked enemies, especially when they are being so wicked. My man is sometimes like that. He is kind and sweet, oh, yes he is, but he smolders at the brazen meanness of what we allow ourselves. And then some days when he has had enough, he explodes at the terrible injustice, and it is terrible (both the explosion and the injustice)."

Sky admired how her friend put the two together and made a sort of joke of it, while still being serious. She added then softly. "And yet love reproaches our anger with incomprehensible kindness."

Sky saw that Lady Winterbourne loved him so much that when she spoke of the Elder's failings, she considered them her own. *That is very interesting*, she thought. *To suppose perhaps that we are so much a part of one another . . .*

The empty chamber

Lady Winterbourne showed her one last thing. Her friend slid her hand along a panel, explaining that at one time it was illegal to celebrate the sacrament of Incarnation. Sky imagined what it must have been like to be a hunted priest or a recusant family stealthily hiding someone who could get you killed. Lots of folks would wonder at risking one's skin and fortune for arcane ritual, but she was not that sort. It was not perhaps the romantic in her so much as an ingrained sympathy if not belief that what matters most is apt to appear silly or trivial to those getting on with life. The folk who knew pain and charity amidst their poverty, they would know better. If there ever was an aristocracy with genuine nobility, they would know this too and protect the heart of the people like a sacred pledge. And there it was. The chamber was not ornate. It was sparsely furnished with a simple wooden chair and a small table upon which a porcelain wash basin was set. A fine grain of sleepy dust told her no one had come to this place in a long time.

The night globe of the child king

Lady Winterbourne went with Sky a considerable way into that night, but she would not treat her as a child who must be walked home. When Lady Winterbourne turned to depart, a shiver came over Sky.

"But really, why are they following me? Is it quite safe?" she asked in a hurry of panic.

Her friend approached her again and spoke a kind of blessing, touching her forehead, her nose and her lips. Her words were perhaps less comforting. "Do not be anxious over that," she said. "It is not our concern, whether we are safe or not. What if the Anointed had chosen to be safe, rather than good?"

Nevertheless, the evening had put off the cloak of malevolence. After some initial uneasiness, Sky discovered her old pleasure in strolling about the city. She came upon what the locals called a rock garden, which was an ancient cemetery. Ordinarily, Sky wasn't superstitious, but a light flickering provocatively amidst the granite monuments made her catch her breath. When it disappeared into a vanishing trail, she resumed her walk, relieved. There had been an open book from Lady Winterbourne's library containing Homilies on the Song of Songs. Sky did not even know she had read from it until words from Gregory of Nyssa introduced a voice far different from the slithering gloom of her pursuers. *The advantage you will gain from having welcomed me and enabled me to dwell in you will be the dew with which my head is covered and the drops of night that trickle from my locks...*

At the Lion's Gate, she gazed down upon the vast desert that acted as an ocean to defend the city. The sentinels could drift into sleep on that wall. And then, she doubted her eyes. She saw it once more, a flicker of light. *"It can't be in both places, can it?"* she asked herself. *"It must be me."*

Yet she was willing to let that mystery be. Adventure, fear, relief, and welcoming caught up with her. Too sleepy to feed the demon of distraught tagging along at her feet, Sky turned for home. How nice it would be to hear Midori complain about the random feminine affections thrown at Mr. Takashima in her absence. It was then, in the corner of her eye, that Sky glimpsed the boy.

The child was carrying what she took for a candle. When she saw better, the taper appeared more like a crystalline flower, its petals soft, translucent, glowing so that a rounded arc of light went forth as herald ahead of him. This was too much for the poor demon, and it fled hapless into the night.

Psalmic resonance

We, he said, and the pure flame danced. There within, she saw the luster of kindness, the light. The women bearing water, they carry the vessels on their heads, the golden glow of the sun dazzles to a point at their feet. Like shadows in the dusk, the sandhill cranes stand in tranquil waters. In order to see, the wigmen paint themselves in gold incarnadine, in the tent of their ancestors, the skulls of the forebears sing, they dream the future.

In the mist, the forests of Bhutan rise in majesty. The Rhododendron flourish, pink and red flower bursts crown green fronds. The rock spires of Huangshan manifest in a nimbus of fog. Slowly, they ponder. Against the dawn clouds of Mongolia, midnight blue and cerulean, the caramel carving of deer in the burnt orange flesh of stone. In the afternoon, the Kazakh hunters train the falcon, its solar feathers sparking in the wind.

The rock wall is the color of sand. Further on, it becomes striated, blanched into faded bone with umber shadows. The skins and pelts of slain beasts adorn the wall, beneath which the dogon hunters of Mali repose in golden caps and robes. This is not arrogance, but tribute and gratitude, releasing the spirits of blessed prey. Lush limestone ridge coated in emerald moss. The waterfall descends in white-blue garments, veiling in springs of thunder the quiet shouts of angels.

The tall spine of the kokerboom reaches up from the Namibian desert. The spongy fiber of its trunk nurses the precious river of life. Slow to mature, at thirty it begins to bloom. In the leaves of the quiver tree the honey of aloe; under cover of the Milky Way it sleeps, a scarf of stars whispering your dream. At the Pushkar fair, the smoke of evening fire rises like incense from the golden dust. White turbaned men chatter and wind down the day, the long necks of their camel mounts drowsing.

In the mountains of Honshu Province, hot springs tender warm welcome amidst the ice. The snow monkeys arrived, settling in for a bath. The mobile flesh of their magenta faces beneath golden fur portrayed according to individual preference varied inclination — serenity, bleary eyed lassitude, mutual regard. It was just like the Romans, they chatted about family, the weather, the prospects for spring.

The sands of Namibia, blazing in the day, the gazelle cross over in the gentler morn, their soft prints destined for the wind. Apart from the parched and suffocating heat, the dunes sway in abstract perfection, a coverlet in vanilla and sepia stretching to the horizon. And the Himba women cover themselves in the rich *otijize*, a mixture of red ochre, butterfat, and resin. The dull master will tell you it is protection from the sun, faithless to radiant beauty.

Long sleeved, in white muslin, the merchant sits in simple linen. Only the red fez upon his head hints at the exquisite chromatic range of his carpets, the woven patterns suggesting the dance of fractals. He waits in solemn contemplation of the fields of fabric. You have entered through the Medina archways in search of his wares. He will not tell you which one has the power to resist gravity. Perhaps the woman at the fountain filling her plastic bottle knows something of enchantment.

The cold earth come to life, five-foot-long caimans scramble from out of the wetlands, their black eyes gawking like over-sized marbles. Amiable fellows, the farmers of Brazil feed them. Bernanos, surfeit with Europe's betrayal, fled there, too, where its primeval forests gave cover to his childlike fury at the injustice of mankind.

The highlanders of New Guinea, the Chimbu men, apply the naked bones of future time onto the living skin. These skeleton men, bearing ancestral memory, weave the tribe as one. Yet empire gobbles up the local ken, the shrewd grow skeptic, the march of legions carries forth despair. Distant tyrants lord it over electronically. *Are we the ministers of death? Of life-in-death? Do we but supervise the world-death being dead ourselves, long since?*

From a distance, the mountain range would seem inhospitable, yet closer in the wild grasses sing verdant life and possibly *Matilda*. The rust of silent rock faces reflect in water pools that collect in deep canyons. Piebald trunks, spotted like a pinto, sculpture the land, the tree known as ghost gum. Upon the low ground, sporting a dorsal display that mimics stone and leaf, the thorny devils craftily play at *Where's Waldo*.

The muskox of Nunivak Island makes a good hoplite. Heads and horns facing outward, the bulls form a defensive circle, careful to sandwich juveniles between veterans. A herd of male walrus rest peacefully on Togiak beach. Close packed; from above they look like yams with tusks, a truce made possible because jousting just isn't fun without females watching.

At the entrance to the adobe building, the Somba children, three brothers, emerge. They come bearing four puppies. The youngest boy stares out with serious face, but his puppy smiles. The middle brother holds two canines in his arms; they loll about in happy abandon. The eldest, to his left, wears a thin necklace of silver. The fourth puppy lies across his lap, sleeping. The blue sandals of the youngest child have escaped from his feet. They lie off to the side, communing with the dust.

The young leopard peers out from her perch in the acacia. No Juliet upon her parapet, she watches from safety not for Romeo, but the delicious impala unwary enough to be welcome. A lone Plains zebra stands awash a throng of white-bearded wildebeest, a bewildered referee dropped into a flash rugby scrum. At the Etosha water hole, the beasts gather at the height of day. Zebra and the little springbok antelope cede access to the aggressive display of the southern ostrich, their periscope necks and squawking faces rise from their bodies like angry fan dancers.

The Bajau are sea gypsies, allied to no land. Their children scout about in narrow canoes, the rough paint already peeled back from the wandering. Thin houses of board shaped like shoe boxes stand on platforms staged above the waters, wash hangs from lines attached to support poles or hooked below a makeshift roof. In the sea of Cortés, long-beaked dolphin sport above the azure sea in playful arcs, a school of hundreds racing the vessels of men.

The giant trunks of the baobab stand like columns against the pale sky deepening into blue. Their modest arms branch into tendrils like nerve endings touching the silence. Below this subtle prayer, the tropical zebus move the oxcart in stride. They follow the human bidding, unconcerned with the invisible Parthenon above. In the Amazonian canopy, the three-toed sloth practices stillness.

The golden eyes of the young lioness meet one with the glow of vivacious health. She could be dangerous, but just now, her portrait is willing to forego violence. Amidst the Pushkar bazaars, a Rajathani woman pulls back the cobalt veil fringed with gold braid, green and pink icicles. Her dress of spangled yellows, rubies, violets, burnt orange, and greens weaves a floral paisley. An enameled necklace of six point flowers alternate petals of rainbow harmony; even the blue band, a lanyard meant for a Nokia camera, blaze against the silky mahogany of her skin. Her lovely face is bejeweled as well. A tiny plate with streaming chains adorns one ear; a delicate burnished miniature pagoda hangs from the other. Most astonishing amidst the constellated fabrics and metals that somehow avoid cacophony, the same golden eyes that burn with leonine grace recur in the woman. An Orient Helen, hard to say who more fearfully takes one's breath away.

Perhaps intended for the eagle angel, certainly only grasped from the skies above, you might puzzle over one of those long patterns cut into the earth shaped like a beast to glyph a mind, some road built into the rock by simple people that never knew bulldozers or surveyor's equipment. Ancient alien theorists suggest . . . The Ord river delta sent its own greeting. In the center of the mudflats the long trunk of the axial tree glows silver blue and purple, its attending aura reaching out to the floodplain, painting the wetlands in brown, orange and yellow ochre.

The flock stands in equipoise, their pink cotton candy bodies atop thin bamboo stalks for legs, the long curling neck and tail feathers flash a touch of mandarin orange. These flamingos find their doubles mirrored in the coastal pond miles from kitsch and suburban front lawns. Aerial artists, sifaka leap and pinball from tree to tree. On the ground, resembling slight, awkward lemurs, they skip sideways rather than walk, their infants cling like needy rucksacks.

The late summer sun of Okavango sits close to the horizon, a crimson giant singing lullabies to the flames of grassfires below. Safe from danger, a herd of African elephants ponders the old ways, tells tales of coming autumn. In Jaipur, during Holi, the elephants partake in the festival of colors. Mahouts drape shining brocade headdress upon the patient head, paint the docile pachyderm slate with vibrant patterns and images beyond the wildest fantasia of a Botswana elephant.

The columns toppled long ago. What's left is a stone fragment here and there, some upright, others on their side, like chess pieces abandoned by giants. Stubby grass surrounds the silent ruins, the horizon low and bright. An athletic young woman in a bathing suit climbs a recumbent pawn; stands on ancient stone inviting the gods to gaze in admiration. A priest draped in black garments bows over the lectern and reads the scripture, memorizing his existence word by word. An iconostasis of saints stands behind him imploring the unknown.

Guanxi fishermen stroke the feathered breasts of their cormorants, whisper words of good fortune to their trained companions. The lanterns atop the shallow timber boats call out to the piscine inhabitants of the river Li, *now is the time to discover the winged death, transfigure into the next world.* Tshechu dancers of Bhutan, from above they appear a colorful whirl of spinning tops; two of their number, Buddhist monks in ceremonial finery, carefully step in the choreography of slowness. Somewhere, on a footbridge over rushing waters, two boys balance their way across, seeking the imperceptible union of the dancer and the dance.

The narrow asphalt road is divided by a broken line of white paint. Trees in the hill country adorn themselves with ghosts, fog shrouds everything in mystery. Two lonely petrol tanks stand guard, Ampol emblazoned diagonally like a sash against their breast. A handmade sign ever hopeful announces "Café Open Now." Another, more ambitious effort is shaped like mountains to proclaim the highest petrol station in Wales. The old men gather in tweed caps, half of them loitering with rude wooden canes. Border collies sit or stand alert, awaiting the serious play of collecting wayward souls. The sheepdog trials bear witness.

Asaro mudmen of Papua New Guinea, the bush demons; each one peers out from a clay mask that covers the head like a deep sea diving helmet. While the Chimbu play at bones, the Asaro cover themselves in the white-gray clay of the spectral dead. The masks are unique, a grotesque panorama of goblins, some grin, this one has buck teeth, whilst others disdain with a frown or stick out a tongue. Thus, did their ancestors abash their foes. On the Galapagos, a giant tortoise charms with innocence. Gregarious, he too lounges in the mud with no thought of death or enemies. *Mozart wrote operas when I was young*, he says.

Mauna Loa and Kīlauea, those fiery sisters, just try to get them to cool it. The very suggestion that one is more beautiful than the other is likely to set them off. And then they disagree on nearly everything, whether plaid should be considered a color, for instance. Though you wouldn't want to be too close, it's undeniable they ravish when they're hot, rivers of molten dragon blood flow in silken streams to the siren song of the oceans. That's where they start to find peace and their discord resolves into new land.

Once there was a lake. The slow sediment of limestone built the towers, a Neolithic forest yearning for its lost sea. A great gray owl perfectly matches the patterned bark of the Douglass fir. Immobile upon a narrow perch, he'd disappear completely were it not for his golden eyes which quiz one with the inscrutable mirth of a Cheshire cat. Close them and the illusion is complete. Minerva's avatar sinks beneath the philosopher's gaze.

Long distance friend

"Everything means itself and something more," explained the lightbearer. "If it did not mean greater, it would not stand within the beyond of our prayer, could not be itself." These words were thick, demanding attention. A foundation invoked in *ora*, discovered in transcendence, identity marked by mutability of addition — Sky was unable to penetrate the import of these words. Her heart was busy with a particular thought.

"Can you really bring forward anything . . . or anyone?" she asked innocently.

The child-king shrugged. "So far, abba hasn't said 'no.'"

Sky was too shy to ask about her boy. She had another in mind. "There's a friend I hear, but never see," said Sky. "She's ever so nice."

The moment she saw her, Vanaya, Sky's heart was pleased. The tawny skin, the thick flames of braided hair, the warm, limpid eyes, it was a face to match the voice of her friend. And the girl knew Sky as well, the one who asked for coffee. They spoke with that swift tongue of happiness so keen in young friends. Naya told her funny tales of Onahyu and hinted at wondrous worlds that made Sky eager to join her on adventures. So quick to tell, it was a shock when Vanaya informed her that much time had passed since they had spoken last.

"That happened ages ago," she said.

"For me, it was only a few weeks," said Sky, suddenly embarrassed.

The pause that followed was hard to fathom, but Sky didn't like it.

"What is it?" she asked.

"They threw me off a cliff for breaking the rules," said Vanaya.

Sky paled at her friend's appalling news. It was impossible to answer. Naya's sad smile tried to comfort her.

"It's alright," she said. "I'm still falling."

Sky did not recall returning home. She felt more than ever the questions in her being, and something in her wished for sleep without end. Mrs. Takashima shook her head at the girl, coming in so late. Boys were always bad news.

A holiday in the Lake district

Perhaps Sky should have been suspicious when Father Bunn showed up the next day dressed in the regalia of the tourist hiker known to hostels everywhere. His comrade, Ratcatcher, maintained the Ansharu preference for brocades and resilient fabrics silky, yet strong, though he sported a new hat which suggested outdoor adventures.

"Nothing like a traveling holiday," said the priest. "The Lake District is truly a wonder, old thing."

"Nindigisch javi etherbod," added Ratcatcher after a brief nudge from Father Bunn.

"Our friend believes you ought to come along. Your aura is looking somewhat peaked."

"Oh, I'd no idea," said Sky, feeling oddly exposed at this fantastical information. "But really, I've got to feed Audrey, she's such a dear. And Feirefiz. He's a dear, too, but you know, a Newf, so it's rather a lot of eating."

"Not to worry," said Bunn, beginning to pack for her. "It's already settled. Benedicta will see to the companions. The Elder's disappeared before, you know, so it's nothing she can't handle."

Moss-On-the-Bridge

They took the train to a little station called Moss-on-the-Bridge which was rather confusing as there was no bridge to vindicate the appellation.

"Might have been a structure back before the rails came," said Father Bunn, "or it refers to a faerie *pontis* that only the few can see."

All the while they were making their way to the hiking trails, the priest was telling outlandish tales whilst sipping from a marbleized flask that contained a magic elixir which turned out to be iced tea mixed with spiced wine. Bunn said his great aunt Alice was an expert on the Druids. According to Aunt Alice, the Druids would roast people alive in wicker cages over a coal fire, though his aunt was somewhat skeptical that this was indeed a feasible manner of cooking. She speculated that if one used green willow and soaked it sufficiently, the cage was likely to outlast the doomed victims. You either like that sort of droll humor or you don't. Sky was on the side of laughter, but once they began the actual walking, the lush green meadows and serene lakes so impressed that everyone became quiet before all that beauty.

After they had settled beneath a lovely old ash tree whose re-flection looked back at them from still waters, Father Bunn de-clared, "*Ex Divina pulchritudine esse omnium derivator,*" to which Ratcatcher assented with the usual polyglot iteration. For Sky's sake, the priest explained that "the Beauty of God is the cause of the being of all that is." It seemed then, in the sweetness of their friendship, that nothing wicked could intrude. Perhaps that is why Sky felt one might bring up the gelid, protean shadows that Lady Winterbourne had dispersed. She was certain the entire reason for the excursion was to protect her from their malign intentions. Yet when she began to touch upon the subject she saw that the priest drew her attention elsewhere.

His reticence confused and worried her. Father Bunn clearly did not think it proper or helpful to even mention the dangerous ones connected to her. Instead, he explained that it was possible her focus was wrong. The enemies of God make a pretense of wisdom, but they know nothing.

Then Father Bunn peered at her for a long time, remembering the odd prophecy of Brother Timothy. "When you are ready, they shall fear you."

Angler's delight

Aside from dark, whimsical humor, the bagpipe is also known to divide the human race. There must be some entangled connection between Anshari and the Scottish, for Ratcatcher had insisted on bringing along his bagpipes, which were rather awkwardly occupying a seat on the train (the ticket was lowered to a child's rate.) So, when Ratcatcher said, "Pisces dunewaver, dunewaver, anah," Sky was and was not surprised that the Ansharu method of angling seemingly required the eerie, spectral winds of the Scotch yodel.

"I don't think the fishies are likely to bite," was Sky's pithy surmise.

But no, it was a steady, almost hidden drone that Ratcatcher evoked. Sky did not know you could play a bagpipes quiet, but that is the Ansharu way, unless at a wedding, in which case even a rambunctious Scotsman will be outdone by the ebullient crash of those tribal bellows. And lo, first one little fish and then another poked its head above the glass of the lake. He was a very pied-piper of the dreaming realm, the waters of sleep and reverie, our Ratcatcher.

Of course, they did not actually catch the fish. The point was the greeting and the applause of presence. When they came back empty handed, Father Bunn laconically commented that even the Lord needed at least one fish to start with in order to multiply for hungry souls.

The second-best scythe

The Lake District was home to various local pastimes of venerable, though obscure origins. No one really remembered why on the first Tuesday after the Spring equinox, the citizens of Tilden-on-Nash were required to prod a wheel of cheese down the center of their village square, nor was it fully known why there was a ceremony in which young men adorned themselves with greenery and followed a winding path accompanied by dancing nymphs and hobgoblins to the top of certain low mountains where they were figuratively sacrificed. In the good, old days, straight literalism might have done. (It had something to do with unemployed chimney sweeps, but that is neither here nor there.)

By chance, Sky's little party happened upon a different ritual performance. A challenge was offered between a local hero and the king's man, in this case represented by the closest approximation, a fella of wealth from one of the nearby houses of prestige. The two were tasked to mow a long row of tall grass using the ancient scythe. There was a rhythmic technique, a balance of blade and swaying body, you couldn't just learn it in a day. The skill favored the hand born to agrarian labor, and so it normally played out. This time, however, the king's man amazed them all, swung the blade in perfect pitch, as they say. Only towards the end, when it was clear who would win, did the local hero begin to gain with a fury.

It might have been scripted, or the wealthy scion knew what was best and pulled back, pretending at an injury. The result, the expected and usual, was met with festivity and communal joy and pride. The ale flowed plenty, paid for by the loser, of course. The priest was thirsty, the Ansharu played his pipes. Sky knew the voice of the second best scythe.

It was surprising how often she ran into Deco.

The summer house

The summer house, as Flavius George and his family were in the habit of calling it, was a rather sprawling Roman villa situated among rolling emerald hills and overlooking a pretty and serene lake. Normally, Flavius George was happy to retreat from market concerns and the riot of urban chatter into its placid confines. The peace of the summer house, however, had been spoiled by the arrival of his sister. Aunt Elisabeth had decided opinions and since she made no distinction between her habitual custom and the ordinary course of nature, she expected unquestioned obedience to her personal convictions as if equivalent to divinely sanctioned laws. How else account for her rigidly stipulated criteria for the proper arrangement of floral displays, the correct style for young women to wear their hair, the superior etiquette for eating ice cream, the ideal frequency and manner for cleaning household linen and glassware?

Since Aunt Elisabeth had a capacious mind extending to the minutest detail of domestic order, the cosmic reach of her demanding exactitude was apt to discover innumerable obnoxious indiscretions in the most ordinary of human actions. Worse, Flavius George, who otherwise was subject to despotic obstinacy, became quite timorous before her preemptive certitudes.

"She is an intolerable cow," said Aurora under her breath.

"I cannot understand papa," lamented Diana.

"Don't say that," admonished Narina. "Cows are actually quite nice."

A matron with an iron-gray coif topped by an old-fashioned lace sat knitting in a small chair near the fire. She seemed oblivious to the girls' dismay, stopping only to observe the swaying pendulum of an ancient clock.

"Deco's come home," she suddenly announced. "Perhaps he'll put her in the pot!" to which the triumvirate of daughters universally attempted to shush and calm her into respectable silence.

Introductions

It was amusing, the way Deco kept glancing back at Sky whilst ardently pleading for someone to come and keep his sisters company. Her chaperones, Deco could not help think of them that way, were compelled to inquire into the propriety of his offer. They could come themselves. The Summer House held treasures to satisfy priest and Ansharu. In the end they trusted Sky's character and the past history of her friendship with the lad. Father Bunn and Ratcatcher would follow the planned itinerary and circle back to retrieve her.

The Great Room to which Deco led her boasted high ceilings, marble columns, and a large fireplace with a massive alabaster mantle. The furniture was sumptuous and tastefully selected. Three young ladies peered at her with varying degrees of curiosity, whilst an older woman, evidently a tolerated old aunt or even perhaps a beloved nanny, sat at the side of the youngest girl. While Deco attempted rapid introductions, the older woman kept glancing with shy diffidence that beat back an urge towards more effusive welcome. The others were equally preoccupied with an equivocal anxiety. All eyes drifted to the singular figure of Elisabeth Grant-Bromley, who stood with magnificent patrician reserve, barely deigning to notice the newcomer.

Aunt Elisabeth remarked upon the generations of Elnarian wealth that was but poorly represented in the little summer house. This was aimed at Deco, who presumed to bring an obvious off-worlder into the sacred domestic space of the family. If the girl blushed, so be it. But Sky did not blush. It was all very lovely, yet somehow prosaic and shallow blooded to one who had walked in the night of childhood, and peered within the round candle of serene care.

The siblings spoke privately after the decidedly chill reception proffered by Aunt Elisabeth.

"Rory, do try to be decent," said Deco.

"I only ever tell the truth," said Aurora. "I don't know why everyone is upset by that." Diana arched a skeptical brow. "Oh, all right," said the middle sister. "I shall pretend to be Narina and talk of nothing but the joy of ferrets and how lovely an alpaca smells."

Deco frowned. "Little steps, Rory. Just don't be beastly. You might try that."

"I suppose you may have been warned. About me, I mean," said Aurora.

"Should I have been?" asked Sky with just the right inflection of innocence and confidence to disarm Aurora.

"I am supposed to be treacherous," said Aurora.

"It's a wonderful thing to have a reputation," said Sky.

The new world

She discovered Diana, the eldest daughter, beneath a canopy of Gothic arches that formed an arcade partially occluded by a fence of finely wrought iron lattice work. Within this seclusion that nonetheless allowed a soft light to illumine the chiaroscuro of the marble architecture, the young woman sat in a dramatic pose, holding before her the model of a Spanish galleon with sails unfurled and emblazoned with a slender scarlet cross. To this mise-en-scène was added an elaborate costume of maroon brocade dress with a high lace collar. The long bodice and narrow waist bequeathed a sea of fabric, upon which rested an open book of illuminated hours.

Diana's baroque coif of layered coils and two long, beribboned braids was offset with a delicate lace veil that revealed a theatrical mask of mauve shadows painted around the eyes and temples of the young woman. She was an elegant and arresting image that was extended to elbow length gloves of a sheer, dark fabric open at the fingers and a large amethyst ring set upon the middle finger of her left hand. For a long moment, Sky watched her with open admiration as Deco's sister contemplated the naval vessel with an enigmatic expression of audacious wonder. Then Diana abruptly dropped the ship next to a tower of stacked books with the sudden violence of a bored child.

"We are doing histories," she said in explanation. "Today I am Isabella of Spain planning to adventure the New World. And here you are. Deco can't stop talking about you."

Sky blushed in the most pleasant manner and Diana decided she liked her.

"Have you seen my sisters? No, you wouldn't have. Aurora will be up in the campanile or the attic with a telescope. She's very keen on the stars, even during the day, which is odd, but no one thinks to ask her about it — and Narina will be wandering the grounds with her animals. She prefers them to people, but don't let that put you off. She'll like you, because Deco does."

It was hard to judge the seriousness of all this information from Queen Isabella both regal and mischievous. Diana led her to an interior room with tall ceilings, tapestries, furnishings of thick fabric and dark wood, so that Sky could imagine she had indeed entered into a world of extravagant royalty. A house maid silently appeared and Diana smartly commanded refreshments.

"You'll have to excuse us," she said. "We are dull here and being by ourselves so often, we slip easily into eccentricity that appears normal without society to look askance upon us."

"Society is often stupid and brutal," said Sky. "Just the same, I don't advise you try dressing up as Marie Antoinette."

Diana laughed with subdued mirth. "You're much too clever. My brother usually goes for another sort." Diana paused. She felt she had inadvertently been too familiar. She was not lying about their lack of company. "Do you like books? Papa buys a lot of them for the library. He doesn't read them, but he thinks a great house must have such things."

"I prefer horses, I'm afraid."

"You're a Narina, but you've lived with people of learning, I think. I'm sorry. I keep prying."

"It's only natural. Only I haven't much to tell you. I only remember fragments. Sometimes, I don't even know I remember them. They just show up unannounced. I'll be rambling along and then I'm telling a story I didn't recall ten minutes before."

Diana smiled. "Papa says that when you are old, you remember everything you did decades ago as if it were yesterday and what you did yesterday as if it never happened."

The maid returned with an assortment of tea, fresh fruit, and light pastries. The young women had barely touched their repast when Sky rose abruptly and stood before a large lithograph set obliquely against a music stand. Diana joined her, intrigued by the evident fascination of the image for her guest.

"Do you like that? Deco bought it from a merchant. He knows I am fond of such works. It is from a book of visions, the *Scivias* or 'Know the Ways.'"

The image depicted two concentric circles of lavender and gold rings, the inner circle encompassing the length of a tall man with sad eyes. "The merchant did not know the meaning of it, but it is called the Man in Sapphire."

"If you're not careful, he'll eat you up," said Sky.

An unorthodox family

They were decidedly an unorthodox family which commended them to Sky's sensibility. The paterfamilias made an appearance. Sky gathered that Deco and he were frequently at odds, so she expected coolness, but Flavius George with his rings and dyed beard captivated her in his aggrandized role of merchant king. Flavius George, for his part, rather liked the girl. He was inclined to fondness for attractive young women on general principle and this one had the good sense to reciprocate with lively humor. He forgave her connection to Deco and pretended that she was only there as a friend to his three daughters.

"You see what he is like," said Deco when they were alone.

"I'm sorry. I think he's quite the dear, though I'm sure he can be a terrible autocrat."

"Of course, you like him," said Deco, who made himself scarce for the rest of that day.

Indiscretion

It soon became evident that the Fates had no idea what to make of a new companion. They were so used to finding their own diversions and so hated the regulatory impositions of Aunt Elisabeth that the best kindness they could think to give Sky was as complete a freedom of the house as possible. It did not occur to them to include her in their peculiar interests. The only stipulation was the unnecessary caution to avoid if possible the Elisabethan presence. And so, Sky found herself wandering the halls in search of an occupation. It was thus that she stumbled upon the vast chamber in which Flavius George displayed his ever increasing collection of art.

The red room with its gargantuan inventory of pictures overwhelmed: the stormy sea and vigilant harpooners, displays of bucolic simplicity set next to fantasias of pleasure palaces or solemn ancestral portraits that appeared disinterested in the living. The cumulative effect produced a dull musky headache of confused, vague threat, as if the entire room was an overwrought potpourri. Sky wanted to close her eyes to escape it. An irrational panic set in followed by a fainting feeling, so that she might have sat down just there on the marble floor. "Distraction, distracted by distraction," she muttered. Then in an oblong mirror standing in a frame of ironwood, Sky caught a glimpse of movement, a wave of taffeta, some glimmer of diffident fabric.

With instinctive flight, Sky hastened her steps and nearly ran towards the perceived source of motion. She stopped short in an alcove barely more than a cupboard. Already, she was feeling ridiculous, but also relieved to be out of that immense chamber of cluttered ocular assault. Sitting before a table and pulling out mementos from a cedar box, the nanny peered up at her.

"It was only yesterday," she said, as if that explained everything.

"Oh," said Sky.

"We can put any number of things in a box, can't we?" said the nanny. "The objects might be there, and if you're lucky, provided you are quiet and don't demand, they might let you in."

"Yes, I see."

"But it's not the object we want. It isn't, really. It's a whole world that the object reminds one of."

"It's strange," said Sky. "I've got a whole collection of little things and they all whisper. I can't always say what, but I love them. But there's always more. I pick them up from places no one else is looking."

"It was like that the day Flavius George brought back Deco. He wanted a boy, you see. He was sick of a household all of girls. I told him there was nothing I could do about it. It's all old wives' tales, the things they say about getting a male child. Melt a little boy charm of silver and add to curds, swing a needle in a circle above your head . . ."

"Wait! Deco is adopted?" said Sky, stunned by the nanny's guileless candor. "Does he know?"

"Now all they do is fight, neither can tolerate the other," said the nanny, ignoring or not noticing Sky's question. A sudden qualm suddenly entered the servant's prolix indiscretion. "Only don't tell Aunt Elisabeth. She doesn't know and Deco is the only one of us she likes."

"I suppose so," said Sky.

"You're very agreeable," said the nanny.

"I honestly have no idea what I'm doing," Sky confessed. "I thought I did, but now I don't."

"Yes," said the nanny. "It's like that. Here, hold this."

The servant of the nursery years handed her a little child's book. It was swaddled in soft white leather and opened to bright, enameled pictures of trees and castles and dressed animals. Close up, the silvered hair hid a face not so old, thought Sky.

"I had that when I was a girl," laughed the nanny. "I used to dream such dreams."

"They never come true, do they?"

"Oh, I wouldn't say that, dear. It's not finished yet, and perhaps it never is."

Narina's complaint

Sky discovered Narina walking in a green pasture populated by a large group of flightless brown birds. They were evidently fond of her, congregating in groups of two or three and craning their long necks, squawking, and turning their oblong, funny little heads to gain her attention. Narina did not wait for the ordinary conventions of polite distance between strangers, but began talking in an affable, intimate manner.

"You see before you the great engine of our family wealth. Papa found out about them when he was a diplomat. I suppose there's more to it now, but it began with the emu."

"You are certainly the queen of their attention," said Sky.

"All creatures respond to love. Of course, it helps if you feed them," said Narina.

"Yes, I suppose that is only natural."

They were silent together, companionable, but soon it became evident that Narina was rehearsing ideas she had probably tried numerous times upon her siblings and was now glad to be able to thrust upon a fresh audience.

"Eating is a problem, though everyone does it and hardly anyone thinks about it."

"I'm not sure I follow."

"Well, death. Something always has to die for another to live. I'm not one of those folks who cry at the pain of a baked potato, but it's dreadful that life should always require death."

"I see what you mean," said Sky. "But if you think about it too much, you might stop altogether and then who would feed the emus?"

"I know, and honestly, we all have good appetites in our family, especially papa. I don't think about it till later and then I feel guilty, just not enough to give up sausage and cake."

All the while they were carrying on this melancholy reflection, the girls were traversing gated fields and Narina was showing off some of her favorites. Narina introduced Sky to a long-haired sow named Galina and a crow named Merlin who was very chatty, though somewhat fixated on something or someone called Smoogs.

"Smoogs is his dog," said Narina. "He's a fat Pekingese that rarely leaves the house."

Then they hid behind some outhouses because Aunt Elisabeth unexpectedly appeared like an ill omen looking about with a critical eye at the haystacks in a neighboring field.

"She has a second sense," informed the youngest daughter. "If she suspects anyone is enjoying themselves, she is sure to come round to twist your guts into knots."

After that, they waited for ten minutes and made up stories of increasing levels of unlikely naughtiness about Aunt Elisabeth before emerging to resume their tour, only Aunt Elizabeth had the last laugh. The sky grew quickly dark and the wind picked up, threatening a sudden downpour.

"She chanted a hex," said Narina with bitter glee.

The rain fell in a rapid, gushing line. The girls made a dash for a long shed that housed tractors and other tools used to maintain the grounds. Standing under its eaves, Narina's gloom gave vent to further recollection.

"Once there was a terrible storm. The lightning was everywhere. When I came out to the fields, I found my miniature donkey and one of my little goats lying on their sides with flies buzzing all around them. The day before, they had come running at the sight of me. I had pet them and told them how much I loved them. And now . . . now burnt flesh, worm food."

"I'm so sorry."

"Even Rory came down from her attic and tried to say something nice. She's not very good at it, you know. I can't remember exactly what. It was something about supernovas and stardust, I think. How we are all star stuff. She thought it poetic and helpful, so I thanked her for her kindness, but it is really cold and cruel, because something alive and loving is now dead forever. Everyone felt sad, but they also thought I was just a child because I wouldn't be reasonable. And I'm still not. What do I care for reason if it doesn't love my loves?"

"I can't accept it either," said Sky, silently reminding herself to ask Rabbi Naftali about all those sacrifices in Leviticus.

They play at Characters

No one was quite sure how the Character game began. Rory said that it was ordained by the stars. It wasn't ever clear when she was joking. The house rules, in any event, were either ramshackle or strict, depending on conditions hard to predict. Diana explained that there was an ancient box with cards. Aurora had found it in the attic when they were children; so long ago it was when she was actually amiable. Each card had a character and each character had an assigned location along with a wardrobe number. When the game was played, the card informed one whose character one would inhabit, the room where the acting should take place, and where one could secure the appropriate costume.

"Often nothing much happens," said Narina with a spark that implied sometimes something did.

Rory advised Sky to take the card with a little bend in it.

"You get to choose between Boadicea or a Zulu queen. Either way, one throws a spear and yells a bit."

Sky, however felt this might be a bit like cheating. The way of it was like this: Aurora drew Marie Curie, which made her happy; Diana was Mata Harie which caused Narina to giggle because the outfit involved an enormous bustle. Narina was George Sand which meant she would spend time brooding in the music room with the piano.

"Unfortunately, Chopin never shows," she said.

Sky rather regretted not taking Rory's advice. The game threw her a card no one had ever chosen before.

"I've never seen it in the deck," said Diana, the card for Eve.

"Wardrobe won't be a problem, but you'll have to run if Deco comes around," said Narina.

It was true; the card did not designate a wardrobe, though it sent her to an ancient wing of the house that looked out upon the orchard.

"Do stay away from, you know," laughed the eldest daughter. "Though I don't think the apples are ripe."

In the end, they chose a sumptuous emerald gown of satin and lace for her. It was the one assigned for Anne Boleyn.

I am black, but beautiful

The room designated by the card was as peculiar as the family. From the ceiling of the great room dark clusters of smoke hung like stalagmites. Here and there, the consistency increased so that swathes of inky cobwebs attached themselves to the cornices and to the mantle of the fireplace. Nearly everywhere, it was like finding oneself in a charcoal sketch of dusty inertia covered in a sepia wash of tranquil indifference. Yet a billowing curtain ushered in a parade of golden leaves determined to announce the waiting earth.

That's odd, thought Sky, that it should be autumn in the middle of summer.

Tiny figures of strange aquiline fauna gathered like curious cats and traced out irregular boundaries of the interior space. These little soldiers spied Sky sitting on the low cushion placed at the edge of the living carpet. The viridian dress of the girl was décolleté, the firm bounce of her lively bosom offset by the Stoic implacability of her expression. The dark burnish of her face bled into the fiery obedience of the long hair that draped her back. In her delicate hands, she gathered a skein of blue thread.

Before the girl, standing lightly upon the carpet, a nimble shadow formed the silhouette of a dancing figure that bowed gracefully at the waist. A vague suggestion of eyes and nose appeared to occupy the figural head of the shadow. As if in compensation to this modest allowance, the torso revealed an arched passageway, from which the azure thread emerged from innermost darkness. Above the blue line, a tiny pair of birds escaped the centripetal pull of spiritual night. The first of blood rose was followed by a pursuing flash of pale white wings. There was something really charming in the lilt of the shadow's limbs.

"He's the Fred Astaire of shadows," thought Sky. She found herself beneath crystalline arches that opened onto darkness. Slowly, her feet descended the path recently described by the avian couple. This, too, is garden, she thought.

"*Nigra sum sed Formosa.*"

A lovely day

Sky played chess badly with Deco and charades rather well with his sisters in one of the Great Rooms. Deco was apologetic without saying so for having allowed his fractious relation with his father to impinge on the warmth he felt towards Sky, while the sisters made a concerted effort to enlarge domestic affections. As the day drifted towards evening, it is true that Aurora was frequently wishing to sweep Sky away and show her celestial events far more interesting than Deco's gossip or Diana's decorous wit, yet the general good will was evident culminating in the minor gratuity of the warm tongue of a rather pudgy Pekingese adding his personal welcome.

"Smoogs is very discerning," said Narina.

Sky was touched, and felt in her heart that she could love them all, though presently she could not stop thinking about the Eve game and the dream that came to her and what it might mean.

An incident

Mrs. Grant Bromley regretted the obstinacy of her nieces, their eccentricity, and reclusive natures, all of which she determined a result of dispositions acquired through the distaff side of an unfortunate marriage. The quality of her prejudices might be indicated by her relative toleration of the farouche tendencies of her nephew. While Deco had the appearance of someone who would never take on the mantle of responsibility, he was adventurous and social and his aunt secretly nourished the hope that his boldness might yet be turned in a more constructive direction.

Lord Raveh, recently returned from the war, was the occasion of yet another disappointment. Aunt Elisabeth had recruited the admirable Miss Angstrom, who graciously consented to accompany herself and her nieces on a visit to Tamberlin. When the coach arrived with Miss Angstrom, the elder sisters, as was their wont, had mysteriously disappeared. Narina clearly sulked as the one yet compelled to join the expedition whose entire purpose was the education of her brother's daughters into proper amiability and decorous behavior. There was, of course, the additional implicit message insofar as the scheming interloper had not been included.

The day, alas, was ill destined. The journey to Raveh's great house was punctuated by the efforts of Miss Angstrom to draw out the taciturn girl. Indeed, Miss Angstrom was keenly interested to share with everyone her admiration for the lands and the manor, though she became becomingly shy when quizzed upon the character and appearance of the prince.

Arrival did nothing to abate chagrin. Prince Raveh was courteous, though he seemed unaware of their intended visit. A secretary had failed to inform him of the letter advising of their proposed audience. Worse, his strange friend, Shadrael, was present, unsettling everyone but Narina who suddenly grew precocious and chatted with naïve and disarming openness. The prince was evidently charmed. They were, of course, asked to lunch and brought to a sumptuous room where the windows caught the sunlight cast through a veil of ash trees. The dappled effect was perfectly delightful. Now Miss Angstrom seemed quiet and abashed. The ride back was sure to be an unpleasant affair.

The conversation, thanks to Shadrael, circled around recondite matters such as the healing powers of certain stones and the gnostic meaning of the yak. All this greatly pleased Narina and this in turn pleased her host. Only once did Miss Angstrom perk up from her social swoon. Her eye caught the shimmer of an unusual, quite lovely fabric which turned out to be the matter of a dress the prince called "the spoils of war." She could not stop staring at it, so much so that the prince was provoked to further commentary.

"I found it in the rustic cabin of an unspeakably haggard old crone," he recalled, provoking an amused smile from Shadrael.

The ruins

Deco took Sky's hand and led her carefully across the precipice to the ruins. The Gothic bones of its beauty stood indifferent to the cold horizon. The vegetal incursions, the little mice and wrens that sheltered in its wreck of time, tolerably parleyed with the human intruders. Deco pointed to a high gap in one of the remaining walls.

"That is said to be the place from which an evil deed was done. Two young brothers, heirs of blood, suffered defenestration. Others tell a different tale. A maiden meek and lovely was kept prisoner there, peering out in lonely sorrow for some rescue that never came. She escaped in the slow way. First, hopeful suitors looked for her only to discover a matron grown sour and prematurely past her prime. And then, a hag with sad eyes took her place. At last, she was free of it; dust well past weeping. No one tells happy stories about a place like this." Deco was quiet then with his thoughts before adding under his breath, "There's no charming happily ever after in truth."

This was hardly amatory talk, but Sky was somehow amused. "You'd make a terrible governess. All your children should throw themselves in wells or ship off with the navy in an effort to get away."

Deco laughed. "Oh, you can't tell these things to children. No one could possibly go on without lying to themselves."

Sky smiled shyly at him. "You remind me of someone. Someone I can't quite remember. Not his face, I think, but his voice, the way he looked at things."

"Shall we go back? I seem to always be taking you to see obscure remnants of lost time."

"No, I like it very much."

Before the ball

Shortly after the failed attempt at raising the social awareness of her nieces, an unexpected second chance intruded into the insularity of the summer house to tempt Aunt Elisabeth. Invitations arrived for a ball that was to be given at Tamberlin. For months, Prince Raveh had retreated into himself, unable to come to terms with what had happened in the field at Kos. Now, however, it appeared he was attempting to renew connections to the local families. A charity ball was to be given with proceeds to benefit the veterans and families of the Sixth Legio, as well as those from the prince's own militia.

This was, of course, a great event for the country, dominating the conversations and plans of many a mother with daughters of suitable age for as everyone knows a ball is a perfect setting to introduce lovely young women with aspirations to eligible bachelors with pockets sufficiently flush. It was a matter of speculation and in some cases, actual betting whether the daughters of Flavius George would make an appearance at this greatly anticipated opportunity.

As it happens, Aunt Elisabeth had a word with her little brother. She also saw opportunities. If she'd had a mind to take advantage of a bit of insider trading, she could have made a killing with the unofficial bookies of the area. And so the daughters of Flavius George found themselves attached to the committee sorting the jumble. Narina, of course, was less than useless. The candidates for charitable redistribution were duly noted and determined utterly ridiculous or promising solely on the basis of how adaptable said item might be as toy or useful habiliment for one of her animals. Aurora pretended not to be there, while Diana made desultory attempts to actually sort items whilst talking amiably with Sky.

Proceedings were thus suitably dull until Phylida Angstrom opened up a box and discovered a brass astrolabe.

"What is it? And who would think to give such a thing?" she asked.

Aurora was suddenly furious. "Put it back," she said, bestowing an angry glance on all around. She was certain her aunt had done it.

"Yes, put it back," said nanny in an unexpectedly firm voice.

Other boxes revealed the usual assortment of clothing and knickknacks once, but no longer fashionable provoking comments more bemused than gently mocking.

"And are you going to the ball?" asked Phylida. She had never quite forgiven Sky for the incident at the hunt, though she admitted none of it was really blameworthy.

Still, it had been unpleasant. Phylida felt vaguely that she had been embarrassed by the ordeal, and since she could never think of it without also picturing Sky, a certain irrational animosity had grown up in her heart. Phylida did not, of course, truly consider the offworlder girl an actual rival, though Deco seemed to like her well enough.

Sky blushed. "I haven't actually received an invitation," she said. "Besides, I've no idea how to dance."

"I'm sure the prince has no idea you are here, Sky," said Diana kindly. "I'll have papa let him know. As for dancing, you see how terrible we are. Flavius George is afraid to unleash us on society, so my sisters and I have often enough danced amongst ourselves. And Deco, you know. We'll give you a few steps. The young men don't really care about dancing, they just want to stare and chat with pretty women whilst pretending you fancy them."

"How terribly cynical," said Phylida.

"You only say that because you fancy the prince," answered Aurora tartly.

It was so easy to be beastly when forced to wade through other people's unwanted junk and listen to silly girls.

A dress for dancing

Sky truly did not know how to dance. Of this she was quite certain. Sky expected to stand apart from any such thing as a minuet or a waltz. All that was "for the others," nor was she sad about it. "I am not a girl for dances," she told them. Still, to be on the safe side, Diana had done her best to offer some rudimentary steps. They lurched about the empty ballroom of the summer house. Deco happened upon them and could not help smiling, they were so comic.

"You never know when a dashing young officer might be quite taken, and then one must not refuse a turn around the floor," said Diana with a meaningful glance at her brother.

The next morning, word was sent to Prince Raveh informing him about Sky. That same afternoon, an express rider arrived with her invitation along with a mysterious package that contained the dress Shadrael had given the prince. When the girls were preparing their finery, it was just like Characters, only real people. Aurora consented to help Sky with the fitting. It was an undeniably beautiful dress, somehow strange and stunning in the way it caught the light, almost a bridal dress of the Fay, so unusual. As she prodded and pulled, adjusting just so, Rory informed her there were certain kinds of dresses they sew you into like the Apsara dancers of Cambodia.

"Those are beautiful as well, silk brocade with intricate pleats in front. We have a card for one, but it's too much trouble, so we just put it back if someone selects it."

But Sky's wit was droll. She thought of another sort, the shrouds they sew you into where no one dances. Aurora smiled at that, their taste in humor being sympathetic. Then Narina discovered a card attached to the dress that had dropped out. It was almost like it had come from the game, though intended for Sky and Tamberlin.

"It's a magic gown," she read. "Sky should only let herself go and the little feet will dance up a storm all by themselves."

"Errant non-sense," said Rory.

"Oh, you heretic," said Narina, certain it was true.

Betrayal

The appearance of Flavius George's daughters was a great coup for the ball. The drama of their entry was followed by quite diverse results. Narina, delightful on the cusp of womanhood, yet still quite a girl, spent all her time talking with a red-faced middle-aged farmer entirely oblivious with regards to the eccentricity of the Fates or even the identity of his conversation partner. All he knew was he had expected to be dull and was utterly gobsmacked, that's the word he used when telling the story later, gobsmacked, to discover a lass so reliable and wise on the best ways to raise guinea fowl.

They had agreed, as how could you not, that guineas do not tolerate confinement. There was studious back and forth on the relative merits of runs versus free range. A run kept the guineas safe from predators, you'd have to allow for inevitable losses with the latter, but what wonderful natural pest control, that was the farmer's argument. Narina would have none of it. The guinea could be trained to roost at night in a coop, provided it were large enough and one started when the man shy keets first hatched. She said three feet square was enough for an adult bird, so multiply that number by how many chicks and wait for the fowl to grow into the space.

The farmer claimed his guinea scared the chickens and Narina admitted they were very cantankerous and territorial, opining that ducks seemed to be an exception.

"Ducks bore them," she said.

Aurora was a different matter. To her surprise, Rory came out rather a stunner. She was shockingly good looking in an opulent white brocade gown that went with the Anastasia Romanov card. To her amazement, the male youth of the area kept lining up like aristos waiting for the guillotine. All night they tried their luck and all night Aurora cut them dead. She had no idea parties were such fun.

Diana was lovely, amiable, and so perfectly sane that she cast a protective veil upon her more eccentric sisters for whom everyone found themselves quite willing to make allowances.

As for Sky, it was true about that dress. All the officers wanted to dance with Sky and Lord Raveh opened the ball by asking her and closed it, too. And everyone thought it quite charming, except for Aunt Elisabeth and one other. Phylida Angstrom screwed up her eyes at the sight of the gown, at the treachery of it.

An unpleasant tirade

Sky and Narina were begging an early breakfast from Cook when the force of nature that is Mrs. Grant Bromley came unexpectedly face-to-face with her misbegotten adversary. Disappointment over everything Tamberlin percolated in the fuming soul of Aunt Elisabeth. The injustice of the world towards her every attempt at foresight tempted this woman of principle to indulge bitterness. She even began to suspect that her indomitable will could fail to marshal obstreperous elements into proper order. That there might be fundamental error in her understanding of the Good never occurred to her. All she felt was uncomfortable and unfamiliar weakness, so there was a hidden vulnerability and desire for self-protection that caused her to shudder at the bodily presence of Sky.

Aunt Elisabeth began to revile the off-world girl as so much shabby lack of decency, having too little sense to feel the embarrassment of overreaching her natural limits. The vehemence of her tirade was beset with ironies, aside from the truth that one cannot impose by dictate what could only reasonably be gifted by love or connatural sensibility. The scullery maid hid behind the shadow of a cabinet and refused to move. Cook was so distressed by the outburst that she dropped an old plate, not especially valuable, but something she had handled for years so that tears came unsought to her eyes.

A truth universally acknowledged

"That was unfeeling," said Narina.

"You mustn't worry yourself."

"I can't abide cruelty."

Sky had such an expression of tenderness for Narina, but also a look as if she might at any moment burst into laughter. Then she said, quite unexpectedly, "It is a truth universally acknowledged, that a single man in possession of a good fortune, must be in want of a wife."

When the youngest daughter appeared confused by this declaration, Sky answered in a gentle voice still tinged with the ghost of Jane's wit, "It's really quite alright. I assure you, your aunt is entirely mistaken."

Narina stared into Sky's face. She was at first puzzled, then simply silent. "I believe my brother is rather fond of you," she said at last.

"As I am of him," said Sky. "But all this —." She gestured towards the gardens and the stately edifice of the summer villa. "What we want, what we really want, is much more than anything that can answer to our calculations."

"Oh, I don't think you are mercenary."

"Lots of girls are. And poor girls can't afford to be indifferent I suppose."

"Perhaps you're in love with someone else?"

Now Sky seemed sad. "All that romance and match-making; and if it turns out well, what of it? A few good years, decades if you're lucky. And maybe you miss out. Something happens and we miss our chance."

"Don't you love Deco at all then?"

Sky struggled to answer. There was a complex emotion in her heart she could hardly name. Then she remembered words from her friend in Regency Park.

"In the ancient days, men and women practiced slowness. It is a joy to be wanted, but the promises made, they promise something we can't grant, or not yet anyway, not the way we think. I'm sure I'm perfectly unclear."

Narina saw that Sky was sincere, but she had no idea what she meant, except that it was going to hurt her brother and satisfy the beastly aunt. She glumly shrugged her shoulders and subtly was glad the new girl had been rebuffed.

Mama lowers the boom

It's funny how a trivial incident can somehow unravel things. They seem pretty stable, it's been going that way for years, then suddenly, nothing much happens, but the whole thing goes to pieces. Often, it happens quietly, without much protest, because the collapse actually occurred long ago and one is finally presented with the hollowed out shell of a long dead thing. The person Sky had taken for the nanny was outraged by the tears of Cook. She was offended on behalf of their guest. It was an utter breach of hospitality. And there was Flavius George looking shame-faced and fumbling about as if he would rather be anywhere but in his own, abundant villa.

"Papa always said she was a bitch. She needs to go, Flavius," announced the buxom kettle.

Flavius George frowned. There would be scenes. He'd have to go on a minor spending spree just to get over it.

"Alright, mama," he sighed. "If you insist."

Chapter Six

Revelation

The madman returns

Ahmed, the watchman, was helpful. It was not uncommon that such men were facilitators of many things for the guests of the pensione. And so, Nuha came and knocked gently at his door. She entered at his bidding, her eyes at first cast down. She could not have been more than fifteen. When she saw him, even though he had bathed and his long hair had been brushed back into a semblance of order, Nuha was momentarily quailed.

"Come here," he ordered in a low voice.

He looked like an Assyrian king or perhaps Babylonian, for he carried still the traces of madness as if he had spent seven years chewing on grasses and forgetting his human face. She approached him with trembling heart. Soren asked her to sit beside him.

"What's your name?"

"Nuha."

"Nuha," said Blake, "I need a shave."

She found then a pan of warm water and soap and a sharp blade and slowly, with great care not to cut him in the least, took the beard from his face. She was surprised at the end. He was younger than she thought and handsome. She was quite willing. She rubbed herself against him and placed a hand under his shirt.

"You are good, Nuha." He smiled, but moved away, looking firmly at her so that she could see he did not want her body. "I have come a long way," he said, "but I am not yet ready for the world."

"I am not the world," she laughed. "I am Nuha."

"So you are." He laughed, too.

She clung to him then, ran her fingers playfully through his hair and listened to the steady breathing of his heart. Chaste as siblings, they slept until awakened by the sound of the muezzins from the Arab quarter calling believers to prayer. She wanted to refuse payment, but he insisted. Nuha parted from him without kisses, yet happy.

The mermaid's song

The water was cool. Lunar light bathed the black-green sea with a soft, glittering ribbon of incandescence. Soren sat upon a dark outcropping of rock, a wet mist striking his body with a mild damp that was not unpleasant. During the days, he hid amidst the poor fishermen and their wives and children, repairing nets or talking gossip with the old women in their tarred shanties. They did not know him. He was not one of them, but he was accepted all the same. Some deep, unworded human code bound them together. He told no tales; they asked no questions.

It was only in the solitude of night that he permitted himself the luxury of unearthing his tangled reflections. How long could he have stayed away? He would have remained in the desert forever, perhaps, if it had not been for the impossible girl. Slowly, he had almost come to forget desire for anything or anyone. The silence that protects, that shields one from infinite desire allowed him seeming endless deferral, though he never supposed it a triumph of the spirit. And yet, here he was, his ear cocked to the murmuring of the waves.

A legend had grown up amongst the fisher folk. It was said that when a mermaid was to die, she sought a deep sea cave, in whose silence she sang out her memories and the secret of man's desire. Should a mortal happen to chance upon her death song, a boon or curse would come measured to the listener. No. He had never escaped. Bittersweet this nearly visceral knowledge or intuition that the soul itself was constituted by contact, something not bounded by the limits of his dust and senses.

"Speak. Speak to me!" he cried out.

The waters of the night received his prayer, but Nothing answered his demand.

Soren smiled grimly. He knew as much. You could not demand. You were heard, of course, if only by that inner spirit that abides with one, making judgment and commentary as if one were separate and apart from one's actions. By this reflection, he allowed his passion to subside,   melted into the long and endless slap of shore and wave. The tides were such inconclusive diplomats, ever supporting the wet, soggy path of sand marking the boundary of incomplete fusion.

Seven stories up

Soren stood before a cracked silver mirror. The four year old son of the hotelier watched him with open-mouthed wonder as he applied a long thin blade to his soapy chin. A dozen half-remembered tales crowded his morning brain. "Seven stories up," he said suddenly, startling the maid who entered the room to refresh the bedclothes, but really, to glance surreptitiously at the stranger, naked to the waist. He didn't explain. He never did.

He was thinking of his pal, James Morissey, who was always up for a laugh, good at pool, handsome, damaged, and alluring to women. Morissey spoke in vulgarisms culled from the babble of psychologists and counselors who sought to give him words to silence the demons of despair. "You gotta get rid of that stinkin' thinkin'" was his favorite spell to ward off the evil. Soren plunged his cupped hands into the basin of water and provided the final ablutions to his face. He looked at the little boy, whose interest vanished with the disappearance of the soap beard.

You are so caught up in discovery, so innocent of concepts. Or rather, the child is ignorant that he, too, must mediate the real by intellect. Things beckon, mysterious, not yet tamed. And this is what it means to get old: to have a thousand fragments of a thousand stories and to ponder whether they go anywhere, anywhere at all.

There was, for instance, the unearthing of Occidental mummies on the Western edge of China. Henry Ellwood had left a record of it in one of his coded notebooks. Archaeologists pondered the tomb of a priestess, a blonde woman of about forty, in which a prisoner had been sacrificed and a baby buried alive. The child had been between eight and sixteen months old. There was evidence of tears and even a hint of mucus still remained, its eyes shut in furious despair, its mouth open, gasping in terror.

One day, Morrisey's mantras gave out. He went willingly where the child was so forcibly dispatched.

Night in terse

"Did you ever notice how often men of intrigue appear at night? Where they go beneath the sun, I do not claim to know. They are a nocturnal species, trading in secrets that are ashamed to be seen in the nakedness of the midday glare, for then all can see the threadbare jacket and the boots falling apart at the seams."

"Night is a mysterious realm," answered the stranger. "In evening dress, the certitudes and duties of the day run off to sleep. Tricksters and con men abound, but they do not master the darkness. In the moonlight there is softness, too, as in dreams that hearken to forgotten depths."

"You speak like a poet," said the bartender, an old pugilist with a bull-neck and meaty hands. "The reckoning of your kind is beyond my ken. The spooks are sharpers, and that is all I say."

The Boxer's words belied his modesty. Soren knew the vatic manner. So he answered with this wisdom. "Mankind cannot exist without the night. In slumber, the agony of their lives is loosened and the soul quickens, even as the body rests like a seed in the earth."

At Boxer's

Simone was blonde, pale, languid. Her voice, her every gesture said "doom, doom." She thought she had peeked to the end of the book, and that nothing was uncertain. It was her despair that made her dangerous to women and appealing to men, because a woman in despair often has no limits to what she will do.

She had noticed him straight off, not seeing so much as sensing with inerrant judgment the presence of a man suffering in a brooding, interesting way, just the sort she fancied. He was not a regular. Moreover, he did not immediately respond to her. She liked him for that, too. His eyes were turned inward, peering upon the unseen, though the regulars, also, often did not flicker an eye. The latter were waiting for the alcohol to make them argumentative, numb, or temporarily animated by the usual banal and lascivious spirits.

"What's your name?"

He looked up at her, startled. Then, in a half second, he discerned her way.

"Mister."

"Just Mister?"

"That's right."

She took this as refusal. Disappointed, Simone began to move away, then stopped just at the edge of his table. She glanced back, treating him to smoldering, tragic eyes.

"You want to drink alone."

It was a statement, not a question, but it had in it the promise of companionship. He allowed her two steps.

"I'm not much for conversation," said Blake, not so much at the woman as to the ghosts hovering in the vicinity of the opposite wall.

Simone turned a chair out from the table, and pressed herself provocatively against its back.

"That's alright," she said. "I'll talk for both of us."

They call me the witch

Simone slowly drew her hand across his chest and down, in a circular motion, across his stomach. She played with the thick, dark hair of his chest.

"You're a monkey" she said laughing. Then, "my memory is not so good."

He looked at the circular scar by her cheek and kissed it.

"I got that when I was a very little girl. I was playing on the sea in Turkey. I ran out upon the rocks and fell. It's from that that I forget. Bah!"

Soren felt tenderness and regret for the little girl who fell.

"No. No one ever hugged me like that. No one did."

Soren could say nothing, but held her like a child. When he tried to move her away so that he could look into her eyes and see her smile, which while rare was a wide, toothy grin, sensual, lighting up her face and making it almost beautiful, she could not bear to be seen. Simone grasped him with sudden fierceness, showering his forehead with kisses and pushing his face down towards her neck and chest.

"They call me the witch," she said, followed by a deep, earthy laugh. Her golden hair askew, her brown eyes moist and inviting, he held to her naked body and breathed in her playful confession. There were rabbits that rambled in the parks near her apartment. She delighted to see them. "Oh, look at the bunnies!" she would squeal with pleasure. Birds also nested near her balcony. She loved to see them feed at the seed she always left for them. She was happy to make the mother's journey easy, that she might feed her young.

Soren understood that these were vicarious opportunities.

"I once had canaries. I was always watching the eggs, to see when they would be born." She told him of the slow tremor of birth, the tapping suddenly pierced by feather and cry. "Poor things," she said, with despairing joy at the joke. "They were born behind bars. They were prison birds."

"I am bad," she said.

"I know you are." He could see that she was rather pleased.

"I'm going to make you bad, too."

A pact

The intensity of their lovemaking was matched by Soren's refusal to give his name. Each somehow arose from a common desire. There were great swathes of time when neither would speak to the other. It was an implicit vow of silence, though certainly not of chastity. What they mutually wanted was to cut off the past, and so much as possible, the future, to live in the bliss of flesh without memory.

One day, he put a name after Mister. He forgot, was all. And that was it. Simone vanished like a ghost. He thought later that probably she was a ghost.

It wasn't really true, though, about forgetting. He had tried to forget, but Simone could not destroy memory. Soren remembered Rachel, and decided to break the tacit terms of an inhuman contract.

In his cups

The fella at the bar was not a spook. He was dressed in a checkered suit with wide lapels. No spy would wear such an outfit, even to save his life.

"There's no understanding woman," he said, leaning back with his fat finger portentously in the air, his round eyes staring at you with a winking, gnostic air of mystery, as if they had recently been in the depths, cast adrift after long employ by a king of whales.

"Oh, sometimes she's easy enough to figure, but what is bewildering about the species, might as well own up that some ways they are quite alien from mankind — what's beyond troubling is that she doesn't know herself, that's her mystery, you see? She knows, but she doesn't know how she knows, and most of the time lives in a sort of muddle, don't you see?"

He waited for a response, but this was only rhetorical. "No, lad, you don't see, and if you did you'd be an imp, a spawn of devils, a whelp born of fly dung and rotten cheese."

The checkered prophet paused and chuckled to himself and looked longingly at the half empty bottle of vodka, but he was drunk on his own words and let it be.

"A woman is a wonderful being. The world could not endure without her, but she's evil too, like the rest of us. That's a thing she doesn't like to admit. Unless she's very attractive to men, then, sometimes, if it's to her advantage, she'll admit that she's no good, but even then, in her heart of hearts, she's crossing her fingers and stipulating, because, after all, at least she's not a brute."

The puppet show

The children peered up with innocent wonder at the familiar puppet show. There was Galdar, the Sorcerer, and Morwen, the lovely queen, for Elnaria was a kingdom then, full of life and power, rejoicing in its wealth and adventure. Everyone knew the story. It was the first tale learned in the crib, how Galdar promised to make Elnaria the pride of all the cosmos, and how all that was needed was a lock of the glorious Morwen's hair. Now Morwen did not trust Galdar in her heart. His plans seemed foolishly ambitious. Elnaria would suffer for such pride. So Morwen refused the sorcerer. There she went, through the little golden door of the puppet theater, refusing him again.

"Confound her! Confound the woman!'" shrieked Galdar on the stage, making a dance of his knees and his elbows that made the children laugh.

But the story did not end there. Next, the scene with the maiden, Shya, wretched girl, she was one of Morwen's servants who often accompanied her as she prepared for bed.

"Bring me a lock of your mistress' hair," purred Galdar, "and I will make you an empress."

"Could you make Sylvester love me?" Sylvester was a flunkey for the kingdom's steward and a tremendous fop.

"Yes, I could do that," said the puppet Galdar, and even in the performance, one could almost discern a sneer at such a girl that would turn aside an empire for the steward's second-best serving m an.

Soren did not stay for the rest of the play, for the predictable cutting of the lock whilst Morwen slept, and the disastrous casting of the spell. It all went wrong. The gods refused Galdar his triumph. The ribbons of time were shredded. Elnaria was cast out from the world, destined to catch the exiles of the earth like spindrift, but never to send forth her own. The very city had been lost from the memories and lips of men so that she might never have existed.

Procuror of lost and disbelieved things

There was a knock at the door. Soren listened to its insistent thud. The third time, he determined it was neither apparition, nor likely to go away. With a sigh, he abandoned the nebulous design for a fountain that had slowly been coming into focus, put down his pencil, and proceeded to reckon with the outer world, come so rudely to his small domicile.

The opened door revealed an extraordinary visitor, to be more precise, a pair of visitors. The first was a tall, lean African dressed in a red robe, Maasai as it turned out. In front of the African, a smallish figure sat in a wheelchair. The chairbound was almost entirely ensconced in fabric. A Navajo blanket wrapped him from the knees to the feet. A shawl adorned with stylized peacocks was draped over his shoulders. Furthermore, one could barely see a ginger-colored moustache and a pair of dark, oval sun glasses from beneath the shadow of an oversized sombrero.

Soren was so surprised, he forgot to offer a greeting. The little man in the wheelchair seemed hardly to care. He held out a closed fist, turned up the hand, and revealed a tiny ivory sculpture of a packman carrying his luggage. There was an expression of profound, almost majestic sorrow on its face.

"Are you the artisan who crafted this piece?"

The voice was quick, bright with boyish enthusiasm.

Soren took the trinket and appeared to scrutinize it, though he knew already it was his. An old couple who had taken an unaccountable liking to his gruff ways sold them for him at their table in the bazaar. Soren wanted time to evaluate his visitors. In the silence, Blake noticed that the African looked neither right, nor left, but stood poised. *On guard.* His charge, on the other hand, was unabashedly curious, peering around Soren at the simple bed, the table, the chisels, hammers, and bits of half-worked marble on the workbench.

Not waiting any longer for confirmation, the man in the wheelchair continued.

"Allow me to say I am most impressed with your work. The good mother and father that sold me the piece were quite unwilling to let me know about you, I assure you. I had virtually to buy them tea and crumpets for a week to manage a name and district. Fortunately, your landlady is far less scrupulous. You might want to note that — about the landlady."

He stopped talking and folded his hands. Soren thought that he might have precipitously fallen asleep. It was hard to tell with the dark glasses, but then suddenly, as if he had never quit, the visitor concluded, "Though I suppose you know. Anyone who smokes that much is craven and easily plied."

"Yes, it's mine," said Soren, suddenly tired and irritated and hoping to come to a point.

"Good." The invalid began to search the folds of his clothes. "I would box her ears, if I were you. I could have Toby do it." He pointed to the Maasai. "This is Toby Jaguar. Well, his real name is unpronounceable in Swahili, but it means Jaguar. Imagine naming your child that. Did you know that a panther is no different than a black jaguar? I say, maybe we should call you Panther, Toby."

Toby made no response, except perhaps to breathe slightly heavy. It wasn't true, by-the-bye, since the Swahili for jaguar is jaguar.

"I had a time of it with the Bureau of Names, but fortunately I have some pull and they let him keep it, Anglicized, of course."

At last, he had come upon what he was looking for. He handed Soren a card which read,

---

Timothy Pigott-Smythe
Procuror of lost and disbelieved Things
Wedding Rings, Birth Certificates, Hope, Virginity,
Winged Horses,etc.

Tim Piggot-Smythe allowed himself a sly smile while he waited for the full effect of his disclosure. "I assure you, it's all true. Except the bit about virginity. I can't really do that."

Soren did not believe him about anything, but he liked him. He knew this because he discovered he was suddenly not tired, nor burdened by principled misanthropy.

"You're lucky. I move a lot. A few weeks back I had a nice place above a bakery. Can't seem to settle. And what is it you are attempting to find here, Mr. Piggot-Smythe?"

"It's TimPig to you, if we are to be friends, and I thought that you might make me a chess set."

Tim removed his sun glasses, revealing steady, gray blue eyes, and something Soren did not expect. Sadness.

"Well, TimPig," he said at last. "I am not much for friends."

"You see," said Tim. "You've already found something lost."

The Lord of Hosts

The man was neither young, nor old. He stood for a while as Beorn attended to the sea worthiness of his toy craft. The boy was at first so absorbed in his maritime duty that he failed to notice that he was observed. When he did, the boy merely redoubled his concern that every aspect of responsibility should be well achieved. Having satisfied himself and given a short speech to encourage the ship, he launched it upon the waters.

Soren silently watched along with the boy as the tiny sail caught a flicker of wind and serenely entered the depths of the artificial lake that graced the property. Only then did he ask the boy if he thought naval power sufficient to answer the strength of Pharaoh's chariots.

"Nana," said Beorn, "told me the pride of Egypt was drowned in the Red Sea."

"I have heard that as well," said Soren. "I notice that your craft is well apportioned, but it lacks any figure at the stern, or even a painted eye."

Beorn pondered this and his brow darkened.

"I mistrust the ship without a spirit guide," added the man.

"The men have spirit enough," said Beorn, assuaging doubt with firmness.

Then Soren smiled at the boy. "You may well be right, if they are noble."

The boy perceived that the man was an artisan by the satchel he carried with him. "Are you here to see my father?" he asked.

"His friend, I think," said Soren.

He reached into his satchel and pulled out a tiny winged figure.

"This," said the artist, "is only an image, for an angel defeats the imagination. There are many such spirit warriors, the most indefatigable army, eternal and good."

Soren handed the angel to Beorn. "You may place the angel on the boat if it pleases you. Only you must remember one thing that is most important."

"What is that?" asked Beorn, already enamored by the bright angel, turning it in his hand so that the sunlight dazzled translucent pinions.

"You must remember," said Soren, "that the Lord of Hosts is a child."

The girl in the Garden

No servant appeared when Soren's water taxi nudged against the shallow steps that led up to a path that ended in a gallery of arches. The walls of the villa were painted a pale, soothing peach color, off-set by narrow oblong shutters, uniformly closed, which kept their secrets in the hue of a deep plum. Uneven patches of thick ivy bearded the walls, adding to the beautiful sleepiness that faced the lake. The base of the structure leading up to the water's edge was masonry of white gray stone. This same material was used to construct a slender elbow of a bridge which reached out with an affectionate, tender arch to a smaller, more modest building whose roof could be espied from an extended terrace set off by a low fence.

Despite its lack of opulence, this other building somehow completed the prospect of the villa, lending a spirit of peasant domesticity that saved its partner from aloof insularity. A small boy dressed in patrician robes carefully examined the accoutrements of a model ship. Soren listened as the boy delivered a sincere and serious oration of encouragement to the craft. Without a trace of condescension, he felt a sprig of delight enter his heart.

As there was no one about to greet him, he joined the boy and watched the prow of the craft bravely cut through the invisible boundary between shoreline and the dangers of the chaotic deep. Soren gave to the boy a small gift, for he sensed in him a pensive, lonely soul. Afterwards, he had taken a few tentative steps when Toby Jaguar emerged from a darkened archway.

The Maasai observed him with detached silence. Soren indicated that he had brought the chess set. The brow of the taciturn factotum rose ever so slightly in acknowledgement. Then Toby turned and mutely led Soren through a winding path of stairs and corridors. When they came upon a terrace situated on the roof of one of the villas' lower buildings, Soren discovered TimPig with slippered feet hanging off the edge of a chaise lounge.

TimPig was regaling a middle-aged nobleman who attended to his speech with a wistful, quiet manner. Soren was momentarily sorry that he had come unannounced, but, if anything, the eccentric collector of obscure items was delighted to see him.

"There you are!" said TimPig. "Soren Blake, may I introduce Prince Raveh? The prince and I have been discussing set theory, a rather abstruse pastime, I admit, though the nature of numbers has always fascinated. You may recall that knowledge of mathematics was prerequisite to enter Plato's Academy."

Soren opened a wooden case and began to line up a veritable animalia of chessman. Ebony stone sported crows for pawns, hippos for knights, with mountain gorillas for rooks and upright crocodiles made to span ecclesial diagonals. The king and queen were paired, cobra and asp. The ivory pieces matched them with rabbits and ibex, elephants and fierce tigers, all ruled by a strange couple, unicorn and hart.

"What is less well known is that Plato was an earthy man and cannot be understood apart from his love of wine and the flesh," said Soren.

"The scholars have him all wrong then?" asked Prince Raveh, surprised at the artisan.

"One must remember that the cave and the divided line are only preliminary gestures. The Good does not appear and is outside the line altogether. There is only ever one image that is meant to explain all the others, and that is Socrates himself."

"What did I tell you?" chortled TimPig to the prince. "I am a magnet for strange beings. They find me."

Soren shrugged, declining to mention how TimPig had gone to some trouble to find the artisan. "We are all strange beings if you are awake enough to see," he said. "Now about my payment."

This was the sort of frankness Prince Raveh was more accustomed to find in those who struggled for their bread, but expectation was again upended. Soren explained that he preferred barter. He had stumbled upon a barn find; a 1941 Indian Four with sidecar, but needed parts. Don't ask how it made its way to Elnaria. There are souls in things, that's why, produced as a mystery of memory. Even those made of machined parts without ontological substance hold a relation to an originating mind.

"I'd like to put in a Qua clutch if you can procure such an item in this world. The exhaust valves on the 441 are surrounded by a lot of iron, so I need a clutch that will shed as much heat as possible. And if you really can find the impossible, a short skirt piston with gas expansion rings would be lovely. Of course, I'll owe you more than the set for all that."

TimPig clapped his hands and asked Toby to bring him a ledger for one of his warehouses. While they were waiting, the prince retrieved the thread of conversation devoted to mathematics. Prince Raveh began to explain some interesting features of Cantor's set theory. It was amusing, the way his tepid aristocratic ennui briefly vanquished. However, Soren's enjoyment of sudden vitality in the prince was subtly troubled by the distinct feeling that he was being watched. This faintly ridiculous sensation persisted as Arco wondered aloud if a certain spatializing logic in sets was not undermined by the paradoxes of infinity.

"Take pi, for instance. It has no exact value. You can never catch up to a real number. The space between integers is literally without end."

TimPig related the curious study of a Cambridge professor who measured the lengths of the earth's longest rivers in a straight line from their sources to their mouths. He then measured them by following their intricate meanderings. Such a laborious measuring revealed a ratio of the wandering route to the straight line that approximated π.

"Yes," said Soren. "The true art of mathematics is symbolic. It cannot be understood by those captured by the appetite for mastery. The engineer often turns the mystery of being into a lust for possession. Mere quantitative measure is ignorant of qualities."

Soren paused, gazing down at an oasis of palms that adorned a small vestibule outside the provincial structure adjacent the bridge. From that distance, a young woman stared up at them. Her white blouse and blue overalls belonged to a working class, though a crimson belt made from a strip of satin declared protest against mere utility.

"The rivers, too, desire perfection," said Soren, half lost in wonder. "And so they prefer the circular to the linear line, though perhaps the spiral is the best path."

What emotion blazed in her almond eyes beneath dark brows? Such playful beauty, but there was iron in her gaze, did she know him without his beard and haggard pain?

"Who is she?" asked TimPig.

"Just a girl."

"It's never just a girl."

"A surprise."

"It's always a surprise."

Faith

When did he see her next? Another man would have dropped everything to find her. Soren waited. He felt in his bones that she would find him when the time was ripe. It was a kind of faith that they were already and always connected. A few weeks after he saw her in the shadow of TimPig's villa, Soren went to visit the Jews. He tried to tell Naftali about her. It was hard to explain. He began by talking of his art.

"I find that I can do many things. They come to me as if from afar, but it is a near far, as if the greatest distance is the closest intimacy. First, there is the resistance of material. It could be stone or wooden plank, or more ethereal, the time of breath, the word that whispers in silence. And yet, that resistance calls to me as invocation, the form of the other bringing to vision the reality I touch but cannot see. Something happens I cannot explain. I must abandon attempts to coerce, the mastery of art is not force. I do not control, but recognize, yes. It is a sort of prayer, Naftali. There is an ecstasy of sheer forgetfulness, and I only attend to the other. Then my hands are discerning, speaking, praising. It is like *that*."

What he really wanted to know is if he had summoned her from the invisible realm. *Did I imagine her into existence?*

In the Hasid Study House Naftali said to him, "I knew when I first saw you that you were like our zaddik, only perhaps you do not know. There is what we call *hitlahavut*, 'the burning.' This is the ecstasy of man when he lives from the other world. I can tell you stories of the holy dancing and laughter and vision, it is the life we pursue whilst the Outsiders can only perceive musty little rooms, cramped quarters, and the poverty of those who are not slaves to idols."

"I am not a saint. I only understand a little," protested Soren.

"But there are zaddik, the wandering ones, whose *hitlahavut* is not yet fulfilled," answered Naftali. "Solitary, these live unfulfilled and fugitive. They enter into exile to 'suffer with the Shekina.' They are like the Shulamite bride who pines for her Lord of night. What does the exiled zaddik do? He lives friendship with God as the stranger in all lands. It is said there are moments when he sees the Shekina face-to-face, that the glory appears in the shape of a woman who laments the husband of her youth."

White Orchid

As it happened, the next time was both profoundly natural and rather strange. Indeed, this is always the case, but only the wise notice. Soren was in the market on a street named after an Elnarian sage whose title means "the White Orchid." Whether this has any significance, well, who can say? It was not the market he usually made use of, but someone had told him of a seller of various herbs and medicinal plants hard to come by out of season and so while Soren was bent over a table covered in ginseng, arboreal radishes, and sambong, the girl appeared at his shoulder.

Rachel was not shy, nor did she remonstrate with him for leaving her at the gate.

"What are those?" she asked.

"That is Angelica," he said, trying not to betray emotion. "And next to them, milky oats."

"Why do folks use them?"

"Milky oats, if taken in the time of the new moon, are said to promote prosperity and abundance."

Rachel spun around so that her long skirt twirled, a ravishing petal in the breeze. "And these here?"

He told her the names of Silver Bush used to treat gout and rheumatism, of Coneflower which was good for wounds and toothache, and of Turmeric and Valerian to lessen anxiety.

Rachel spoke then in a soft, but steady voice. "Sometimes, when we think we can't do anything for the other, that all we can do is suffer, it might seem a burden."

"Yes, it can seem that way," he said.

She looked him clear in the face. Her beauty nearly stunned him. She was even more beautiful than when he had admired her in the stark desert.

"And some people soak up sympathy that is really only self-regard under a thin veil. They sop themselves in it and think themselves good."

Soren wasn't sure if she was making an accusation, so a note of hesitation entered his voice. "Well, I've never been mistaken for that," he said.

"It's really best not to worry about it. Love isn't something you can balance in an account book," she said with the clarity of almost a child.

"I see your point," he said firmly to parry her sincerity, because he had no idea where she was going with it.

"We forget ourselves in love. It goes beyond willing. This gift from what is deepest in our hearts. Then we still offer, we give ourselves, but not as a possession. It's part of the gift."

He looked at her then, astonished at the wise in the girl. She was telling him what was hardly to be expected. "When that happens, the burden is light," she said.

And suddenly, he realized she was taking the lead role in the proposed drama. He had thought she was blaming him for abandoning her or trying to convince him to care for her when she was explaining how easy it was for her to love him.

A fairy tale

"The people tell this story of the City. They say the Guardians and even the kings before them were never the true rulers, but only the servants of the actual prince. The true prince is a nasty, hungry rat, older than time, that lives in sewers and mazes beneath the City. Prince Rat puffs himself up and sells false dreams in exchange for man's spirit. They say the City is sad, because men feel their bondage, even when they believe that they are most free."

"That's a fairy tale I can believe," said Blake with a short, bitter laugh.

"Oh, that's not the end. What would be the good of a story that ended like that?"

"It might be true."

"If it was, it would be better not to tell stories at all," chided Rachel. "Only bad men would tell them."

She was silent then and he could not see if she was angry with him or lost in her own reflections.

"I told you. I shouldn't be around people," he said sulkily. "How does it end then?"

"I'm sorry. I can't tell you now. You'd only laugh at it. I was trying to think how to tell you, but I can't."

He saw then that she was not angry with him at all, but sad and warm and a little pitying. He couldn't stand the pity in her, but forgave it because she was honest and beautiful and he was such a brute.

A postcard

When he drove up in the Indian, it was spit polished and shiny as a parade horse with flanks brushed and ribbons in its hair. The engine purred. There was a small woven basket warm with baked quail and filled with figs and a bottle of wine. It was nestled in a blanket waiting for her in the sidecar. She felt happy. It made her happy to grab his hand and to hold it. She was wearing a white dress with blue polka dots which reminded her for no clear reason of the light in Tuscany and childhood romps in the apple orchard.

Rachel felt his regard, the way he couldn't stop looking at her. And then they were humming along the road. He took her out of the city, rumbling past golden seas of wheat and new forest. They turned onto a narrow trail that climbed into hills. The hairpin turns would have vanquished a different girl, but she was brave. Her heart smiled because he knew it. Then they were descending. The road broadened slightly and the lulling break of the sea began to whisper to them.

Soren slowed the Indian and brought it to a stop at the edge of a promontory overlooking a beach. The westward slope declined steeply for many hundreds of feet to a rocky shore. Even the gulls that pierced the air were so far below them they seemed silent. The water slapped against the rocks in grays and dark fuscous greens still bearing a frisson of the depths. Further inland, the white sand kept solitude with the wind-lapped waves. One could believe one had come to the end of the world.

"It would make a melancholy postcard," she said.

"I like just this sort of beauty. Everything really beautiful is sad, ever notice?"

"Oh, that's a lovely thing to say, Scout."

"Is that what you're calling me?"

"Why, yes. It's what I called you before. Don't you remember?"

She smiled, thinking she might blush. They were silent, watching the dance of water and rock. "You don't," she said after some deliberation and, she had to admit, trepidation, "have a name for m e?"

Soren gave the barest hint of a wry grin. "Boss girl, Getsherway, Imperious . . . no, not really."

I hate you. I hate you, she thought, wondering how long they would be allowed to be so lovely together.

A request

There was a dapper old gentleman who lived in Soren Blake's building. He must have known better times at least. His beard was always neatly kept. The fedora he wore matched the ancient suit he had chosen in brighter days. In the afternoons, if it wasn't too chill, he would seat himself at a bench located near the entrance to the building. There, he would play upon a darkly stained cello with the graceful aptitude of a gifted amateur. Children, especially, were drawn to his performances. They would gather in little groups and forget their antics and little disagreements while listening to pieces from Vivaldi, Zani, or the easier of Bach's suites. If the fellow was feeling more ambitious, he'd make a fair effort at the sixth.

Adults, too, would call out for favorites or drop coins at his feet. But the old man did not play for money. It was whispered that he gave away whatever largesse he received to widows and older pensioners who desperately needed it. Yet he was clearly poor himself. Then one day, the old man settled onto the bench, as usual, but did not play. He appeared confused and fumbled with the bow. Then he smiled with the guileless candor of a child and looked back with mute incomprehension at the questioners who asked if he was well.

Some of the residents helped him back to his small rooms. Later, Blake heard that the fellow was ill. One evening, when the night air was frigid and a small animal was whimpering outside, Soren went down to investigate, feeling foolish and angry that a poor beast was suffering. The creature was not in sight, but the dark cello lay forlorn, propped up against a motley collection of trash. That was how Soren learned of the old fellow's demise.

When Rachel saw it, she wondered aloud if he could play.

"No. It belonged to a friend who no longer has need of it. I felt it should be looked after, is all."

"You will learn to play," she said.

"Is that an order, boss?"

She glanced shyly at the instrument. "It is a request."

Ghost of a chance

The old peasant kept looking into his empty purse. He'd raise his head and wipe his brow, then peer down with profound concentration as if the very act might change the impoverished belly of the money pouch.

"There was a silver coin, señor. I swear it," he said at last in a voice barely above a whisper.

"There was," said a voice that belonged to one of the bohemian stragglers standing at the bar. "But that was three, maybe four years ago."

"The fella don't know he's a ghost," explained a spook who had decided the way to be unobtrusive was to wear a Hawaiian shirt. "All he wants is a drink. Boxer tried giving him a free shot once. Didn't work. Seems he has to pay with that missing coin or it's no good."

"Anyone try giving him a new coin?" asked Soren.

"Yeah, we tried that, too," sighed Boxer. "Placed a shiny bit right next to him on the table. He put it in his wallet and damme if it didn't go disappear. That bag has a curse on it."

Soren sat down across from the ghost. "Boy, I'm parched," he said.

"I am alone in the world," said the old man.

"I'd like to drink, but I've got an odd habit," said Soren. "I just can't drink without a partner, know what I mean?"

"No one cares," said the old man. "Even I don't care. When I speak, the ears are shut."

"Tell you what," said Soren. "Why don't you drink for me and I'll have a drink for you? That way no one will notice."

The sad peasant looked up from his gloom with a bemused, astonished expression. "Might work," he said.

"I personally favor single malt scotch, but today I'm not feeling particular. You go tell Boxer what I'm drinking."

"It's so dry," said the ghost. "Even a little drop of water would be a kindness."

"That's right," admitted Soren.

Later, after the spooks and the artists and the pugs had all gathered round and gawked while Soren and the ghost drank toasts to one another, followed by doggerel songs with everyone joining in, they could hardly recall when the old man had snuck away with his empty money bag.

On the table where he had sat, Soren discovered a silver coin.

A little night music

She was waiting for him on the landing when he got home. He had been thinking of her all day and of the stories they had told one another in the Chora Makra. He was pleased to see her — and surprised, for she was wearing a thick white cotton robe, the kind they used to include with a room in the better hotels on another world. She took in his questioning glance, but averted her enchanting eyes. Once inside, she fluttered about, chatting with sporadic energy about her day. Then she sat down in the corner where he had placed the old cello and stared for a long time.

"Tell me," she said, "one of the stories you told then."

He knew the one she liked best.

"Pretend," he began, "that on a day where the doves swim and the fish fly, there is a knock at your door. When you answer, there is a liveried footman who delivers into your hands a parcel. He tells you that it is a present from Prester John, the great and mysterious king of the East. The gift is a book written in the ancient language of the heart, from before the days of sorrow and fear, that is, from before the time when men were men.

You are pleased and honored to receive such a book, but when you open its pages, you discover it is full of symbols you cannot read. The footman is already retreating into his coach. You cry out after him that the language is unknown to you. A hand brushes aside a fabric curtain from the window of the carriage. A face hidden in shadows looks out at you.

"The words will come clear, little by little," says a voice like a sad violin from within the vehicle. "As you live your life, the book translates itself."

"Imagine that you are walking along a busy, city street. It is early spring and the boulevard is filled with lovers. Your thoughts are wanderers, full of memory and expectation. An old woman sits on a bench feeding the pigeons, which, one must excuse, are *her* pigeons. A little further on, there is a vendor selling flowers, hoping to entice some coins from those inebriated on love, those who one can always tell by a certain blush in the cheek, a skip in the walk, as if there were no such thing as hunger and death and disgrace. Yes, my friends, what is one to do with lovers?

You walk on with a shy smile perhaps — and if it is a dream, it is a beautiful dream, no? – past a little fountain, perchance, and past a dozen men dressed in gray suits and grim faces and, forgive me, also, several women dressed likewise in gray and grim, you walk past these important people, undoubtedly important, for why else chain oneself to such a spectacle? And now you are a little tired. It is a long walk and a small rest, some lemonade . . . it would do you good, but you hear quite distinctly the sound of a child crying. It is such a bitter distress that you cannot look away.

There. Yes, next to the juniper, there is a young boy with a smudgy face and he is looking so disconsolate and alone. Where are his mother and his father? How should they have left him? You look around, but there is no one to pay attention to the little fellow who has stopped crying. For now, he has set down at the edge of the street and he is looking out at his fellow travelers, sad, but wary, as if one might be an enemy or a long lost friend.

What will you do? He has quieted and that is good for the nerves. Better to leave him there and to find your shady lemonade. So, what shall you do?

You may leave. Nothing shall be said against you. He had stopped crying. Perhaps he was only at a game. Perhaps he was a pickpocket. But if you leave, you must close the book."

"We certainly shall not leave," said Rachel.

"Imagine, if you can, a man who is deaf and dumb and blind, for I have been that man. Imagine, also, that while this man has been to the world a kind of surd wrapped in impenetrable darkness, all the while, he, himself, has been listening to, almost seeing, a kind o f story.

He will have seen many faces, a multitude of plots, and an almost dizzying array of wonders, the meaning of which he does . . . and does not know. Now imagine what is more difficult, that for many years, to all outward appearance, there has been nothing wrong with this man. He can see as you do. He may walk about the country or in town as well as any. He hears and takes part in conversation. To all eyes, he is an ordinary member of the human species. He is a little nervous, given to sudden moodiness, but none of this is beyond the normal range of human behavior.

On an expansive night, especially if he is amongst his friends, he will try to tell what cannot be told. He will advert to the faces, to the stories that roil in his blood like a poison he cannot purge. He will grow hysterical, likely as not fight over a nothing. Then he will part from his company. The fit will be upon him and you will not see him for many days. He will be exiled, self drawn into the cocoon of the single room where he lives. The lights will be dimmed, the shades pulled down. Imagine, if you can, a man who is deaf and dumb and blind."

"He is a brute, but I love him."

"Who are you, young fellow, and why are you here?"

For a long moment, the boy does not answer. He is distracted or perhaps he is simply reticent before a stranger. One approaches near to face him and in order to better ascertain the possibilities when he suddenly, without preamble, brings the matter to hand.

"There was a rich man. And he said to me: 'See this flower? Pluck it and a princess will die.'"

"That was certainly a very odd thing to say."

The boy wept.

"Chin up, young man. Flood gates, I'm afraid, must remain closed. You can never tell with rich folk."

"But do you believe it?" he asks between his sobs.

I did not want to say to him, "it is ridiculous." For one, he would not have believed me. And secondly, there is something charming – that every flower should have its princess. "It may be true," I said cautiously.

This sent him into a new paroxysm of misery. "I plucked the flower!" he shouted. "I did it! I killed the princess!"

"Enough!" you say. This charade has been allowed to go on too far. Tell him the truth. There is no connection between flowers and princesses. The rich man, knowing a small boy could never resist such a provocation, has played a cruel joke on him. Yes, yes. I see your point. All the same, I did not quite know what to say. This reasonable solution is a safe truth, and hence, this boy and I mistrust it.

We sat in silence for some time. Indeed, we both had a bit of the glums.

At last, in desperation, I said, "Your princess shall live."

I said this as decisively as I could. I hoped he would accept my authority as an adult — he was not yet grown enough for that idea to be silly — but he was still worried about the words of the rich man.

We sat silently on the curb. If you have chosen to come along and if you have not peremptorily quashed the possibilities with a dose of impatient law such as "there is no connection" — you will be party to the most extraordinary event. The small boy turned to us who are his friends, friends by the seriousness of the issue, by our shared sense of understanding, that if we do not have answers, we are, at least, mutually before a very great mystery, he turned and asked in a hushed, quiet voice: "Is love stronger than death?"

"Unless you have loved, there is nothing magical about this question. Once you have — and many may fool themselves into thinking they have acquaintance with the event when all they have experienced is the instinct and imperious urge of biological imperative — once you have loved, it must, inevitably, become the question of questions.

There is not just the macabre, disastrous death of the body, but the much more despondent and incomprehensible death of the soul. How does the shadow begin, the growing apart of lovers, of parent from child, brother from brother, friend from friend? The presumed eventual heat death of the universe into an immensity of breathless chill is nothing to the brief, painful actions, the long, eventless spaces where ineffable life is allowed to fall into inanition. Mutual recrimination, abandonment into the separateness of our individual truths — tempers and sorrows grow, until all that is asked is that some impartial spirit enter into the game and declare our wounds real, our enmity just.

And still we have not said all and can never say all. Love cannot be preserved, but must be squandered, upset, put at risk. Love is adventure. Fidelity is the dance of love, not an unchanging substrate of iron. I have said all this for the sheer joy of descrying the unfathomable. And if you have heard all this before, recollect that to speak truth is to remember one's human face."

She was quiet.

"I told it better in the desert. I am tired, Rachel."

"No. You told it just right. Are you really tired?"

Something about the way she asked made him reconsider. "Just a little. Not very tired."

Rachel stood and stretched. She removed the robe and used it to polish the cello. The flash of her naked flesh flowed and shimmered in the warm lamplight. Somehow, perhaps she had help, she had drawn two perfect sound holes in charcoal above the small of her back. She knelt then and allowed him to compare the old instrument to the nubile form. She heard him gasp with the pain of desire. Standing up and turning, she asked while falling into his embrace if he would play adagio for her.

Inexpressible stone

He wanted to tell her, speak the inexpressible stone, the one that she could strike, and bring forth the waters of life. These elements of earth, of celestial rivers, Soren felt them as heaviness, mute darkness. He'd fallen asleep with his head resting against the marble waiting like Michelangelo for a dream of form. *Only say the word and I shall be healed.*

Jacob discovered a ladder to the heavens, angelic portals, ascent by degree to the azure throne whatever that meant.

He awoke to find her near, Rachel.

Incognito

On the one hand, there is *the body in the world's truth*, which people take as the real body, and in fact as the only body, the one you can see, the visible body, the body-object ranked alongside all the objects of the universe and sharing its essence, that of having extension: *res extensa*. On the other hand, there is *the body in Life's Truth*, the invisible body . . . it is from the invisible that the unique person comes. This is the no place that intimacy is always trying to touch, the sacred garden lovers seek and that the torturer would despoil.

Here, this body that is real gathers in the fabric of dreams waiting for the eschaton when all shall be revealed, while the visible body is only its imperfect, exterior representation.

The House in the Forest

They went rambling. That's what they called it when he had the Indian purring and she'd crawl into the sidecar with a scarf tied around her neck and he put on a silly leather cap as if he were preparing to fly.

There wasn't any plan. They just found a road and kept going. Sometimes they followed the twisted turns of the old city until they happened on something interesting: an old fountain with sculpture he wanted to examine or a confectioner that made a sponge candy she liked. Often, they ended up at a second-hand shop where he'd look at old books and she'd bring him ceramics and lamps that he mainly told her to put back.

But mostly they'd try for a path away from the City where the land became spacious and free and they would glory in the wind rushing past them and the sheer burst of their speed. On this day, they came to a forest. It had its share of new growth, but the bulwark trees were tall, foreboding bearers of tradition, they'd seen a lot.

Soren parked the motorcycle and they wandered a bit before a clearing provided the perfect spot for a picnic. After their meal, he drowsed while she followed a trail dotted with wild strawberries.

Rachel was concentrating on the berries, so when she looked up, she was astonished to see the house.

When she ran to get him, Soren had drifted into that pleasant state of reverie where the tinge of dreams softens every sharp edge with twilight. Rachel tugged on his arm with the breathless impatience of a child. He rose and followed her, still caught in that mental dusk that whispers of sleep.

All the time she was dragging his ponderous steps towards her discovery, Rachel tried to explain what she had found, but he could not keep up with the rapid flurry of her thoughts, and besides, he didn't quite grasp the sense of it until she suddenly stopped and pushed him hard against the chest to stop his mechanical lurch forward. It was all rather comic.

Soren was still looking stolidly into her eyes with no more spark than an ox, so she raised his head with delicate hands before pointing where he ought to look. Then his eyes widened, and he started asking questions she couldn't answer, already leaping up the steps that led to the wide porch.

The main lines of the building were Victorian with architectural embellishments that sometimes shaded towards rococo extravagance. Above the second floor landing, light filtered through tangled arboreal pillars to reach a large glass dome set within the slanting roof like a pellucid jewel. And although it clearly had been abandoned and gone to seed, Soren believed the bones of the structure remained sound.

Rachel danced from room to room, shouting for him to come see the many facets, from cozy to aristocratic that had gathered within that enchanted place.

They would have liked to stay longer, but they had to drive back to the City and the light was waning.

The days that followed, it became a shared secret, a happy shore where the lost things came to land. They talked of putting it back in shape and building a life together, though it was too large and too expensive a project, supposing the noble wreck was not a bound, but forgotten property of someone ignorant of its decaying beauty.

Still, on weekends and sometimes during the week, they'd sneak off to "their house." She'd clean a few rooms. He did a bit of carpentry. It wasn't much, but they had the distinct feeling of sympathetic acknowledgement. The spirit of the house cooed to be once more loved and cared for.

The strange creature joy

The brightness of things astounded Rachel. She wondered how she could have missed the radiance that announced itself with unassuming beauty. Her love shot forth towards everything and everything bowed to the courtesy of her gaze. She looked at simple things: a flower, a puddle of muddy rain in a patch of cobblestone glistened by the sun, the way an old man swung his umbrella, and they all sang to her. Each said, "I do not have to be here, but I am."

It was a language whimsical and bemused. Even the dark things that used to scare her, the night scrawls and spiders, appeared to wink at her, as if she had seen behind their masks and was in on the secret. Everything was the same, and yet completely different.

She was happy with her man. It delighted her to make the child return to his eyes, to see the flush of pride he had in her. It was good to be loved. She longed to tell her man, to share the way that had been opened up to them by the amity in their hearts.

Just so, in the glow of her felicity, Rachel wrapped herself in soft, serene sorrow. It was not an ache. It was not bitter or angry or cynical. It was precisely in the perfect pitch of her contentment untainted by fear of loss or cowardly suspicion of illusion that she discovered a little creature nestled against her breast. It looked up at her with large, famished eyes and clung not fiercely, not demanding, but with a gentle trust that it would not be dropped or discarded or treated badly.

She could not tell her man about it. He would not see it and if he could, he would not understand. He would think it was a threat to them or that she was touched a bit in the head. He wouldn't mind that, because he loved her, but he'd still be mistaken. What she knew in her heart, but did not have the words, was that it was joy calling her, joy beyond happiness that had come disguised as danger and covered in little claws that were sure to scratch and tear.

She could not explain, but a bold trust had come to her. It had come freely, unexpected, yet plainly necessary. She knew that their love could not flourish and live without it.

In this moment of growing awareness, Rachel discovered a young woman leaning over one of the city's derelicts. He was far gone, debased in body, his time unraveled, clothing dirty and torn, and yet the concern in the face of the woman glowed as if she saw beauty everywhere. Rachel strode over to them with expectant joy.

Benedicta smiled back at her as if she recognized a fellow sister in spirit.

The essence of a cherry tree

"There are different ways of explaining all this," said Benedicta. "Mine is only one, though perhaps it will be helpful to you.

I stand in the cloister garden and gaze upon the blossoming cherry tree. I cherish the bright flowers, see that some are yet buds with promise, whilst others have done with the gift of love's blush, gather in soft dust upon the ground. If I imagine further back, I can begin to see a seedling shyly announce in fragile grace a desire to one day perform the blooming dance. My imagination touches the essence of the cherry tree.

However, were I to suddenly ask it to bear figs, the essence disappears. It cannot thrive in falsehood. Only the nothing is utterly pliant to willful suggestion. Here, the meaning is given, something irreducible that constitutes the tree, though it is also multiple, capable of infinite variety, supposing I do not break faith and ask of it a lie."

That sort of girl

When he came back from the agora, Soren threw the remains of a haphazard lunch down on the table: a baguette, several plumbs, and a thin wedge of cheese. Then he perused the work from his day, a tablet of sketches showing men-at-law, merchants, children, beggars and pickpockets. Soren had remarked them all.

Paging through the faces and the proud, abject, devious bodies, he stopped at one of the lawyers. The fella had a sharp chin, a haughty eye that viewed everyone through the lens of a predatory shark whilst imagining mere objectivity. And then he found the likeness of a beggar, his thin flesh covered in misery. Soren's discerning vision came first through the hands, discovered mysterious grace in poverty, grandeur in that wrecked flesh lacking to the perspicacity of the law.

He found Rachel ensconced amidst various piles of his books. She was wearing an old pair of spectacles he sometimes needed. She smiled at his silent enquiry.

"Otherwise, I cannot read the tiny writing," she said.

He'd forgotten she was the sort of girl who reads the footnotes.

The full quid

"There are other levels, perhaps an infinite number of them. I suppose it gets a bit difficult. If you think about it well, there is never an object isolated and by itself, just as there is never a thought without language. Every object of your intentional consciousness, I mean by that what you choose to focus upon, brings with it a tacit dimension. The object dwells in the context of an expanding circle of relations.

And these are what we are apt to call time, which is the mutable dance of event full of contingent, accidental connections. Part of the essence of the cherry tree was the possibility that one day in 1936, a nun named Benedicta might gaze upon it. And part of Benedicta's essence is that she was born in Breslau on Yom Kippur in the year of our Lord 1891 and that she was so reserved her sisters called her "a book sealed with seven seals." But you see I grew past that.

There is another aspect of the unique for the unique; that whatness of the tree includes what I call the 'full quid' which is just those transient moments of contact that supply dramatic openness to newness. The inspiration of the artist, I think, takes hold of this. The artist allows herself to be moved by the peripheral relations that are attendant upon any object, often feeling connections remote to a merely analytic intellect.

Is this necessary to an understanding of the cherry tree or not? While it may appear unimportant for a metaphysics that prescinds from the historical as not pertaining to essences, the wholeness of the uniquely singular is not known integrally apart from the apparent gratuity of what need not have been."

Rain

They both liked rain. Maybe not always, you could see how that would oppress and discourage. Nor was their affection the great neediness of the desert where life is particularly precarious. The rain they liked best was propitious for love making, for reading, for the joy of being together under a roof that served as floor for dancing angels.

On a day of rain, she cooked for him, making pasta from scratch and marinating beef purchased from the kosher butcher on the corner with fresh zucchini thrown into tomato sauce mixed with mushrooms and garlic and a touch of cut lemon.

Not for the first time, he wondered at her, the miracle of her existence. "Who are you?" his eyes asked with simple gratitude. And just as simply, she answered in all her inflections that she did not know so could not answer him, but that none of that was worth worrying over. She was a gift from God who told her what was needed to know in its proper season.

Ralph is unrepeatable

"You must understand," said Benedicta, "that as I conceive it, there is mutual dependency between an essence and its object. It is not correct to think of a needy object and a pure, perfect essence complete all by itself. While it is true that there could be no cherry tree without a corresponding essence, without a cherry tree, the essence is mute. The object unfolds the essence as an expression of intelligible meaning.

Further, I am inclined to see in particular objects a concatenation of many essences. Every quality that contributes to the singular being has its essence, the color crimson, the smooth touch of velvet, the sweetness of honey, for example. And I suspect, beyond what Plato and Aristotle surmise, that there is a unique essence for Socrates and perhaps for Ralph, the Doberman Pinscher.

Every individual object shares universal essences; all dogs are alike in that respect, but only Ralph can be Ralph. He is unrepeatable."

A crack up

One day while on a ramble, the road became clogged with all sorts of vehicles and pedestrians, too. Peddlers with carts and bicyclists stopped and stared. Some folks jumped into the air as if brief levitation would enlighten them as to the cause of the backup. While everyone around was asking the same questions and protesting ignorance or speculating an accident, Soren became quiet. He was starting to simmer. Soon he would boil over and start to hate the whole noise making, vulgar, imbecile lot of them.

Rachel kept glancing over and trying to console him with her warm eyes. He felt the power of her gaze and looked away, because he didn't want to absolve the so-called rational animal of the stain that crept into everything it did.

When they got closer, the flow was wintry molasses, a crack up was revealed as cause of the delay. A cart driven by a nag of a horse had collided with a pair of teen age boys who had been sharing a scooter. The horse was in a bad way. The old man sat astride the toppled cart and waved his cap into the air, gesticulating with frazzled energy, the wisp of his thin beard shaking. You couldn't tell if he was savagely angry with the youths or lamenting the horse.

One of the boys yelled back at the man, while the other watched everyone passing by with a melancholy, distracted face.

Soren turned to Rachel. He wanted to warn her not to look, but she was already climbing out of the sidecar and running to the beast. She placed her hand upon its heaving sides and made soothing sounds that only occasionally rose to the level of ineffective words.

In the long, circuitous route back, an icy silence erupted between them. Soren was silent because he began to sense that things were not right. The place was not right. The old wound, the wretched gash of existence would catch them yet in its endless net. She was quiet because her love longed to endure anguish, to taste the wounds to the depths in order to live the life of the luminous dark.

Rachel and the Geisha

It is odd, how perfectly ordinary things become difficult under duress or high feeling. She simply had gone to the wrong sleeper. It was inane, really, and she might have berated herself several times and remonstrated with him later for causing it all. The compartment door opened. It was the Geisha, though she was no longer dressed to impress. The white lead paint of oshiroi was removed, as was the expensive silk kimono.

Seeing her now, Rachel recognized that she was older than she had imagined. The woman took in the situation with a glance and beckoned her within with a gracious smile. Her name was Ayaka, though this was a sign of her profession. Her birth name was hidden with her childhood poverty. Her parents were poor farmers and she had been sold to unscrupulous men who scoured rural villages for young girls. Fortunately, she promised to grow into a beauty and had sufficient wit to impress the okasan who was in charge of the geisha house in Kyoto where the zegen had sold her. All this biography was related in the most charming manner as if it were a story in a book.

"If you were a patron in a tea house, we would burn incense to mark the time. It would be very expensive to converse with Ayaka. Would you like sake?"

Rachel shook her head. She felt obliged to apologize and retreat, but there was a sheltered intimacy, as between children, that had arisen between them so that she also wished to prolong the encounter.

"You do not marry?" she asked tentatively, conscious that it could be a painful or inappropriate topic to broach.

"No, but there is a formal union marked by ceremony possible to us. It would be a long conversation to explain dannas to you, but men are good and bad everywhere."

"My man is good," she blurted out, her eyes tearing again despite her wish to remain calm.

"And you are good, too, I think, but you are hurting one another."

Rachel sighed and ran her hand nervously through her hair. "Something is happening. I can't explain it to him because I don't understand it myself. He feels I am betraying him, but I am not. I'm not. If anything, I cherish him more."

"He is indeed fortunate. And yet, men often hate themselves and cannot believe in love. Some are very timid because of this, but even those artful in seduction are already plotting violence because their desire is secretly masochism."

"He calls me brat and I call him brute, but it's only just a game we play."

"I have an idea," said the Geisha. She pulled from a white leather travel case an ornate, lacquered box which contained a dip pen and a bottle of ink. From another compartment, she withdrew a stationary of brightly colored paper and a small delicately engraved knife.

"Do not gush and do not explain. Just write quickly and from your heart what most you wish to tell him."

Rachel pondered for a moment, pouting with innocent concentration, her natural beauty suddenly glowing so that Ayaka had to restrain herself from laughing admiration. Then Rachel wrote what was given in her heart to say. The Geisha creased the paper and cut a thin message bearing ribbon.

"Now you must trust me. I shall send this at the right time."

"But how will you know where to send it? Our names, our address? And surely it will change."

Ayaka may have told her, but Rachel heard the brute talking in the corridor. She felt as if there ought to have been a kind of magic circle around this moment. She did not want to explain, so she made a hasty, if heartfelt goodbye.

A clock that shows all times

"An actual thing is not merely itself, just as temporal beings are not only temporal. In addition to their matter and their time, this is only a way of saying the same thing, there are timeless, immaterial structures that accompany every actual being. Essential structures bear an inexhaustible multiplicity of meanings and possibilities in excess of anything that could be instantiated in any particular moment. This excess is a flourishing that calls to actual beings as the lure of perfection.

And yet, the actual manifests a vividness that the essence itself lacks. This allows for a tensional mode, neither a static, lifeless concept, nor the dynamic of temporal movement. Essentialities are the simultaneous unfolding of essential possibilities. Every musical variation is contained as a clock that shows all times. You relate within yourself to the expressed past and the unexpressed future as a score that continuously varies, self-transcending in order to become yourself.

Because of this inherent openness, essentialites cannot be defined and closed off as a concept may be comprehended. As Max Scheler used to say, the words only possess the value of a pointer: 'look for yourself, and then you will understand what I mean.'"

Lord of the Sabbath

The fields of golden wheat, the soft breeze, the horizon open and whispering of freedom, they'd parked the Indian and kicked back. Somehow they happened upon a stretch of happiness where it was pleasant to be with one another, to feel the vibrant hum of lazing nature, as if the entire world joined in the body at ease, the Sabbath rising from the depths. He left her to get a closer view of the river and to sketch its abundant life. So she was alone when they surprised her walking through the fields, bending an ear to sate their hunger, the Man and his disciples. She heard the tone, but not the words of the men in sumptuous clothes who questioned him on matters of the law. Rachel would have been offended by the umbrage in their flesh, the way they stood and accused. He answered them calmly, matter-of-factly, slowly explaining what they could have known had they humbled themselves to receive revelatory beauty. But they could not give up their precious Necessity, the thing that balks at divine largesse. She fancied the Man acknowledged her gaze, a wry resignation to the vanity of human nature much diminished by lack of love. When they retreated from her vision, Rachel was suddenly dismayed that Soren had not been there to capture in art the natural, unassuming sovereignty of the true Lord. But when he returned, she grew shy and could tell him n othing.

Reverence

He slept peacefully beside her. Rachel watched the even breath, that gift of spirit. She seemed to see the little boy he once was and the old man he had yet to become. She was glad to see there was still fire in him, the old man. *We must pursue the Good, even if we appear foolish in the doing*, she whispered in a prophecy. She longed to rush forward and to hold him, to cover him in kisses, but some feeling held her back, it was hard to explain why, reverence for the unique, lonely path that cannot be shared apart from something she could hardly name. And then he murmured slightly in his sleep, and she saw only her Soren, the precious, vulnerable flesh. Quickly, she turned her face from him lest he wake and ask her why she was crying.

A fairy tale

"What I say now will sound like a fairy tale, one of those stories of a Golden Age that somehow folk remember, though no one has ever experienced it. That's because the essence of gold is not limited to anything you've ever seen. The gold watch or ring is not yet what gold will be.

If you want to know, this is the meaning of the Auric Age: matter was originally not like we experience it today. Take a plant or an animal. You apprehend without great difficulty that there are complex structures that manifest as outward form. The more developed the organism, the more it is pointed towards exterior display as communication of interior being. About the minerals and crystalline world, it seems as if radiant show is a function of interior uniformity and external regularity. The stonecutter shapes the rock from without.

But Michelangelo was closer to the truth when he said that he discovered the form hidden in the marble. Dead matter as brute fact is desolation. In the beginning, form and matter were harmonious; the matter was not prior to form, but spun out, as it were, as the dynamic clothing of living spirit. The minerals of geologic ages sleep and dream of when they danced to the music of love."

Rachel's smile

They went to the outdoors café because it was easier to be together surrounded by strangers. Each was solicitous of the other. Neither wanted to hurt the one they loved, yet somehow it kept happening. Miserable that ache, so gutting of the joy of life, and so weakly vulgar, almost embarrassing that it should also take the form of petty exasperation, along with draining, persistent anxiety, a chore to avoid the hidden mines.

Anonymous antagonists seemed to be involved. No one recalled burying them in just that place. Someone else must have buried them long ago. Soren was once again at the precipice, feeling tired and on the verge of just letting go into abandoned despair. The Chora Mokra threatened to overwhelm him, fighting through the frail boundaries of his heart. Already, he'd escape by taking long walks without her. When he returned to the apartment, Rachel was kind. She said she understood that he needed time away from her. An artist requires solitude, which was true, but they both knew it was a lie.

So to make up for it, he'd suggested an evening out, though the streets were uneasy. Unrest had taken hold of the city. Differing parties ostensibly committed to freedom and the common welfare were simmering partisan vengeance. The Anshari watched it all with strange indifference. Perhaps they'd be glad if both sides were successful, wipe the planet clean of human history. You could hear shouts and breaking glass in a neighboring district, but the patrons of the café remained in their seats.

Weirdly, it felt almost cozy. The waiters came by with exaggerated courtesy. The music was louder, the jokes more vigorously laughed at, even as they sat at their tables and prognosticated the future that was happening one street over.

Later in the night, a song started up and everyone joined in. A middle-aged couple rose from their seats and danced. Rachel nearly grabbed Soren's hand to pull him into the dance, then decided better of it. Soren's jaw tightened, his eyes peering outward with intense concentration. He wanted to go home. He desperately wanted her to be safe. Yet they lingered, neither able to summon the strength to be alone together.

There was a furious exchange, closer now, followed by loud shouts and moaning. It was time to go. Soren stood, and grabbed her by the shoulder with preemptive command just as an angular, rail thin man in dark work clothes came round the corner. The fellow shambled about in half-conscious torment, and then sprawled across their table. More partisans appeared in a crowd behind him. Whose side, did it matter? Too late to flee, Soren unconsciously made fists to defend her honor. And then there was the otherworldly siren, that shrieking across the sky that made everyone freeze.

During all this, Rachel was not shocked. Had anyone been free enough from the anxiety of self-preservation to observe her, they would have remarked that she was exceptionally serene. She held the stranger while blood oozed from his brutalized face. The man's eyes stared upwards in unfocused agony. Was he more innocent than others? Probably not. No doubt, he'd felt hope, frustration, perhaps love. He'd endured fears, the dryness of boredom, and his own and another's human foibles like everyone else. Perhaps it was a trick of light, but his features softened. In Rachel's smile, the dying seemed to forgive everything of the world. Here was beauty trailing the immemorial peace of another world. For a clear second, the image was burned into the retinas of his unseeing eyes.

Then the shadow of the dark sun fell. The sound of spectral wings, the Shiriloth breaking through the insubstantial matter of their lives. Swift as the guillotine, it fell. Her eyes met the desperate seeking of her lover's face. Soren felt the intimate touch of her love.

And then she was gone, leaving him again in her impossible game of tag.

The fevered city

A low, solemn tremulous drone proceeded from the horn of the didgeridoo, a kind of chthonic whale song. Soren was hungry, ravenous. He'd known the dull apathy that could starve for a week and feel no ache of the belly. He thought himself strong then, useless with an aimless strength, but above the compulsion of tongue and guts. Now he was weak. He would soon lose the last bit of will, the last drop of insolent hatred. Then he would become passive, withdraw into himself and stare out at the shrinking world with the dull eyes of a child too resigned to fan at the relentless, stinging fl ies.

He found himself by some accident of the jostling mob at the edge of a quay. The fervid stench of the sick, of rags stale and sticking to the body, of muttering complaint and soft sobbing welcomed his flesh as brother. Rocking lamentation gave to the ghetto the appearance of a corporate life that subsumed individual existences. The beast was a confused creature of the shanties, somehow wounded and dying into the night. It whimpered before a mortality it could not understand or imagine, but which lurked, terrifying, pitiless, casual and perversely neutral.

Soren Blake stood at the docks and contemplated the sea. It was not possible, he thought, to be infinitely sorry. Infinitely sorry was an exaggeration and an indulgence. Only a god could be infinitely sorry and the gods, though subject to passions, were too remote, too separate from human frailty to be really sorry.

"To hell with it," he said, turning and striving forward between the rows of broken carts and hovels made of boxes and tin, "the hell with it all."

Maybe we are responsible to learn to love even the unlovely. He could not feel that, even as he was swept up in a compassionate rage, for both the good and the evil, but mostly for the innocent; the child, the simpleton, and the poor beasts. He longed to die. In spite of its impossibility, he was infinitely sorry for the born.

And the wives of fishermen knelt among the briny rocks taking with violence the beak-headed, lubricious, flagellated squid life.

Quotation References

pp. 2- 4: The Australian author is Gerald Murnane. The quotes are from Murnane, Gerald. *Border Districts*. New York: Farrar, Straus, Giroux, 2017. The abstract mode imitates Murnane's own rhetorical gestures towards reference in that text.

p. 5: Quote from Isaiah 13:12, 20 – 21. KJV *The Holy Bible: Old and New Testaments in the King James Version*. Nashville: Thomas Nelson Publishers, 1976.

p.13: Source unknown.

p.27: The Lafferty quote is from Lafferty, R.A. *Arrive at Easterwine: the Autobiography of a Kristec Machine*. New York: Ballantine Books, 1971.

p. 29: The Hopkins' quote is from Hopkins, Gerard Manley. *The Journals and Papers of Gerard Manley Hopkins*. 2nd ed., Ed. Humphrey House and Completed by Graham Storey. Oxford: Oxford University Press, 1959.

pp. 29 – 30: The Woolf quotes are from Woolf, Virginia. *The Death of the Moth and Other Essays.* New York: Harcourt Brace & Company, 1970.

p. 34: The quote regarding the Texas panhandle is from Hart, Ray L. *Unfinished Man and the Imagination: Toward an Ontology and a Rhetoric of Revelation.* Louisville, KY: Westminster John Knox Press, 2001.

p. 37: The Goethe quote is taken from Bortoft, Henri. *The Wholeness of Nature: Goethe's Way Toward a Science of Conscious Participation in Nature.* Great Barrington, MA:Lindisfarne Books, 1996.

P 37: The Rosenstock-Huessy quote is from Rosenstock-Huessy, Eugen. *The Fruit of Lips or Why Four Gospels.* Ed. Marion Davis Battles. Eugene, Oregon: Pickwick Publications, 1978.

pp. 39: The William Blake quote is from Blake, William. *The Complete Poetry & Prose of William Blake: Newly Revised Edition.* Ed. David V. Erdman. New York: Vintage Books, 1988.

p.42: The Milbank quote is from Milbank, John. "The Soul of Reciprocity Part Two: Reciprocity Granted", Modern Theology 17, no. 4 (October 2001).

p.43: The Stephen R. L. Clarke quote is from his essay "How to Believe in Fairies." https://www.scribd.com/document/326909031/How-to-Believe-in-Fairies

p. 44: Paul Claudel, the quote is from The Fourth Ode in Claudel, Paul. *Five Great Odes.* Trans. Jonathan Geltner. Brooklyn, NY: Angelico Press, 2020.

p. 48: Quote from Revelation 3:1 is from Hart, David Bentley. *The New Testament, a Translation.* New Haven: Yale Univ. Press, 2017.

p. 67: The tale is told in Boulad, Henri. *All is Grace: God and the Mystery of Time.* Trans. John Bowden. New York: Crossroad, 1991.

p. 78: The poet's line about an animal hunted is from Jones, David. *In Parenthesis.* New York: The New York Review of Books, 1937.

pp. 79 - 80: The Milosz poem, "A Portrait with a Cat, Berkeley, 1985" is from Milosz, Czeslaw. *New and Collected Poems: 1931 – 2001.* New York: Harper Collins Publishers, 2003.

p. 84: Matt. 26:13 is from the Hart translation. Ibid.

p. 86: The italicized lines are from Traherne, Thomas. *Centuries of Meditations: Compiled and Edited by Bertram Dobell.* Pantianos Classics, 2017.

p. 93: The Bulgakov quote is from Bulgakov, Sergius. *The Apocalypse of John: An Essay in Dogmatic Interpretation.* Trans. Mike Whitton. Revised Michael Miller, Munster.Aschendorff Verlag, 2019.

pp. 93 - 94: The quotes from Rev. 1:5 and 1:18 are from the Hart NT translation. Ibid.

p. 104: The quotes from *Parzifal* are from Wolfram von Eschenbach. *Parzival and Titurel.* Trans. Cyril Edwards. Oxford: Oxford Univ. Press, 2009.

p. 112: The line "it is useless to teach those who do not expect to be transformed" is by Rosenstock-Huessy. I specific textual source is unclear.

p. 116: The philological etymologies are taken from Florensky, Pavel. *The Pillar and Ground of the Truth: An Essay in Orthodox Theodicy in Twelve Letters.* Trans. Boris Jakim. Princeton: Princeton Univ. Press, 1997.

p. 118: The Before all oreogenesis quote is Jones, David. *The Anathemata.* London: Faber & Faber, 1952.

p. 147: Claudel quote is from the Third Ode in *Five Odes*, translation by Jonathan Geltner. Ibid.

p. 151: "He weeps for the land that dreams his bitter dreams" is from *The Sleeping Lord and Other Fragments.* London: Faber & Faber, 1974.

p. 184: The lines from Gregory of Nyssa are taken from Clément, Olivier. *The Roots of Christian Mysticism: Text and commentary.* Trans. Theodore Berkeley and Jeremy Hummerstone. Hyde Park, NY: New City Press, 1995.

p. 184: Much of the inspiration for Psalmic Resonance is taken from Wolfe, Art. *Earth is My Witness: The Photography of Art Wolfe.* San Rafael, CA: Earth Aware Editions, 2014.

p. 187: "Are we the ministers of death?" quote is from Jones, David. The Sleeping Lord and Other Fragments. London: Faber & Faber, 1974.

p. 195: The story about the druids is inspired by an anecdote in Ellis, Alice Thomas. *A Welsh Childhood.* Pleasantville, NY: The Akadine Press, Inc., 1990.